Adrienne Nairn was brought up in East Yorkshire. Travelling extensively, she has worked in South Africa, England, Australia and New Zealand. Adrienne wrote her autobiography *My Brother My Enemy* in 2013 and has spoken on the subject of elder abuse in New Zealand where she now lives with her husband, carrying out voluntary work. She has one daughter and two grandsons living in Sydney.

To my father, Maurice Lobb.

Adrienne Nairn
with Maria de Jong

THE INHERITANCE
THIEF

Best wishes

Adrienne Nairn

AUSTIN MACAULEY PUBLISHERS™

LONDON · CAMBRIDGE · NEW YORK · SHARJAH

A CIP catalogue record for this title is available from the British Library.

ISBN 9781788238113 (Paperback)
ISBN 9781788238120 (Hardback)
ISBN 9781788238137 (E-Book)

www.austinmacauley.com

First Published (2018)
Austin Macauley Publishers Ltd™
25 Canada Square
Canary Wharf
London
E14 5LQ

Acknowledgements

To Maria, without whose help this book would never have been written. Whilst researching ghost writers to help me with my novel, I was fortunate enough to find Maria de Jong and I shall be eternally grateful for her expertise in turning my autobiography into readable fiction. Her patience and advice have been invaluable. We spent long days working together, building a great rapport and countless emails passed between us. Maria has worked tirelessly and her experience in writing biographies, memoirs and family and business histories was much needed.

Maria provides ghost writing, editing and publishing services through her business, Life Stories New Zealand, and has produced a number of books of the highest quality. My sincere thanks to you, Maria.

My wholehearted thanks also to Maria's team of readers: Howard Johnston, Nina Molteno, Fred de Jong and Kay Hurley, who gave valuable feedback on the story. You have all helped craft a compelling story based on true events.

Thanks to Tom Lodge for his advice on digital marketing and e-books.

Anna – always there, still there.

My many friends, who have listened, offered advice and been there for me, too many to mention for fear of leaving someone out, but you all mean so much to me.

Bernie Hanvey, a new friend, who gave me invaluable tips and advice on publishing in the UK.

Les Hunter, my distributor in Scotland, who is still a calming influence, offering his expertise when required.

Last but not least, to my husband, Ian; daughter, Rachel; and son-in-law, Jamie. You all know the truth, thank goodness for a real family.

Chapter 1

Cathy stood outside the gracious old apartment building in Lyme Regis. Frowning, she looked up at the windows on the top floor, the late afternoon sunlight gilding the fine wrinkles on her soft skin. She had travelled all the way from New Zealand to England to pay her stepmother a surprise visit, but now she was here she hesitated, not knowing what kind of welcome awaited her.

Before emigrating, Cathy had often spent weekends with her father, Renton, and his second wife, Lucille. After a late blooming romance the pair had enjoyed 15 spectacularly successful years together. Visiting them had always been such fun; their happiness had seemed to throw a circle of golden light around them, and Cathy had basked in the glow. Standing now below the apartment, she had a fleeting image of Lucille in one of her loose silk dresses, straw-coloured hair freshly set and drink in hand, laughing at one of her father's jokes.

But that had been some time ago. Cathy's relationship with Lucille had been soured by a dispute ten years after her father's death and she hadn't seen her stepmother for a long time. She desperately hoped that on this summer's day in 2008 they might put the past behind them and be friends again

She took a deep breath and ran a hand nervously through her wavy blonde bob. Then, with a determined step, she entered the lobby and took the lift up to the penthouse on the fourth floor. At the front door she paused, staring at a small rectangular impression on the wood where once there had been an engraved brass nameplate with the lettering "R.J. & L.M. Coleman". The nameplate was missing. Only the screw holes remained. Her heart beat faster. There was something wrong. Cathy swallowed and pushed the doorbell. A moment later she heard muffled footsteps within the apartment. The door swung open, but instead of her stepmother, a middle-aged man, a complete stranger, stood eyeing her quizzically over his brown-framed glasses.

'Hello, I've come to see Lucille. Does she still live here? I'm a friend of hers,' Cathy said.

The man's expression changed. 'Just a minute, I'll get my wife − Helen!'

There was the sound of another door opening and more footsteps, before a woman, with a friendly smile and a brown pony tail, appeared.

'This lady's come to visit Lucille,' the man explained.

'Oh!' His wife's face fell. 'Perhaps you'd better come inside. We have some bad news for you, I'm afraid.'

Cathy stepped into the penthouse. She was immediately dazzled by the transformation. Gone were the floral patterns, the chintz and antiques favoured by her stepmother. Instead, the apartment had been redecorated in a neutral palette of cream and beige tones, with sleek modern furniture.

'I'm sorry to tell you that Lucille died 18 months ago,' said Helen apologetically. 'We're renting the apartment.'

'I see, I didn't know... could you please tell me what happened?'

'We understand she was in a nursing home for the last ten months of her life. I think she just grew weaker and weaker. I'm very sorry; were you a close friend?'

'You could say that. I live in Spain and haven't been in contact with Lucille for a while,' lied Cathy. She felt it was safer not to reveal her true identity.

'It must be a shock to you, then.'

'Yes, I hadn't expected it. The apartment has all changed − it looks lovely. But the view is still the same.' Cathy gazed out the full length windows at the boats moored in the harbour and the green expanse of Lyme Bay. 'Do you mind if I ask who owns the apartment now?'

'A family member bought it from your friend a few years ago,' explained Helen. 'Would you like a cup of tea?' she offered kindly.

Cathy shook her head, the sea view blurring through her tears. 'I'd best be on my way, but thank you just the same.'

On the train back to London, she chose a seat next to a young man wearing sunglasses too busy listening to his iPod to take any notice of her. She dabbed her eyes with a tissue, blew her nose and stared past him at the fields and towns rushing by. Cathy wondered how after so many years of caring for Lucille their relationship had come to this. Lucille had had no children of her own and for a long time Cathy had been like a daughter to her. Yet now she hadn't even been informed of her death!

She had an idea who might be behind this. As the fields sped by, her mind slipped back 20 years to the happy weekends with her father and stepmother in Lyme Regis before her father had died. Before everything had changed.

Chapter 2

The sun rose golden, tinting the light layer of clouds pink and casting a rosy glow over the smooth sea as Cathy stood gazing out of the penthouse windows.

'Good morning, Luvvy,' Lucille said cheerily, 'it's a beautiful day for the car boot sale. Your dad's just packing the car.'

Cathy turned away from the view. 'Good morning, Lucille. Tell Dad I'll be down soon to give him a hand.'

As soon as she had finished her tea and toast, Cathy hurried downstairs to the garage, where her father was lifting boxes of crockery and knickknacks into the back of the station wagon.

'Look at these cane walking sticks, cost me 50p in Spain and I'm selling them for £30 each.' Renton held out an elegant stick for Cathy to examine.

'Very nice.' Cathy felt the smooth grain. 'How many did you buy?'

'Fifty, and I've only got ten left.'

The heavily-laden station wagon pulled into the already packed car park at 6:15 am. Once the stall was set up, Cathy and her father settled themselves in deck chairs, while Lucille whipped around the market to see what bargains she could find. She arrived back, puffing a little, hauling a large basket of treasures.

'Look at these brass candlestick holders – only paid a pound and I reckon I can get a tenner for the pair. And I found this Victorian perfume bottle for Emma.' Lucille held up a crystal bottle with a glass stopper.

'That's pretty.' Cathy's daughter, Emma, had stayed at home in Glastonbury with David. Usually Emma loved coming down to see "Gran" and Granddad, but this weekend the 13-year-old had tennis lessons and a birthday party to go to.

Lucille carefully arranged a long necklace of intricately carved cream beads on black velvet.

'The woman who sold me this necklace thought it was bone, but I reckon it's ivory and at least 100 years old.'

Cathy admired the necklace. Lucille had a good eye, often beating the antique dealers, who did the rounds at seven, to the best pieces. Sure enough, it wasn't long before a dark-haired woman in a green dress stopped to admire the necklace.

'It's beautiful, isn't it?' Lucille held it out. 'Here, try it on. It's an Edwardian ivory necklace. I believe a captain in the army brought it back from India to give to his fiancée.'

'How much is it?' enquired the woman, admiring herself in the silver-backed mirror.

'Forty-five pounds – it looks lovely on your olive skin.' That clinched it; the ivory necklace had a new owner. The woman slipped it into her black handbag and merged with the crowd. Lucille whispered to Cathy, 'I only paid £10 for that necklace.'

Renton was having an animated discussion over a walking stick with a tall, dignified woman.

'Handcrafted in Spain. If you look closely, you'll see that each stick is a little different.'

The woman pushed back a loose strand of silvery hair as she chatted to Renton. Though in his mid-seventies, he was still a handsome man, with twinkly, blue eyes and a head of steel-grey curls. 'I've only got a few left – they've sold like hot cakes. For you, I can make a special price of £25.'

Smiling, the woman pulled out her wallet. Cathy headed off to buy coffee with some of the proceeds. She loved seeing her father and Lucille in action at the car boot sale. They were masters in the art of wheeling and dealing. Honestly, her father could hold his own with the wiliest of rag-and-bone men.

The couple had shown the same shrewdness in their property deals. Lucille, a former estate agent, and Renton, a handyman, had formed a dynamic duo with skills ideally suited to buying, renovating and selling properties. Cathy was delighted with their success. Her parents had split up when she was six. For many years, her father had struggled financially and had difficulty paying maintenance to support Cathy and her elder brother, Alex. Renton had met the recently widowed Lucille in his hardware store. He'd helped her out with a few handyman jobs around the home. Lucille was the kind of woman who imagined every man to be in love with her and sure enough, Renton soon fell under her spell. It was during the repair of an elaborate ruched pink blind in her bedroom that the two had got on more intimate terms.

They married in Spain, Lucille in peacock blue with a matching hat and a spray of white carnations. A flamenco guitarist played at the reception, which was held on the upstairs *terraza* of a small hotel in the mountain village of Mijas. Afterwards, they drove to Granada for a brief honeymoon.

Back in England, Lucille demonstrated her knack for buying houses at knockdown prices and Renton used his DIY skills to renovate them. Lucille was adept at on-selling the houses for a handsome profit. After several years, they were able to buy the penthouse apartment and retire. Cathy was grateful to Lucille for her part in the transformation of her father's life. Right now, he was chuckling with Lucille as he boxed up the leftover bone china to take home.

The car boot sale over for another week, they drove back to the penthouse for lunch. Lucille handed around pork pies from the market. They were all tired from the early morning start and happy to relax in comfy wicker chairs on the balcony. Cathy munched quietly on her pie, enjoying the view of Lyme Bay, while her father dozed in the afternoon sun.

After a spell, Renton opened his eyes and said, 'Your brother rang last week.'

'Yes, I saw Alex when he was home on leave,' answered Cathy. 'David and I had a weekend away with him and Sonia in Cornwall. He doesn't seem to think he'll be working in Oman for much longer. It sounds like the Sultan's cutting back on his private security force and getting rid of the Brits.'

'The expats are too expensive now the price of oil has fallen. But Alex sounded pretty confident about his severance package. Knowing him, it'll be a good one… he's a tough negotiator.'

'When I spoke to him,' Lucille said, 'he sounded annoyed that I hadn't told him earlier about your father's heart condition. But it's not really my fault if he's home on leave for a month and doesn't bother contacting us until he's at the airport about to fly back to Oman!'

Renton sat in silence, contemplating the sea. After a while, he said, 'It's hard for them to adjust to normal life again when they come back from the Middle East. You experience some terrible things in war. I remember when he came back from Oman one New Year's Eve, with a bullet in his shoulder. His ribs were sticking out because he had lost so much weight sweating in the 40° heat.'

'The sacrifices they make...' Lucille sighed, closing her eyes.

Cathy chose not to comment and took another sip of her tea. Her father knew all about a soldier's life. He had fought in the Second World War and been wounded in the D-Day landings in France. Like him, Cathy was proud of Alex, a hero who had been decorated four times for gallantry. But she wished her brother would take more of an interest in the lives of her father and stepmother. He rarely visited them. It was the same with her mother and her second husband, Henry. Alex was far removed from their lives. Her mother could have done with more help now that Henry had motor neurone disease and was stuck in a wheelchair. Only last month, Cathy and David had looked after him for a week to give her mother a break. Though it hadn't been easy nursing Henry, they had managed. But Cathy suspected that helping Henry on to the toilet was a task beneath the dignity of an ex-SAS soldier.

Chapter 3

The next morning, Cathy opened her eyes to see the striped Roman blinds illuminated by bright sunlight. She had slept late. Renton and Lucille had gone to church, so she decided to go for a walk to Monmouth Beach.

Holiday chalets crowded against the shore, while rugged cliffs rose up in the distance. The tide was coming in. Cathy slipped off her sandals and paddled in the shallows, her gaze drifting from the wavelets lapping at her white feet to two children playing on the wet sand.

'Quick, Libby! Stop the water coming in!' yelled the boy, hastily scooping sand into a breach in the dam. A little girl with blonde pigtails ran to help him. She knelt next to him and began shoving handfuls of sand onto the wall.

The pair reminded Cathy of outings to the beach in Scarborough as a child. Some of her happiest memories were of building sea walls with Alex. Her mother's family had a beach hut for storing deckchairs, an umbrella, buckets, spades and a kettle. Sometimes her grandmother would come with them. Despite being a very elegant woman with impeccable grooming, Grandmother Milne had often changed into her bathing suit in the beach hut and swum with the children in the North Sea.

Grandmother liked to remind the children, 'How lucky you are to have a nice beach to swim at. Lots of other children would love to go to the beach for the day.'

Picnics at the beach were bright scenes in Cathy's store of childhood memories. In reality, things hadn't always been so idyllic and looking back, Cathy realised her parents were an ill-matched couple. Her mother's family, the Milnes, had been well-to-do and owned a fashionable department store in Scarborough. Cathy's mother, Margaret, was indulged as a girl and accustomed to getting whatever she fancied. During the latter part of the war, Renton's regiment had been stationed on England's north-east coast and he and Margaret had crossed paths at various social gatherings put on by the locals to entertain the troops. Margaret was soon infatuated with this dashing soldier, whose company brought welcome relief from her grim duties as a trainee nurse in Scotland. Before the 24th Lancers embarked to France, Grandmother Milne sought to assist her daughter in acquiring a husband by summoning the object of her desire to the house for a private audience in the drawing room. Not one to beat about the bush, Grandmother Milne began, 'I hear that you are moving away.'

Renton was shocked. 'Even if I knew such a thing, I could not confirm or deny the movements of the regiment.' It was a serious offence for a soldier to disclose troop movements.

'You don't have to say anything, because I know what's happening. But Mr Milne and I would like you to give your future plans with Margaret some serious thought before you leave.' Grandmother Milne regarded him with cold blue eyes.

Renton began to stutter out a reply, 'I'm… I'm sorry, madam, but I hadn't really… I've been quite focused on my training and going to France.'

'But not so focused that you haven't enjoyed my daughter's company,' replied Grandmother Milne. She continued rather haughtily to suggest that if Renton held her daughter in high regard, he would not want her to go back to emptying bedpans in Edinburgh.

'You will never want for anything if you marry her, I can promise you that. Do have a think about it and let us know.' With that, Grandmother Milne swept from the room, leaving Renton feeling quite stunned. Margaret soon appeared, blushing and smiling, bearing a tea tray.

Some days later, Renton had visited Mr Milne to express his concern at the prospect of marriage when he could easily be killed in the war. But Mr Milne did not appear to be bothered by this possibility and the pair was soon engaged. Renton was 30 when he married 19-year-old Margaret. Mid-way through their honeymoon in Scotland, Renton realised he had married a child who answered his questions in monosyllables. The marriage stumbled on, discontent on both sides, until eventually there was a bitter divorce. Renton was relegated to the financial wilderness of a single man on low wages, struggling to meet the hefty maintenance payments extracted by Grandfather Milne's lawyer. With her parents' support, Margaret fared well. Grandfather Milne purchased a bungalow for her and the children and found a job for his wayward daughter in the lingerie department – the irony of the solution escaping him.

With their mother working six days a week, Cathy and Alex often found themselves in the chilly atmosphere of their maternal grandparents' house, in a fashionable quarter in Scarborough. Filled with fine furnishings from the store, the house had no fewer than three grandfather clocks. Grandmother Milne was very strict and insisted on lady-like behaviour. She would never allow her granddaughter to lick an ice cream on the street. Heaven forbid! Licking was vulgar – ice cream should be delicately nibbled, even if it hurt the teeth, and only ever eaten at the beach.

The stiffness of the Milnes' household contrasted with the love and warmth in Granny and Grandpa Coleman's bungalow. Granny Coleman loved having her grandchildren to stay in the holidays. She would play board games with them and help them flip pikelets on the wood stove. Cathy loved sitting on Grandpa's knee. He would fish his gold fob watch out of his waistcoat pocket and ask her to blow on it. When she did, the watch would magically open so that she could see the time. Cathy was too young to realise that Grandpa had worked the little lever without her noticing.

The memory of the fob watch faded from Cathy's mind. She looked up to see grey clouds racing across the sky; a cold onshore wind had sprung up. Zipping her jacket up tightly, she turned for home. As she started back along the beach, she saw that the little girl was crying. Her brother had tipped a bucket of cold seawater over her. It reminded Cathy of the way her own brother had sometimes been nasty to her.

Like the time they had pooled their pocket money to buy firecrackers for Guy Fawkes. Cathy loved the pretty ones: Golden Rain, Mt Vesuvius and Snow Storm; Alex preferred bangers. Hurrying home from school one afternoon before the big day, she had been hoping they could go to the shop to choose their fireworks together. They had been invited to a bonfire at her aunt and uncle's house.

As she came closer to home, she saw her brother and his friend were letting off loud bangers and penny rockets on the footpath. Alex held up a penny rocket in a bottle and aimed it straight at her.

'What are you doing?' she screamed, ducking as the rocket shot over her head.

She soon discovered that Alex had spent all the money they had saved together on noisy crackers, jumping jacks and sky rockets. She remembered how angry and indignant she had been. To make matters worse, her mother had refused to take sides.

Generally, though, Cathy and Alex had got on well, and she'd missed him when he'd gone to boarding school at the age of 11. The house had seemed oppressively quiet without him.

Alex had hated boarding school. He was a loner and the bullies preyed on him, sensing his insecurities. In one particularly humiliating incident, senior boys had cornered him in the toilets. They had forced him into a stall and made him kneel, shoving his head into the toilet bowl. Alex had fought hard, chipping his tooth on the porcelain rim, but he was held down and the cistern flushed. It was this incident that prompted him to run away. He planned his escape carefully, hoarding food from his meals. The night before he left, he packed a small duffel bag with snacks, a raincoat, some clothing, a comb and his pocket money. He hid the duffel bag under a laurel hedge, near a side gate. His escape was planned for the last class of the day, when a rather doddery Latin professor was in charge.

Towards the end of the lesson, Alex put up his hand.

'Yes, Coleman?' said the master, peering at him over half-rim spectacles.

'Sir, may I go to the toilet?'

'You may, Coleman,' nodded the master, returning to his marking.

From the toilet block, Alex walked straight to the nearby hedge, retrieved his bag, slung it over his shoulder and walked swiftly out the side gate, without looking back.

Chapter 4

One night Cathy woke up to find her mother sitting on the end of her bed, crying helplessly.

'What's wrong?' asked Cathy anxiously.

'The police have picked Alex up again – this time on a train. The conductor found him asleep in his school uniform,' she uttered between sobs. 'I don't know what to do.'

Cathy hugged her.

'Will they take him to Dad's?'

'Yes, and then back to school, but he'll only run away again. And the stealing – he's out of control. They found some things he'd stolen in his satchel.'

Before long, Alex was expelled. Drastic action was needed. Renton applied for custody of his son, and in an unusual move by the courts at the time, custody was granted to the father. Renton wisely enrolled his errant son in the Boy Scouts, which proved to be his salvation. Alex loved outdoor adventures, tramping, camping, cooking over an open fire and being trained to understand nature and live in the wild. Renton encouraged him to apply for the British Army. He felt the army would "straighten him out", giving him some much needed discipline and a career path. At age 15, Alex entered the Junior Leaders Regiment, then progressed to the army, eventually serving in a peace keeping force in West Germany. It was the height of the Cold War.

On one particular winter's day, Alex had come in from routine border patrol duties to see the men gathered around Lance Corporal Buckingham. Grabbing a mug of tea, he had joined the circle. Buckingham was regaling them with stories of the latest exploits of the Special Air Service (SAS). Alex knew this elite corps of soldiers was specially trained to operate in small bands and act independently in the most hostile of environments. He decided to apply.

The selection process for the SAS tests human endurance in the extreme. Soldiers have been known to die on the timed marches in the Brecon Beacons. In the first weeks, Alex found himself tramping over that same tough terrain with a 45 lb pack, a water bottle and a rifle. Over the next few months he was subjected to constant physical exertion, aptitude tests, jungle training, survival courses, and escape and evasion. The selection course was designed to break the applicants and less than ten per cent ever made it through. Alex showed the grit and determination to be an SAS soldier and made it.

Cathy was immensely proud that her brother was in the SAS, but she also felt anxious when he announced that he was leaving for Oman.

***

In Oman, SAS troops and British officers contracted to the Sultan's army faced mountainous, rocky terrain and extreme heat, while at other times it was cold and wet, with thick fog for five months of the year. After only a few weeks, Alex put on his khaki shirt and the armhole tore – the fabric was rotting from the humidity.

In the evenings, he would wander through the narrow alleyways of the souks. He glimpsed veiled women and robed men leaning against doorways, softly lit by oil lamps. There was no electricity, no hospital and very few schools. Alex soon learned that the people were living a feudal way of life, as they had done for thousands of years, because their previous leader, Sultan Sa'id, had feared change. The old Sultan had been overthrown by his son, Qaboos, in 1970. Sandhurst educated, Sultan Qaboos had asked the British Government to help stamp out the communist rebels and modernise Oman. The British Government was motivated to help the new Sultan because of Oman's strategic position on the Straits of Hormuz, a narrow passageway through which the world's oil tankers must pass to reach the oil fields of the Middle East. The British feared the growing influence of the communists in neighbouring Yemen.

Before travelling to Oman, Alex was informed by his commanding officer that British soldiers were to be restricted to support and training roles, but he soon discovered they were involved in combat on the ground.

***

Alex was based in a small settlement with a cluster of flat-roofed, adobe houses and a medieval fort in Dhofar. The SAS soldiers were training local militia, *firqas,* and every two or three days repelling attacks by small bands of communist guerrillas.

One morning he opened his eyes and stared at the mud brick walls of the hut where he slept with the other soldiers. It was just getting light and he could hear the men stirring on their mattresses around him. Today he was on patrol and needed to sort his kit. Next to him, Mac, one of his patrol mates, hit the play button on the cassette recorder. The light-hearted lyrics of Jimmy Nash filled the room, *'I can see clearly now the rain has gone...'* Wearing only underpants, Mac was singing along, swaying to the beat.

Alex looked up at the tanned young soldier, 'You're in a good mood.'

'It's my birthday,' said Mac.

'Oh, that's right. Happy birthday, what are you, 25?'

'Twenty-two, you old fart.' Mac joined in the chorus, 'It's gonna be a bright, bright sunshiny day.'

A patch of blue sky filled the window. *Well, that makes a change*, thought Alex. It had been drizzling for days.

He crawled out of his sleeping bag, turned over his boots and tapped on the soles to knock out any scorpions that might have crawled in overnight. Then he downed a quick breakfast of dates and cereal, before setting about filling water bottles, packing rations and ammunition for the day ahead. All around him the mood was cheery. Mac was popular with the lads and they'd been saving their rum rations to celebrate his birthday that night. The Omani cook had promised to roast some chickens for the occasion. Their four-month tour of duty was due to end soon and this added to the men's good spirits. Alex planned to stay with Cathy in London for part of his leave. One of Cathy's flatmates was a good looker and he hoped to get to know her on more intimate terms.

Shouldering his heavy pack and automatic rifle, he headed out with his patrol. The band of four soldiers tramped in single file along a rocky trail, across the plains, towards the mountains in the north. The first stop was to check on the guards loyal to the Sultan, who were keeping watch on the approaches to their headquarters. Then they climbed to higher ground for a spot of reconnaissance. The patrols had a monotonous sameness to them. Most days were quiet, but there was the occasional skirmish and the odd mortar bomb or shell fired in their direction. Great swathes of the land were controlled by the Adoo rebels, and Alex wondered if they were making any real progress in routing them. It was hard to say.

After checking that all was well with the guards and spending a few hours on reconnaissance, the patrol followed a steep path ascending the mountains. They were aiming for a high rocky outcrop with a bird's eye view of the surrounding area. The landscape was like no other Alex had ever seen. The austere Rocky Mountains were beautiful at sunset when they glowed in rosy hues, but now it was hot and the noon day sun beat down on the men from a cloudless blue sky. Perspiration dripped down his back and legs. He paused to take a swig out of his water bottle. Looking through his binoculars at the plains below, he saw no suspicious activity. In fact, there was no sign of movement at all. At this time of year, the shrubs were green. Everything was quiet. He put down his binoculars and continued trudging up the path. As usual they kept 20 metres between each man. He was tail end Charlie. Mac was in the lead.

Suddenly, there was an ear-splitting explosion from up ahead. A geyser of dust and stones spurted into the air. Heart pounding, Alex broke into a run. When he rounded the bend, he saw Mac sprawled on the ground, his legs a bloody mess from the shrapnel of a mine.

Tom was already kneeling beside Mac, searching through his first aid kit. He pulled out a field dressing and used his teeth to tear off the plastic wrapping. 'Stay calm. You'll be all right. We'll get you out of here. Alex, radio for help!'

Alex dropped his pack on the ground and yanked out the radio. While he radioed through their position, Tom applied tourniquets and dressings, and injected Mac with morphine. Malakai, a powerfully built Fijian soldier, assisted him. Alex watched them as he worked the radio. Poor Mac – one of his legs was missing below the knee. The other was a pulpy mess. Poor Mac – it was some birthday.

'We need to find cover. We can't stay out in the open,' said Tom urgently. 'Nothing more I can do for him right now anyway.'

Alex said, 'Jesus, can he be moved? Look at his legs.'

'He'll have to be. The rebels would've heard the mine. They won't be far away. Malakai, let's get 'im over there.' Tom pointed towards a cave-like opening. Mac screamed as, one on each side, Malakai and Tom hoisted him up under the armpits.

A spray of machine gun fire sent bullets ricocheting off the rocks a few metres away. As Tom and Malakai carried Mac to the cave, Alex grabbed his rifle and dived behind some rocks. He twisted and lay flat, pushing his rifle between two boulders, then panned the terrain with his rifle sight. A turbaned head popped up briefly from behind a low mound 100 metres away. Alex kept his sight trained on the spot. It was kill or be killed and he was going to pot the bastard for Mac.

Another burst of machine gun fire; sand and dirt kicked up short of where they lay. *Untrained*, Alex thought, *Just wasting ammo*. Once more he peered out from between the boulders and trained his rifle on the mound where he had seen the rebel. The turbaned head popped up again. Alex exhaled slowly and squeezed the trigger. The rebel's head jolted back.

'Fuck off,' snarled Alex.

Tom and Malakai were firing off rounds too.

Movement in the rocks to the right caught Alex's eye. He raised his rifle. There was a bullet crack and he felt a sudden searing pain in his right shoulder. His grip failed; the rifle clattered to the ground.

'I'm hit!' he yelled to Tom and Malakai.

'Keep your head down!' Malakai yelled back. 'I've got you covered.'

The Fijian opened fire, raking the rocks with bullets. Then suddenly there was silence. They waited a couple of minutes, but nothing moved.

Alex crawled over to where Mac lay propped against a pack and collapsed onto the ground next to him. Tom reached him, tore open his shirt and pressed a field dressing against the bullet wound. 'Hold this in place.'

He held out his water bottle and Alex took a swig. 'Guess you're going to make it home before us, you lucky bastard.'

'Yeah, there'd better be some nice nurses on my ward,' said Alex, his ears ringing after all the rifle fire.

It looked as if they would be in for a long wait before the chopper found them. His shoulder burned with pain. He glanced at Mac, who was lying with his eyes closed, face beaded with perspiration, looking ashen despite his tan. Tears had made runlets through the dirt on his face. Alex closed his own eyes. The song Mac had been playing that morning came back to him and stuck in his head.

Yeah right, he thought. *Sunshiny day.*

***

After the Dhofar War ended in 1975, Alex had chosen to return to Oman to work as a mercenary for the Sultan. Like many former British Army personnel, he was paid handsomely to work in security. Compared to his time with the SAS the work was tedious, but he was motivated by the financial rewards.

It was another stinking hot day in August 1988. There was very little to occupy Alex in the royal security offices in Muscat that day.

'Tariq, why isn't this air conditioning unit working?' Alex asked his colleague.

'The chief said to turn off half the air conditioners. We have to save money; the electricity bill is too high.' Tariq looked back down at the accounts he was studying, running his finger down the columns of figures.

Alex shook his head. He'd lived in Oman for the best part of 15 years now and seen the country undergo explosive development during that time, but he was still baffled by this kind of false economy. The remaining air conditioners would have to work doubly hard to maintain a cool temperature in the building – this would drive up maintenance costs. In fact, he doubted the Omanis were saving any money in the long run. It was 40° outside in the shade – the humidity made it unbearable.

As all was quiet, Alex thought he might finish writing a letter to Cathy. He took the letter out of his drawer and added in black fountain pen:

I think most of the news here is to do with the economic crisis in the Arab countries at the moment. The budget here is connected to the price of oil, which was worked out at $20 per barrel. For most of this year, the oil prices have been around $12 per barrel, so things are tightening up in the Arab world. They have to cut back on us ex-pats because we're expensive to employ – houses, cars and everything provided. I have four air conditioners in my house and the electricity bill is horrendous. My position here has changed – I have much broader responsibilities now. I'm renegotiating, and rest assured, I will get the best possible deal. I've got the added responsibility of a wife to provide for now and Sonia seems to have fallen in love with a manor house in Surrey. Lucky my BP shares and other investments are doing well! For the rest, we're both well. The only minor hassle is that Sonia's been having a few problems with the electronic ignition of the MG – I blame it on the mechanic at the local garage.

Alex stood up, stretched and strolled over to the water cooler. Valentine's Day was coming up, he thought he ought to send some flowers to his wife. He'd met Sonia in Oman, where she was working for Telecom. She had been sitting cross-legged on top of her desk, a tall, leggy blonde. Just the kind of girl he liked. When she'd spoken to him, he'd liked the sound of her home counties accent. For a few weeks, Alex had made a point of personally checking on the security guards at the Telecom offices. Soon they got chatting and he invited Sonia out to dinner at one of the new hotels.

She arrived looking smashing in a black dress and gold high-heeled sandals. They sipped "mocktails" from hand-blown glasses, sitting on a four-poster bed next to a turquoise coloured pool. Only the Middle East could offer such an opulent setting for wealthy Arabs and expats to play in. On closer inspection, Alex realised that Sonia was around the age when a woman is very keen to tie the knot, but unlikely to conceive a child – this suited him perfectly. For her part, Sonia was rather flattered by the attentions of a handsome, former SAS soldier. She felt safe with Alex.

Alex carefully rested his arm with the gold Rolex wristwatch on the cushions of the four poster, which was inclined so that they could sit comfortably. Sonia seemed quite happy to sit with his arm more or less around her. She looked up at him.

'What are you thinking about?' she asked.

'Nothing much.' He remembered thinking to himself that Sonia would have to learn that he wasn't a man who discussed his work or feelings. The secretive habits of the SAS were deeply ingrained in him.

'Shall we go in for dinner at seven and then take a 30-minute stroll along the corniche?' he had suggested. 'If you like, you could come back to my house for some Turkish coffee.'

'Sounds good to me.'

They were married quietly in Oman. Alex chose not to invite his family, though Sonia's mother attended the small ceremony in a registry office. Sonia had taken an instant dislike to her new father-in-law and his wife, but wisely kept her feelings to herself until after the wedding. For his part, Renton considered his new daughter-in-law to be "snobbish".

'I don't know why Sonia gives herself those airs and graces,' Renton said to Cathy. 'We drove past the house she grew up in when we were in Oxford; it's a dingy little terrace house.'

Alex knew that Sonia considered his family "common" and wanted as little to do with them as possible. But he didn't mind. He'd joined the army at 15 and had lived in the Middle East for so long that he felt quite removed. However, he was determined Sonia would not damage his relationship with Cathy. His little sister had been a loyal ally, looking after his rental properties in England, and he had no intention of letting his wife come between them.

Alex was looking forward to his leave and seeing Sonia again. He finished off his letter to Cathy:

As you have probably noticed, I am enclosing a £10 cheque. I wonder if you could please order from Interflora the Summer Special I have seen advertised in Punch magazine. The Summer Special is a bouquet of pink carnations and pink roses, I believe. It costs £9.99, if you can manage that, super, and if not, then just flowers of your choice, whatever one can get for £10. Could you please have the bouquet delivered to my wife with suitable greetings of "Miss you, Sweetheart" or something appropriate. That's all for now. I'll say goodbye, looking forward to seeing you all again in about three or four weeks' time.

Alex

Chapter 5

Cathy scrubbed new potatoes, then set them on the stove to boil, adding a sprig of mint. Before walking to the bank that morning, she had shoved a hunk of corned silverside into the crock-pot, so now it was just a matter of whipping up mustard sauce, slicing carrots and washing a bunch of spinach freshly picked from the garden.

The phone rang. She put down the tin of mustard and picked up the receiver.

It was Lucille. 'Hello, Luvvy, are you still planning to come down from Glastonbury this weekend?'

'Yes, I am. How's Dad?'

'He's been very weak, really. He's mainly stopping in bed, no energy at all. It's his poor old heart. I think it's because he had that bout of rheumatic fever when he was a child – his heart's weak.' Lucille's voice sounded a little hoarse.

'And how are you coping, Lucille?'

'I'm fine. It's just a bit hard being so housebound. I don't like to leave him on his own.'

'Look, I'll ask my boss if I can take Monday off. It sounds like you could do with a break.'

'That would be wonderful,' chirped Lucille.

Cathy put the mustard sauce in the microwave and called for Emma to set the table. 'I'm going to have to go down to Lyme Regis this weekend and stay on a bit longer, until Monday.'

'But you were only there last weekend,' complained Emma, rattling through the cutlery.

'I know, but your granddad's getting weaker and I want to spend some time with him and give Lucille a break.'

After supper, Cathy got out her ceramic mixing bowl, dried fruit, butter, flour, brown sugar, spices and eggs. Her father was fond of fruit cake and she liked to take him one each time she visited.

At midday on Saturday, she rang the doorbell of the penthouse. After a short delay, the door swung open and Lucille, wearing a floral apron, pulled her into a bear hug. Cathy breathed her light, powdery perfume. 'It's so good to have you here, Luvvy.' Lucille released her from her ample bosom. 'Come in, come in, the guest bedroom's ready for you. I'll put the kettle on.'

In the living room, Renton, sitting in his pyjamas, looked up from his newspaper. He was grinning from ear to ear.

'Dad, how are you?' She gave him a kiss on his stubbled cheek.

'Can't complain. Lucille is taking good care of me. You look well. Sorry to drag you away from your family.'

'It's all right, Dad. I bet David and Emma won't even miss me. They'll be happy as sand boys, sitting in front of the telly tonight watching the All Blacks play Wales and eating their takeaways.'

Cathy helped Lucille make sandwiches in the kitchen.

'I thought I'd duck out to the hairdresser's, if it's okay with you. I haven't had my hair set for ages.'

'Of course, this is a good chance. You go – I'll look after Dad.'

After lunch, father and daughter sat in armchairs looking out over the iron grey English Channel. A strong northerly was whipping up white caps.

'Remember when we sailed to France, Dad?'

Renton smiled, his eyes twinkling.

'That was an adventure and a half, wasn't it? When we struck that thunderstorm just off the coast of France! The sea was wild, just like today, and then the lightning and rain hit. I remember I could hardly see a thing and I was confused by the lights. I couldn't make out where the harbour entrance was! Were you scared?'

'No, I had complete faith in you, Dad.' Cathy laughed. 'It was exciting! But I was disappointed we couldn't reach Cherbourg Yacht Club for the night. We had to sail up the coast until dawn, then come back again for another go.' She grimaced at the memory. 'Dad, remember how you had to rescue that woman?'

'I do,' Renton smiled as he recalled it. On the journey home, their motor had spluttered and almost died, but they had managed to limp to Jersey in the Channel Islands for repairs. While waiting for the motor to be fixed they had got talking to a middle-aged couple on a big launch, *Pipella*. Once the engine was ready, they prepared to set sail. *Pipella's* skipper warned them not to sail against the incoming tide, but Renton ignored this advice because they had a long day's sailing ahead and he knew if they got a little way out, the tide would turn.

Sailing away from Jersey was slow going. Early in the afternoon they hove to and brewed a cup of tea. The sea was calm, the breeze a mere puff. Renton started the engine. Just then he saw a launch altering course and coming towards them. It was *Pipella.* The launch came alongside and offered to tow them to Guernsey for a night ashore. Cathy was keen, so Renton agreed. Once under way, they could sit back and relax.

It was a lovely day with clear blue skies. Suddenly, Renton noticed that *Pipella's* engines had stopped. Then he saw that 40 yards astern a woman was thrashing about in the water.

'Are you OK? Can you swim?' shouted Renton. The reply was gurgled. Without hesitation, he yanked off his jersey, dived into the sea and swam straight towards the floundering woman. When he reached her, he turned her onto her back and towed her to the launch. With a mighty heave, he managed to get her up onto the ladder and her husband hauled her aboard.

'She was so grateful to you, Dad.' I don't how she lost her footing and slipped off the deck into the water.'

'Mmm, and that was a beautiful three-course meal she cooked us that night.' In his mind's eye, Renton saw the candlelight glowing on their faces as they sat cosily around the table in the galley, eating eye fillet steak and mushrooms.

They sat in silence for a while, thinking back.

'I loved being on the boat.'

'Me too. Pity Alex wasn't interested in sailing. But you loved it.' Renton smiled fondly at his daughter. His reveries were interrupted by the phone ringing. It was Alex. Renton chatted with his son for a while, then put the phone down.

'How is Alex?' asked Cathy.

31

'He's fine, busy trimming the yew hedges at the Manor House. He's got a fancy new trimmer. I told him that property would be too much work. I haven't seen him in weeks. Sonia's never keen to visit, so I guess that's why.' Renton pursed his lips.

'Is that Sonia you're talking about?' asked Lucille, coming in with freshly set hair. 'That girl's got a mouth like a pussy's bum!'

On Monday morning, Renton stayed in bed.

'He's tired today,' observed Lucille. She switched the kettle on and sliced up some fruit cake. 'We'll take our morning coffee into the bedroom.'

Lucille and Cathy sat in chairs on either side of the bed. Cathy looked at her father propped up on the white frilled pillows. His face had a grey pallor and his eyes were a little sunken looking. He looked pensive. Cathy took one of his big calloused hands, lying on the floral duvet, in her small ones. It was hard leaving when she knew he only had weeks to live.

'So you're planning to go at 12:30?' he asked.

'Yes, Dad, I don't want to be late home for Emma.'

'You know, I've got a few regrets in my life,' Renton suddenly told her in his deep, gravelly voice. 'I wish I'd tried harder with your mother, perhaps we could have made it work.'

'But she would have had to try hard too, Dad, for that to happen,' Cathy gently reminded him.

'And I wish I could have given you a big wedding, dear. I'd have loved to have walked you down the aisle in New Zealand, then a big party at a hotel afterwards.'

Cathy squeezed his hand.

'But I just didn't have the money to go to New Zealand,' Renton went on, 'let alone pay for a wedding.'

'That's all right, Dad, I'm not bothered.' Cathy pushed back the memory of the low key affair in a registry office in a nondescript concrete building in Auckland. She had met David, a technician from New Zealand, while working there. They'd lived in Auckland for a couple of years, before returning to England and buying a modest, semi-detached house in Glastonbury.

Renton took a sip of his coffee. 'I wish I could have helped you buy a house, too. It was such a struggle for you and David after Emma was born. You had to go back to work to help pay the mortgage. A mother should be able to stay home to look after her child.'

'Most women work now, Dad.' Cathy thought back to those stony broke days when their account had been overdrawn most weeks. It had been hard. Her mother, who was a wealthy woman, had never offered them any assistance at all other than to send a few household items like nappies and linen from the shop, somehow seeming to forget that her own parents had fully supported her.

'Well, I regret that I wasn't able to help you as a father should.' Renton looked straight at his daughter. Their eyes met and he held her gaze. 'I want to do something for you now.'

Reaching for the old black Bible he kept on his nightstand, he took a slip of paper from between the pages and handed it to his daughter.

Cathy drew in her breath quickly. The cheque was for £50,000.

'But, Dad, you don't need to give me money. We're fine now. We're comfortable; we've both got good jobs.'

'I want you to have this now,' Renton said firmly.

Cathy studied the cheque. It was written in her father's neat, slanting hand and it was signed by him.

'But this cheque is drawn on Lucille's account? I don't want to take money from Lucille.'

Renton replied calmly, 'The Jersey account is in her name, but I have signing authority. This is what we both want to do. The money is ours, Cathy. I've made all the arrangements for my death – I've even got a quote from the funeral director. Everything is now in Lucille's name – that way there will be no probate. It's all taken care of. The money is ours and we both want you to have it.'

Cathy looked across the room at her stepmother, who had sat quietly all the time, nursing her cup of coffee in her lap. Lucille looked her in the eye and said firmly, 'This is what we both want to do. Absolutely, this is what I want.'

'I know you'll always be there for Lucille. You'll look after her like a daughter.'

'Yes, of course I'll look after her.' Cathy smiled at Lucille, who beamed goodwill back at her.

'A couple of months ago, you and David saw a bigger house with a nice garden you liked. This money will help you to buy that house. I'd like Emma to go to a private school – one that will give her all the advantages.'

'I think Emma is quite happy at the comprehensive,' Cathy murmured.

'Well let her have the option of changing to a private school if she wants to,' said Renton. Then he raised a forefinger. 'Listen, there's one thing,' he warned. 'Don't tell Alex. It's none of his business and I don't want him to know.'

'I won't tell him then, Dad.'

Later, Cathy would question the wisdom of this decision.

Chapter 6

On Friday, Cathy found a letter from her father lying on the hall carpet when she came home from work. After supper, she brewed a cup of tea and settled in an armchair to read it.

Lyme Regis
26 September 1989
My dear Cathy,

I want you to know how much I appreciated your visit. You give us both so much, firstly sheer joy and pleasure, but so much of your time and effort too. To keep a house, home and family and also to go to a job is a wonderful effort and does you immense credit. But you still find time to support us!

If in any small way my gift can help you, then I will be satisfied. I was so pleased to have the opportunity, as any father would be. I just wish I'd had the chance over the years to do more.

Now dear, thank you for everything you have done for me and especially the love and kindness you have shown Lucille. When one considers what she has done for me, to pick up a very disillusioned man and to give love, trust and encouragement, despite her own physical challenges, she deserves love and all that word means.

Thank you for everything,
Your loving Dad
P.S. The fruit cake is beautiful! Lucille xx

In October, Cathy returned to Lyme Regis to help Lucille nurse her father in the last week of his life. It was Renton's wish to remain at home in the apartment he loved. Giving 24-hour care to a dying man proved to be exhausting, so a night nurse was employed.

On Sunday morning, the nurse gently woke Cathy to tell her that her father had died in the night. Cathy rushed into the bedroom. Her father looked as though he was sleeping. He lay on his side with his eyes closed. Cathy knelt at his bedside, her hands clasping his cold one. She felt her grief welling up inside. A huge lump formed in her throat. Her dad was gone. The father who had given her so much love and who, after the divorce, had driven for hours to Yorkshire just to take his children out for lunch. The one they had always stayed with in the school holidays, though it had meant having Granny Coleman look after them while he kept working in the hardware store. She could remember as if it was yesterday, all the board games they had played in the evenings when he got home and the fun they had had, just the three of them. She had a clear image of her father at the helm of his yacht, the Red Ensign flying as he stood there, shirt off, grinning in the sun. In his element.

'*Bon voyage*, Dad,' she whispered, and kissed him on the cheek.

It was time to phone Alex. He had planned to visit their father on Monday. He hadn't seen him for six weeks. Cathy assumed her brother would drive down immediately.

'When are you coming?' she asked.

'I don't think there's really much point in me coming now. I've got a busy week at work with 15 new recruits to train in firearms safety.'

'But I thought you'd help with the funeral arrangements.'

'Didn't Dad organise all that before he died?'

'Yes, he's done a lot, but there are still a lot of decisions to make and people to contact.'

'Well, I'm sure you and Lucille are quite capable of handling it all. The police will struggle to find a replacement for me here. I'd prefer to wait and come down for the funeral service.'

'Don't you want to say goodbye to him?' Cathy's voice caught as she spoke.

'I've seen a lot of death, Cathy. Dad's gone now. I just don't see the point.'

Cathy burst into tears and put the phone down.

The next day the doorbell rang. *Another delivery of flowers*, thought Cathy wearily, taking the bouquet of salmon pink roses and gypsophila from the delivery man. She read the attached card.

'Who are they from?' asked Lucille.

'Alex.'

Lucille read the card.

Sorry to upset you, little sister.
Alex

'How odd. Is he giving a eulogy at the funeral?'

'No, he said he'd prefer not to.'

Lucille shrugged. 'I've asked your father's old mate, Eric, from the yacht club. The Padre from his Regiment has agreed to take the service.'

'That sounds really good, Lucille.'

On the day of the funeral, it bucketed with rain. The train tracks were flooded, so the Padre was unable to travel down for the service. Cathy felt wrung out from all the crying, but calm, soothed by the beauty of the dark wooden interior of the Anglican Church, which had been decorated with large arrangements of yellow chrysanthemums, and the presence of David and Emma next to her. Afterwards, she warmly greeted her father's old friends and relatives. Renton had a strong faith and was always happy to help others; many shared memories of times he had given them support. It was a big funeral, despite the rain. Alex was stiff and formal with everyone, as was his habit. Sonia was smartly dressed in a navy suit and spiky court shoes. Cathy attempted to talk to her, but she appeared disinterested and vanished halfway through the reception. Cathy was holding an umbrella over her elderly aunt, escorting her out to the car park, when she noticed Sonia sitting quietly in the MG.

A month later, Cathy travelled down to Lyme Regis. The penthouse seemed oddly empty without her father, like a ship without a skipper. She noted that Lucille had lost a little weight, which wouldn't hurt her, but she seemed to be coping. They went through the funeral bills together.

'This is much higher than was quoted.' Lucille's eyes narrowed. 'I'm going to call that funeral director and ask him to explain himself.'

Cathy heard her stepmother on the phone.

'You're telling me that the bill is higher because my husband died on a Sunday?'

There was a pause while she listened to the reply.

'Well, if he'd known that he would have hung on for an extra day!'

Lucille put the phone down firmly.

Chapter 7

About six months after her father died, Cathy and David bought a spacious detached house with a beautiful liquid amber tree in one corner of the back garden and a bird bath encircled by ivy. The house was only a mile away from their old home, so Emma could walk to the same comprehensive, as she had not wanted to change schools.

A few months after the move, they were invited for lunch at Alex and Sonia's manor house on the outskirts of Godalming in Surrey. Emma hadn't been keen to come. Privately, she referred to Sonia as "the witch", but the thought of Sonia's menagerie of animals enticed her into the car. After driving for two hours, their blue Ford Escort turned into a narrow driveway lined with tall beech trees. At the end of the avenue, an 18th century brick manor house came into view.

'I see they've got company,' observed Cathy, nodding at the black Mercedes parked near the fountain. 'Sonia didn't tell me other people were coming.' She glanced down at her favourite blue sweatshirt and comfy skirt; judging by the gleaming Mercedes, she was underdressed.

Emma pushed on the brass doorbell next to the solid oak door. The tinkling of the bell was followed by loud barking. Alex opened the door, flanked by two excitable Dobermans.

'Sit, stay Rufus! Sit, Cesar!' he commanded. 'Hello, Cathy, David… come in.' He ruffled Emma's blonde hair. 'My, you have grown; you're almost as tall as your old uncle.'

Sonia glided across the marble floored entry in a floaty cream shirt and black pants. She frowned at the sight of Emma.

'I wasn't expecting you. I've only got six pork chops. You'd better come into the kitchen.'

They followed Sonia into the large kitchen with its smart chequerboard tiled floor. She reached into the butler's pantry for a packet of crisps.

'Here, Emma, catch!' She tossed her the crisps. 'You had better eat these in here. There's some coke in the fridge, help yourself.' With that she swept out of the room. Emma looked at her mother with raised eyebrows, her mouth an 'o' of indignation. Cathy shrugged her shoulders, shook her head, and followed her sister-in-law's lean figure to the living room.

Alex was handing gin and tonics around on a silver salver. He paused to introduce his sister to a new acquaintance, Tiffany, who was smartly dressed in a white shirt and navy blazer. Her husband, James, nodded at Cathy and then looked away. Tiffany deigned to make conversation. 'Do you ride at all?' she asked, smoothing her short red hair with a diamond encrusted hand.

'No, I've always been scared of horses.'

'What a shame.' Tiffany turned to Sonia. 'Darling, I was appalled to read that article in the newspaper about a fox being killed here by the hounds.'

'It was shocking,' replied Sonia. 'That poor fox! I often see foxes playing in the garden and I think that fox ran here looking for a place to hide. Well, the next thing the hounds were all over it, tearing it apart. I couldn't watch. I must say, the behaviour of the huntsmen was very rude and boorish.'

Tiffany made tut-tutting sounds.

'I looked up,' continued Sonia, 'and saw the Master of the Hunt climbing over my back fence. I thought he must be coming to apologise, but the next moment he was walking away swinging the brush! After a while, I thought I'd better go and check all was safe before I let out the cats and dogs. Well, I found the fox's head and entrails lying in the grass. It was horrid!'

'Are you against hunting, then?' enquired Tiffany.

'It's not the sport itself I'm against, but I do think they could show some respect for private property before they go making a mess ripping the wildlife apart on our lawn. I can't abide people just walking on to my property. The other day I caught a couple of nosey parkers with a Labrador strolling up our driveway. I gave them what for! Rufus had a good time growling and snarling at them.'

The lunch seemed to be an opportunity for Sonia to show off her new dinner service. But not her culinary skills, thought Cathy, chewing on a dry pork chop. The fruit tart that followed came from the village baker. The other guests departed soon after lunch. Emma slouched in from the kitchen, looking sulky.

'How about we all go for a walk?' suggested Alex. 'Rufus! Cesar! Heel!' The dogs followed them out to a stone terrace, with steps leading down to a large, spreading lawn, flanked by stately trees. Emma was delighted when a peacock strutted across the lawn, dragging its magnificent tail feathers behind it.

'I was worried one of the hounds might chase the peacocks, but they were only interested in the fox,' Sonia told David.

Emma picked up a stick. 'Can I play with Rufus, Uncle Alex?' Rufus was the friendlier of the two dogs.

'Sure. Rufus, at ease.' Rufus swerved away from Alex, running towards the trees. Emma loped after him. She caught up to him and waved the stick in his face. At first, Rufus shied away, but then, realising she was only playing, he chomped down on the stick. Emma pulled on her end and Rufus tugged hard, baring his sharp teeth. 'Drop, Rufus,' she said. The dog instantly dropped the stick and Emma threw it across the lawn for him to fetch.

'Cathy, come and see the pear trees in the walled garden,' suggested Alex. 'I've had them pruned by an arborist.'

Cathy followed her brother through an arched doorway in the brick wall. Pear trees grew around the perimeter of the enclosed garden. Cathy was glad of the chance to talk in private.

'So have you made any friends in the village?' she asked.

'Not really. Sonia's so high and mighty that none of the villagers want to have anything to do with her. Now she's got her name plastered all over *The Sun*, with a picture of the house, because the Hunt cornered a fox in the garden. That's one way to fall out with the local gentry. I wish she'd kept her mouth shut instead of blabbing to the papers.'

'Have you seen Lucille lately?' asked Cathy.

'No, the police work keeps me busy during the week, and there's always something to be done around here at the weekend. To be honest, last time they visited, before Dad died, it wasn't a success. Sonia saw a car she didn't recognise coming up the driveway and went out and shouted, 'Where the bloody hell do you think you're going? This is private property!' Then she saw Dad and Lucille sitting in the back seat – we had invited them up for coffee and Lucille's cousin, Tom, had driven them up with his daughter. I tell you, she's worse than the bloody dogs when it comes to guarding the place. Sonia really doesn't like Lucille.'

'I think the feeling's mutual,' commented Cathy. 'It's hard for Lucille though, now that Dad's gone – she misses him. She's struck up a friendship with an old man who lives in the same building, so at least she's not lonely.'

Sonia popped her head through the archway. 'Would you like to come and see my Shetland ponies? They're down by the woods.'

'Cathy, you go with Sonia. I'll see if David wants a game of chess,' said Alex.

Cathy knew David wouldn't want to play chess because Alex always had to win. 'Actually, David might want to see your guns.'

'That's an idea, in fact I've just bought a pair of Churchills,' said Alex. 'I'll go and find him.'

In the middle of the field, a hairy little chestnut pony rolled blissfully on its back, hooves pawing the air. Another black and white Shetland pony trotted straight to the fence to nibble a carrot from Emma's hand.

'Can I lead Freddie around the field, Aunty Sonia?'

'Yes, I'll put a halter lead on him. He needs some exercise because he's a lazy little pony and he's getting fat from all that lush green grass. Aren't you, Freddy?' Sonia rubbed his neck affectionately.

If only she was as nice to people as she is to animals, thought Cathy.

Cathy and Sonia watched Emma lead the Shetland pony around the field.

'It's not easy living with Alex, you know,' Sonia confided. 'He gets in these filthy tempers. Look!' She pulled up her shirt sleeve, revealing a nasty, greenish bruise on her upper arm. 'He punched me.'

'Why did he do that?'

'We were arguing. He told me to shut the fuck up! I wouldn't, so he punched me.'

'Really?' Cathy's eyes widened in shock as she looked up at her sister-in-law's angular face. Sonia gazed fixedly at the ponies. 'He's a real Jekyll and Hyde... I'm afraid of him when he gets angry. Living out here in the country, no one would hear me scream.' She flashed Cathy a look with her veiled green eyes, then shifted her attention back to the horses.

Cathy didn't know what to think. Her first allegiance was to her brother, but she could never condone violence. A grey cloud blotted out the sun momentarily.

'Have you thought about marriage counselling?'

'Alex isn't interested. He told me, when we got married, that he didn't like that kind of thing. You know, stiff upper lip and all that. I think he blames me for the lack of children, but it's him who falls asleep on the couch most nights after watching one of his violent movies or he just sits in front of the computer, playing chess, plotting his moves for hours.' Sonia's expression was desolate. 'There are six bedrooms in that house – we've got no hope of filling them.'

'I'm sorry to hear all this. I don't know what to say.' Cathy looked around hopefully for David, but the men were still back at the house. 'Emma, I think you'd better give the halter rope to Sonia now,' she called out to her daughter. 'Freddie's had a good walk. There's school tomorrow so we'd better be heading home soon.'

Chapter 8

Cathy hurriedly finished putting the mugs in the dishwasher, shook some powder into the dispenser, closed the door and pushed the "on" button.

'Are you ready?' asked David, walking into the kitchen with his black overcoat on, car keys in hand. They were driving to Lyme Regis to take Lucille and her companion, Bertie, out for lunch. It had been five years since Renton had died.

'I'll just say goodbye to Emma.'

Cathy looked in on her daughter, who was having a lie in, enjoying the deliciously lazy languor of youth. Emma looked up at her mother with sleepy blue eyes. 'Are you going now?'

'Yes, we're off. There's some leftover pumpkin soup in the fridge for your lunch. Make sure you get lots of study done.'

'I will. Say hi to Gran and Uncle Bertie for me.' Cathy dropped a kiss on her daughter's soft cheek.

It was a grey, wintery day so they chose a restaurant with a large open fire. David opened the glass door and stood aside as Lucille swept into the warmth. Bertie tottered after her, looking dapper with his little white moustache, trim white hair and red tartan bow tie. He was older than Lucille, and, like Renton before him, he clearly adored her.

'I think I'll have the lobster today.' Lucille chose the priciest dish on the menu. 'Now tell me, young man, where was it caught?' she asked chattily as the waiter wrote down her order.

'I'll have to ask the chef, madam,' he replied.

'I'll have the seafood mornay,' declared Bertie, who didn't have many teeth left.

Cathy chose ravioli, while David opted for chicken chasseur and ordered a bottle of chardonnay – Lucille's favourite.

'I saw a show about Salzburg on the telly last week. We had such a fun holiday in Austria, the four of us, didn't we?' began Lucille, taking a sip of wine.

'I remember taking the chairlift up in the Alps. The views were spectacular,' continued Bertie.

'You were no sooner up in the chairlift with me than you were missing Lucille and wanted to come down again,' David reminded him.

Cathy smiled. The pair had a close, platonic relationship and Bertie couldn't bear to let Lucille out of his sight.

'I remember how we almost missed the bus to the airport. I've never seen you move so fast with your sore feet, Lucille. You and Bertie practically leapt on the bus and left David and me miles behind lugging four big suitcases!'

'But David's got such strong arms,' said Lucille, raising her eyebrows coquettishly and inclining her head towards him. 'It's a pity not to use those muscles!' She gestured towards her plate. 'I'm struggling to finish this lobster; such a pity to waste it. You'll finish it off for me, won't you Luvvy?' Not waiting for an answer, Lucille forked the remains of her lobster on to his plate.

After dessert, Cathy paid the bill and they walked slowly back to the penthouse.

'I think the lobster wasn't as fresh as it might have been,' complained Lucille. 'I feel a bit queasy. How was your chicken, David?'

'My chicken was fine, I quite enjoyed the sauce.'

'I thought the meal was disappointing,' said Cathy. 'My ravioli tasted like they were fresh out of a tin.'

'But the company was excellent,' countered Bertie cheerfully. His taste buds had dulled long ago. As long as there was a salt cellar to hand, he was happy.

Back at the apartment, Lucille busied herself preparing a tray in the kitchen. Bertie nodded off in an armchair while David immersed himself in the Sunday paper.

Cathy walked into the kitchen just as the kettle whistled. She took a thick wad of notes in a small plastic zip lock bag out of her handbag.

'I've got some money here for you to help out with expenses.' She knew Lucille preferred cash – it left no trace in her bank account.

'Thank you, Luvvy, that will certainly come in handy.' Lucille switched off the kettle and took a green tea caddy off the top shelf of the pantry. She stowed the money inside, then put the caddy back. Cathy had done her best to look after her stepmother since her father had died. From the money gifted to her, she had put £30,000 towards the new house and invested £20,000 in a building society account. Interest on that account was calculated at 10–12 % per annum and she happily spent that money on taking Lucille on holidays, for outings and on maintenance of the apartment. The arrangement worked well. Cathy enjoyed spending the interest on her stepmother, who understood the arrangement and appreciated the extra cash and outings.

A year after Renton's death, Lucille instructed her solicitor to draw up a will leaving Cathy two-thirds of her estate and Alex one-third. She showed it to Cathy, who questioned the fairness of this arrangement, but Lucille reassured her.

'I want to give you two-thirds because you do so much for me. Plus you've got Emma to provide for. I hardly ever see Alex. I only get a phone call from him once in a blue moon.'

***

A couple of weeks after their dinner together, Cathy was chatting on the phone with Lucille.

'Guess what, I've scored a free meal at that restaurant we went to,' boasted her stepmother.

'How did you manage that?' asked Cathy.

'I complained that my daughter had come all the way down to Lyme Regis for a special lunch on her day off, and I was most embarrassed because the meal hadn't been up to scratch. Well, the manager invited us back on Saturday for a meal on the house!'

After Cathy had put the phone down, she thought about the conversation with her stepmother. It didn't seem fair that she had paid for the meal, yet Lucille and Bertie were to dine again for free. She dialled the restaurant and spoke to the manager.

The following Saturday, Lucille and Bertie were sitting at a table by the window, studying their menus, when Cathy and David walked in. Lucille looked up from her menu. 'What on earth are you two doing here?'

'I thought we'd join you. I rang the manager and he invited us to come along too, since I'd paid,' explained Cathy, breezily. The waiter pulled her chair out and she sat down.

They all agreed that the food was much improved on their second visit. Cathy ordered a couple of bottles of wine.

'Cheers, drinks on the house!' Lucille raised her glass.

Cathy clinked glasses with her stepmother, 'I think we should pay for the drinks at least. Don't you?'

Lucille agreed. But when it was time to go she sailed out with Bertie in her wake, leaving David at the till.

Chapter 9

Cathy's boss, Andrew, called her into his large airy office on Friday morning.

'Sit down, Cathy. I've got some good news for you. Your application for early retirement has been approved. It's taken a bit of work, but I've got it all signed off by head office, so you can finish in a month's time. Congratulations!' Andrew smiled warmly at his personal assistant.

'That's wonderful news, I'm thrilled! Thank you so much, Andrew. I'm off to Lyme Regis for the weekend, so we'll be able to celebrate.'

'You deserve it, Cathy, after 24 years of service.' Andrew stood up and picked up a bouquet of flowers from a side table. 'Happy birthday for tomorrow! 29 is it?'

'Fifty-one, actually!' Cathy laughed, taking the fragrant bouquet of yellow roses and white stock.

Barclays was centralising many of its services. This, coupled with the increased use of computers, meant staff numbers were being slashed in all branches. Andrew would have to type his own letters in the future. *But you can't halt progress*, thought Cathy. Having reached the bank's pensionable age of 50, Cathy could opt for an early retirement package. Her payout would be a bonus rather like winning a prize in Lotto.

Cathy arrived home fizzing with excitement. David was already packing the Escort.

'Great news! My retirement application has been approved!'

David dropped the sports bag he was carrying and gave her a hug. 'That's wonderful.'

'New Zealand, here we come!' shouted Cathy.

On the drive to Lyme Regis, they talked excitedly about their plans to travel to New Zealand and Australia for a three-month holiday. They would visit Emma, who was now grown-up and working in Sydney. So immersed were they in their future plans that David nearly missed the turn off on the A303, and was forced to circuit the roundabout a second time.

'Perhaps we should ask Lucille and Bertie if they'd like to come with us to New Zealand,' suggested Cathy.

'I don't know about that,' hesitated David. 'It would be hard work for us – they can't walk long distances for a start and Lucille does prattle on.'

***

Lucille pulled a bottle of champagne out of the fridge. She loved an excuse to break open the bubbly.

'Well done, Luvvy,' she said. 'What wonderful news on your birthday. Cheers!'

Lucille clinked her champagne flute against Cathy's. 'Your father would have been so chuffed. He always wanted you to be able to stop work and now finally that day has come. And you've done it all under your own steam.'

'I'm looking forward to stopping work. There are so many projects I want to get on with,' gushed Cathy, her blue eyes shining with enthusiasm.

'Well, I've got another one for you, Luvvy.' Lucille put her glass down on the onyx coffee table and disappeared into her bedroom. She returned with a brown shoe box. Cathy took off the lid. Inside lay a thick sheaf of papers, covered in her father's neat, slanted handwriting and tied in a bundle with a black shoelace.

'Dad's autobiography. I'll have time to type that up now and get it bound.'

Cathy sat quietly for a while, thinking about her father. She looked around the room. The apartment was unchanged since his death ten years ago. Still the same Persian carpets and antiques Lucille had collected over the years. On a shelf, stood a small photograph of her father and Lucille, next to a large photo of Alex in his SAS uniform. Lucille liked to brag to her bridge friends that her handsome stepson was a former SAS soldier. She encouraged the coterie of old ladies with false teeth and pearl necklaces to "ooh" and "aah" over his photo. An oak display cabinet held special family mementos and war medals. Cathy's eyes rested on Grandpa Coleman's gold fob watch and Albert chain. The five-pointed star medallion was missing from the end of the heavy chain because Lucille had detached it to wear as a pendant around her neck. She had an eye for jewellery.

***

The next morning, Cathy went down to fetch Lucille's newspaper. As she crossed the lobby, one of Lucille's neighbours, Mrs Haycock, recognised her and they stopped to chat. After a minute or two, Mrs Haycock lowered her voice and leaned towards Cathy.

'I think you should tell your stepmother not to forget her stick when she goes out walking in the mornings.' She raised her eyebrows knowingly. 'I've seen her striding out along Marine Parade and it's not a good look for someone on a disability benefit. Just tell her to be careful, you never know who's watching.' After giving this advice, Mrs Haycock nodded her head sagely.

'I'll tell her, Mrs Haycock. Now, you take care, won't you.'

***

Cathy carried her tea and toast to the kitchen table, where Lucille was reading the newspaper. Suddenly, Lucille looked up, and said, 'Oh dear, that's a real worry.'

'What is?' Cathy asked.

'This poor old pensioner is going to prison. Apparently he wasn't eligible for income support and he's been claiming it for ten years. Someone must have dobbed him in.' Lucille frowned.

'You look worried, Lucille. That reminds me, do be careful when you go out for walks – you should always take your walking stick with you. Mrs Haycock just told me she's seen you on Marine Parade without it, lately.'

'That nosey parker. It bothers me that some of these "holier than thou" types go meddling in other people's affairs,' Lucille grumbled. 'I wonder if she knows I'm on income support, too.'

Cathy looked at her stepmother in surprise. For a minute or two, she digested this revelation silently.

'But Lucille, are you sure you need to have income support when you and Dad could afford to give me £50,000? That doesn't seem right. You're already on a disability pension because of your feet, plus you get the old age pension.'

Lucille stood up and carried her breakfast dishes to the counter.

'Well, my circumstances have changed. A lady from Social Services visited after your father died to see how I was managing on my own.' Lucille faced her stepdaughter, dishcloth balled in her hand. 'I showed her my bank statements and she said my savings were below the threshold so I qualified for income support.'

'Did you show her the statement for the Jersey account?'

'Of course not, I've closed that account.' Lucille turned back to the sink, huffily.

'Then I don't know what you're worried about. You've given me the money from the Jersey account and they don't know about that money. You've shown them your bank statements and they say you qualify. But if you're worried about it, then why don't you come off income support? Tell them you don't need it any more. After all, you're getting top-ups from me.'

Lucille clattered about, clearing up the breakfast dishes. Cathy quietly finished her tea. *Income support indeed,* she thought no wonder her stepmother's conscience was pricking her! Lucille wiped down the bench and sulkily announced, 'Well, I'm going to get dressed to go out.'

Lucille's mood lightened when Bertie joined them for a stroll along Marine Parade to Ocean View restaurant. On the way, they passed a picturesque row of whitewashed houses with turquoise front doors facing the sea. The tide was in and there wasn't a cloud in the sky.

Drinking champagne in the middle of the day wasn't part of Cathy's usual Saturday routine, but it was her birthday. 'I'm so looking forward to our trip to New Zealand. David wants to take me trout fishing on Lake Taupo. I think we should have a night at Huka Lodge to celebrate our retirement. How about it, David?'

'It won't be much of a retirement if you start throwing the money around like that – we'll soon be broke,' grumbled David.

Lucille took Bertie's arthritic hand in her warm plump ones. 'Bertie wants to take me on a cruise around the Scottish Isles for my 80th birthday. What do you think of that?'

'How lovely!' Cathy smiled warmly at the pair. 'It's a beautiful part of the world.'

On the way home, Bertie walked ahead with David, while Cathy accompanied Lucille, who insisted on whacking her Spanish walking stick onto the pavement with great gusto at each step. At the end of the parade, Lucille slowed her pace and leaned towards her stepdaughter to share a confidence.

'I'm a bit worried about this cruise around the Scottish Isles.'

'Oh, why is that?'

'Bertie said he'd pay for me. Well, he was showing me the brochure and he pointed out that double cabins would be half the price. It's a very expensive cruise and I'm afraid he wants to save some money. But I really don't want to share with him. I need my privacy. Besides, he's bound to snore and keep me awake.'

Cathy knew from previous trips that Lucille and Bertie always had separate rooms; an arrangement that did not seem to suit Bertie quite as well as it suited Lucille.

'Well, would you like me to talk to him in private about the accommodation?'

'Would you? It would be good if you could just have a quiet word on the side with him. I don't want to hurt his feelings. He can be so touchy.'

'Leave it to me.' Cathy patted the older woman's arm, reassuringly.

Back at the penthouse, Lucille busied herself in the kitchen making afternoon tea. Cathy noticed that Bertie was alone on the balcony, so she sat down in the wicker chair next to him.

'It's very generous of you to take Lucille on a cruise for her eightieth birthday,' began Cathy, 'I'm sure you two will have a wonderful time.'

'I was stationed on the Isle of Skye during the war.' Bertie's blue eyes took on a faraway look. 'I've always wanted to go back. It's a rugged, wild place. The locals still spoke Gaelic in those days. They were a dour bunch, didn't like the English being there. They talked about the rise of Bonnie Prince Charlie as if it were yesterday.'

'Well, hopefully they're a bit friendlier these days. Lucille was telling me on the way home that she's looking forward to going there, but she's a little bit anxious.'

'Why is that?'

'She's worried about sharing a cabin on the cruise. She likes her privacy.'

Bertie digested this, then replied slowly, 'I know her thoughts. I'd never do that to her. Separate cabins are just fine with me.'

Cathy changed the subject to Bertie's family and they chatted for a while, before she got up and went to help Lucille, who was buttering scones in the kitchen. She whispered in her ear. Lucille put down the knife and clasped her in a great bear hug; Cathy breathed in her stepmother's familiar powdery scent.

'Thank you, Luvvy. I'm so relieved. With my own cabin, everything will be perfect. Except for that drizzly Sottish weather. But we can't do anything about that now, can we, Luvvy?'

That evening, after she had got home and unpacked, Cathy phoned her stepmother. Lucille was a talker, but Cathy knew she'd be off the phone quickly this time because *Coronation Street* was due to start in five minutes' time.

'Lucille, I just phoned to thank you for a wonderful weekend.'

'Is that so?' said Lucille coldly.

For a moment, Cathy was taken aback by her tone before she recovered and said, 'David and I enjoyed ourselves so much.'

'Well, I'm glad you two had a good time – at least *someone* did,' said Lucille, waspishly.

'Lucille, is there something wrong? Has something upset you?'

'Yes, as a matter of fact, it has.' Lucille's voice rose angrily.

'What's wrong?'

'I don't know how you had the cheek to discuss my sleeping arrangements with Bertie!' shouted Lucille.

There was silence. Stung by the unexpected attack, Cathy struggled to comprehend the cause of her stepmother's anger.

'But Lucille, you *asked* me to talk to Bertie about booking separate cabins.'

'I did not ask you to go poking your nose into my private affairs. Really, you need to show more sensitivity.'

There was an uncomfortable silence.

'Lucille, please think about what you've just said,' replied Cathy quietly, 'Are you being fair? I know you want to go and watch *Coronation Street*, so this isn't the time, but have a think about our conversation and call me back when you've calmed down.' She put the phone down a little too sharply.

Feeling dazed, she wandered out to the backyard, where, she found David watering the beans. 'I've just had the most horrible conversation with Lucille. She accused me of interfering and speaking out of turn to Bertie about booking the cabins for their cruise. She was absolutely furious with me. I can't understand it. She *asked* me to talk to him.'

David aimed the hose at the tomato plants and ruminated on the situation. He wasn't one to speak hastily. Cathy swatted at gnats while he moved on to the lettuces, then the wilting spinach. Finally, he spoke. 'Maybe Bertie was annoyed with her for talking to you about it, so now she's decided to blame you.'

'That would be typical,' agreed Cathy. 'I'll give her a call tomorrow if I don't hear from her tonight.'

'I wouldn't. She's in the wrong, so let her call you to apologise. Just let her stew. You wait, she'll call. You've looked after her for ten years and she'll come crawling back for another hand-out before long.'

It went against Cathy's instincts not to call Lucille. She hated quarrels. For years, she'd played the peacemaker in the family. However, in this instance she decided that David was right. This time she would wait for Lucille to come to her senses and apologise. But would she?

***

A couple of weeks later the phone rang at the manor house. Alex answered it in his study, a gloomy den with wood-panelled lower walls and the upper half painted dark green.

'Lucille, I'm really astounded by this news,' he said after a while. 'I'll get in touch with Cathy and call you back later. Bye for now.'

He walked into the lounge. Sonia was stretched out on the buttoned leather couch watching *Antiques Roadshow*. Alex stood tensely, waiting for her attention. After a minute or two, she looked over at him.

'Who was it?'

'Lucille. She wants me to pay the glazier for repairing her balcony windows. Remember how I paid the glazier's bill just after Dad died?'

Sonia muted the TV. She always listened closely if money was involved.

'Well, she reckons more work needed to be done,' Alex went on. He narrowed his eyes. 'She wants me to cough up another £2,500. I asked her if she was short of money, and she said yes, because she'd lent Cathy £50,000. She says Cathy refuses to repay her.'

'Really?' Sonia sat up. 'You mean she expects us to pay to have her windows fixed because Cathy has all her savings?'

'That's what it looks like. Lucille said the loan was made to Cathy just before Dad died, but now Cathy wants to keep the money.'

'Well, I don't think we should give her any money. It's up to Cathy to repay the loan. And she can jolly well pay for the glazier too!'

'That's what I'm thinking. And I'm angry I paid that first bill when Cathy's been sitting on £50,000 all this time. I'm going to call her right now.'

'No, hang on a minute,' said Sonia, 'let's not rush into anything…' She thought for a moment. 'You know,' she said eventually, 'this could be the right moment to start getting yourself into a position to manage Lucille's finances. After all, the old girl is getting pretty long in the tooth.'

'Good thinking.' Alex sat quietly. His face took on a dark, scheming look. Sonia might be potty about animals, but she was smart when it came to money. Their combined business acumen was reflected in their financial portfolio, which showed they were slowly and surely amassing a fortune. He thought with satisfaction of his gun collection and the rows of wine bottles in his cellar, sourced from all the best wine growing regions in the world.

Half an hour later, Sonia heard him shouting down the telephone in the study. She muted the television to listen.

'What do you mean, Dad gave you £50,000? He never told me! Why would he do that?' There was a moment's silence while he listened to Cathy's reply. Then his voice rang out again. 'That money by rights belongs to Lucille and you need to give it back NOW!' he shouted. 'Why should I pay her bloody repair bills when you're sitting on 50,000 quid?' There was another pause, before he erupted, 'If you won't pay back the money, then on your fucking head be it!' Alex slammed the phone down. He was shaking with anger.

That night Cathy woke up in terror, feeling as if something cold and metallic was pushing against her temples. She lay frozen with fear, unable to move a limb. Was it her brother holding a pistol to her head?

No, only a nightmare, she realised. The dark shadows in the room began to fade. It was almost dawn. She knew she wouldn't get back to sleep, so she shrugged on a dressing gown and slipped downstairs. When she pulled back the heavy green curtain that hung across the French doors the garden was dewy, the sky tinted apricot. Feeling calmer, she put the kettle on.

Her brother was being totally unreasonable. How could he turn on her like this when for years she had been his loyal ally? When he had been living in Oman, she and David had looked after his rental properties, inspecting them regularly and making sure small repairs were carried out and the gardens maintained. He'd even bought a property in Glastonbury just so they could keep an eye on it. And Lucille's lack of gratitude after all she had done for her was completely bizarre; surely her stepmother would come to her senses and call her soon. 'I just have to be patient,' Cathy murmured. She unlatched the French doors to let in Leroy, her Persian-cross. Leroy rubbed his thick charcoal fur against her legs, meowing for breakfast.

Chapter 10

Alex stood looking over the back fence. Evening was approaching and a broad streak of mist blanketed the fields. Out of the mist, a big white barn owl swooped silently in search of moles. Hands in pockets, Alex watched it, considering his plans for the next day. He knew from his experiences with the SAS that planning and impeccable timing were essential for a successful campaign. Tomorrow he would pounce and take control of his stepmother's finances. The owl glided away into the dusk as Alex turned his back on the fields and walked towards the house to phone Lucille.

The next morning dawned cloudy and bitterly cold. But that didn't bother Alex, who preferred cold weather to the heat of the Middle East. As he reached for his overcoat, Rufus and Cesar joined him at the front door, whining and eagerly wagging their stumps. Alex took their leads off the hook, slipped a satchel over his shoulder and opened the front door. His sturdy boots crunched on the gravel of the driveway as the dogs ran ahead. At the end of the lane, he turned on to a busier road that led to the village. 'Sit!' he commanded, attaching the dogs' leads. Alex walked a few paces along the road, then shouted, 'Rufus! Cesar! Heel!' He yanked hard on their choker chains. A lorry rumbled past. Startled by the noise, Rufus surged forward. Alex brought the baton down hard on his rump. Rufus yelped. 'Heel!' growled Alex. Rufus dropped back to walk meekly by his owner's side.

In the centre of Godalming, they passed the Pepperpot, a quaint white stucco building with a little turret. Alex turned the corner and continued down High Street, stopping outside a stationery shop. He tied the dogs to the drainpipe before entering.

'Good morning,' he greeted the young woman, with nose and eyebrow studs, at the counter. 'Do you have any forms for making out a will and for arranging power of attorney?'

The shop assistant went out the back and returned a short while later holding some papers.

'Here they are. Now this is the form for making your own will,' she explained. 'Here's a form for general power of attorney. Do you want them both?'

'Yes, please.'

Alex paid and left the stationer's, congratulating himself on avoiding costly solicitors' fees. He whistled as he walked briskly home. In a few hours, he and Sonia would be at Lyme Regis. Soon everything would be sorted. The brown satchel carrying the forms bumped against his thigh. He ran through his plans for the day: five minutes, to change his clothes, ten minutes to pack the car, five minutes to put the dogs in the walled garden with bones; depart for Lyme Regis with Sonia at 10:15 am, allow two hours 40 minutes for the drive, including a ten-minute stop for coffee.

Lucille appeared flustered when Alex and Sonia arrived at the penthouse. She was wearing a long navy skirt and a billowy, rose coloured blouse, with matching lipstick and nail polish. Alex forced himself to return her hug, though he usually held back from physical shows of affection. Lucille didn't attempt to embrace Sonia, who made no effort herself either. She stood back stiffly, wearing a pencil skirt and heels.

'Cheerio, Luvvy! How are the little highlander ponies?'

'The *Shetland* ponies are fine, thank you, Lucille. How are you?'

'Me feet have been a bit sore of late. It was those army issue boots during the war – they were too tight. Otherwise I'm fine and dandy. I'll just ring Bertie. I thought he might have been here by now. I'll give him the hurry up.' Lucille picked up the receiver and dialled the number. She listened for a while. 'No answer. Maybe I've got the number wrong… now where did I put my address book?'

Alex and Sonia exchanged annoyed glances. They hadn't expected Bertie, and now Lucille was making them wait while she searched the drawers of the sideboard for her address book. Alex couldn't abide tardiness. Five minutes later the doorbell rang and there was Bertie, looking festive with a red, white and blue striped cravat knotted at his throat.

'Bonjour! Did you know it was Bastille Day?' he chirped.

Lucille gave him a relieved smile. 'Bonjour, Bertie! We must kiss twice, on each cheek, like the French do!' The little man was soon swamped by Lucille's ample figure. 'I'd have worn red, white and blue too if only I'd known.'

'We are going out for lunch, not a fancy dress ball,' remarked Alex, drily.

At their table in the boutique hotel, Lucille looked around, appreciating the atmosphere of subdued luxury; the white tablecloths, heavy gilt mirrors and vases of fresh lilies.

'This is very nice, Alex. You're really spoiling us,' she remarked.

'Very posh,' added Bertie, breaking off a piece of bread roll.

Alex looked up from the wine menu. 'I'm glad you like it.' His glance fell on the five-pointed star medallion hanging on a long gold chain around Lucille's neck. He recalled his fury when he had first recognised the star and realised that Lucille had detached it from Grandpa Coleman's fob chain to wear around her neck. Really, the woman had no sense of propriety. It was outrageous. She was like a magpie picking through the family heirlooms, pocketing bits and pieces. Once, he had tried to discuss her behaviour with his father, but he had seemed unconcerned.

Lucille looked up from her menu and he quickly averted his gaze. As usual, she had a question for the waiter. 'Now young man, can you tell me what the fish of the day is?'

'Mackerel, madam.'

'Do you go down to the Cobb when the fishing boats come in?' asked Lucille.

'No, madam, I'm usually serving breakfast in the morning.'

'Well, you should go down some time on your day off. I love going down and seeing what they've caught.' As Lucille prattled on, Sonia rolled her eyes and Alex gritted his teeth. He hated the way Lucille chatted with the waiting staff. He considered it inappropriate – let them get on with the job.

'The Lyme Bay scallops,' he said briefly when it was his turn to order. It was time to get down to business. He cleared his throat, 'Lucille, you seemed rather upset with my sister when we spoke on the phone last week.'

'Yes, we've had a falling out. You see, before your dad died, we asked Cathy to put £50,000 in a term deposit for me. It seemed a good idea at the time because then the money wouldn't be sitting in my account if Social Services came sniffing about. She was to pay me the interest and keep it safe for me. But now she's changed her tune. She says the money is hers and she refuses to give it back. I'm having trouble paying my bills, which is a terrible thing for a woman of my age.' Lucille's voice trembled. 'I don't know how I'll find the money to pay the glazier.'

'You've been very worried, haven't you, dear?' said Bertie, patting her hand.

'So I thought if you could speak to Cathy, she might see sense, and I might have a chance of getting my money back,' finished Lucille.

'Well, I've tried speaking to her but she insists that the money is hers. In the meantime, you've got a bill for the windows that needs paying. I would pay it for you, just like I paid the last one, but under the circumstances I really don't think that would be wise.'

'Definitely not,' interjected Sonia. 'Cathy has Lucille's money – it's up to her to pay that bill.'

'My suggestion,' said Alex, topping up Lucille's wine glass with chardonnay, 'is that we go back to the penthouse after lunch and draft a strongly worded letter for you to sign, demanding that the money be returned. I could have the sum invested on your behalf by my financial advisers, and that would certainly be in your best interests. I can show you the returns I'm getting on my portfolio – much better than having it sitting in an account. Have you still got the typewriter?'

'Yes, it's in the cupboard in the spare bedroom. I hung on to it because I was hoping Cathy would come down one weekend and type up your dad's memoirs on it.'

'Good, Sonia can type up the letter.'

Alex looked around the table authoritatively. Lucille dabbed her mouth nervously with her napkin. Bertie looked down at his shellfish soup, while Sonia looked smug. They ate in silence for a few minutes. Lucille was the first to speak,

'These scalloped potatoes are delicious, but I'm having trouble finishing them. You'll help me, won't you, Alex?' She proceeded to scrape the leftover potatoes onto Alex's empty plate.

'Please, Lucille, don't…' Alex tried to stop her, but Lucille could not be dissuaded. He frowned – it was yet another of his stepmother's annoying habits. The war was long over; there was really no need to eat each other's scraps.

'A big man like you needs to eat up. C'mon, don't waste it,' chided Lucille. As Alex groaned inwardly, Sonia smirked at him across the table.

He decided to broach another touchy subject. 'Lucille, it's been ten years since my father died. Do you think it might be time to take a look at your will, see if it needs updating?'

'Actually, I went to the solicitor's a few months ago to change a few things. My friend, Jean, doesn't come to see me anymore so I don't see why she should get my Minton dinner service. But I would still like to leave my engagement and wedding rings to my goddaughters.' Lucille took a sip of her chardonnay before continuing. 'The way things stand at the moment, Cathy is to inherit two-thirds of my estate, and you get one-third.'

Alex could hardly believe his ears. He was glad that his SAS training allowed him to maintain a poker face. Not only had Cathy received £50,000, but she was also the major beneficiary of the will! Smothering his outrage, he drew himself to attention; that always calmed him, and forced himself to focus on the rest of what Lucille was saying.

'I worked it out that way because Cathy had Emma to provide for. Emma has been like a granddaughter to me, but now she's grown up and lives on the other side of the world, and I don't know if I'll be seeing much of Cathy either. I think I'd better talk to my solicitor about it.'

Alex let out his breath slowly. All was not lost, he thought. In fact, the battle had only just begun.

'No need for that, Lucille, There's no need to waste money on a solicitor. I had a feeling you might like to change a few things, so I took the liberty of bringing a pro forma will down that I picked up at the stationer's this morning. All we have to do is fill it in.'

'It's a good idea to revise your will as circumstances change,' advised Sonia, eyeing Lucille as a cat might eye an ageing thrush hopping about the garden.

'It's definitely time for you to make a new will,' Alex said firmly. 'I'm afraid my sister can't be trusted. I don't expect her to come back from New Zealand.'

'Really?' Lucille's eyes widened in surprise. 'I thought it was just a trip.'

'Well, they're looking at emigrating. And knowing what I know now, I'd say it's for the best. But I'm prepared to look after you, Lucille. My father would have wanted that. I'll pay any maintenance bills for the apartment and give you spending money.'

Lucille's face brightened.

'But Lucille,' Alex went on, 'if I'm to put pressure on Cathy to give you back your money, I need your authority to do it.' Alex paused, looking intently at his stepmother. 'You really need to give me power of attorney if I'm to act on your behalf.'

Lucille gulped down some wine. She twiddled with her napkin, thinking about what Alex had said. Bertie looked uncomfortably from Alex to Lucille. He cleared his throat as if he was going to say something, then stopped.

'We can't really help you unless Alex has your authority to do so,' said Sonia softly.

Lucille nodded her head slowly. 'All right then, if you think it's necessary.'

***

Back at the apartment, Lucille set the electric typewriter on a mat on the cherry wood dining room table. The oval table had been the focus of many a birthday party celebrated in style with her favourite platters from the caterer – whole smoked salmon, scallops cooked in wine and cream, lobster, salads, and vol au vents filled with mushroom and bacon, to name a few. She considered Moët & Chandon an essential lubricant for partygoers. Lucille would preside over the table wearing a new outfit and the star medallion necklace, surrounded by her bridge friends. But today she watched soberly while Alex drafted a letter to Cathy on her behalf, demanding that the £50,000 be

63

returned forthwith. Sonia speedily typed it up. Lucille felt sad that it had come to this, but hoped that Alex could use his knowledge of the law, gleaned from police work, to persuade Cathy to return the money.

When it was ready, Alex laid the letter in front of her, alongside the forms for general power of attorney and the will. 'I'm the eldest and I'll be taking care of you from now on,' he said matter-of-factly. 'So I imagine that you'll want to make me the sole beneficiary of your will.'

'Well, I'm not sure about that.' Lucille looked startled. 'I haven't thought about it like that.' As Alex leaned on the table and fixed her with an unblinking stare, she saw the darkness in his eyes and averted her gaze.

'And there's something else you should consider,' Alex went on. 'Cathy told me you've been claiming income support... Why have you been claiming income support if you say the £50,000 in Cathy's name is yours? You do realise you could be had up in court for benefit fraud? It happens all the time... one phone call is all it takes. You know the government is cracking down on benefit fraudsters. I'm in the police – I see it all the time and believe me, you don't want them sniffing around. If they catch you, they'll whack on the cuffs and knock up a "For Sale" sign as quick as a wink. How else are you going to repay the government?' He let Lucille stew on this for a minute or two. On the sofa, Sonia studiously read a magazine. Bertie was hidden behind a newspaper.

Alex passed Lucille his black fountain pen. 'Where it says "I give and bequeath", you need to write: "All my real property to Alex Coleman, my stepson". Alex repeated the words slowly as Lucille wrote them down in block capitals.

'Bertie, is there a neighbour you could call to come and witness the documents being signed? It won't take a minute.'

Bertie put down the newspaper he was reading. 'Sorry, were you talking to me?'

'Yes, is there a neighbour who could pop up to witness this document being signed?'

'Well, I guess I could call my friend, Harold. I don't think he's got golf today.'

'Right then,' said Alex cheerfully, 'let's do it.' He passed Bertie the phone.

Chapter 11

Cathy came home to find two letters propped against the green vase of white silk lilies on the hall table. She immediately recognised Lucille's distinctive, curly scrawl on the first envelope; the second envelope was addressed in black ink in Alex's slanting, narrow hand.

Here comes trouble, she thought, kicking off her court shoes and dumping her oversized handbag on the armchair. She tore open the first envelope and unfolded the typed sheet of foolscap. A quick scan of the contents revealed that Lucille had signed a typed letter requesting that Cathy return the £50,000 which she held in "safekeeping" for Lucille.

'Not bloody likely,' muttered Cathy.

She opened the second envelope and read the typed letter signed by Alex:

I wish to inform you that our stepmother, Lucille Coleman, has requested that I take over the management of her financial affairs and I now have power of attorney. I request that you abide by her wishes and return the sum of £50,000 owing to her, currently in your possession. Lucille requests that you forward the sum forthwith to my financial advisers to be invested for her. The account details are below. This is a matter of some urgency as Lucille finds herself short of funds and is unable to pay maintenance bills for her apartment.

Cathy felt her chest tighten. David was watching the news in the lounge.

'Can you mute that for a minute? Take a look at this.' Cathy thrust the letters into his hands, then walked into the kitchen, pulled a bottle of wine out of the fridge and filled two glasses. 'This is madness. Those two are ganging up on me,' she said, handing David a glass. 'I think it would be best if we all got together and discussed things properly. It's getting out of hand.'

'Yes, it definitely needs to be thrashed out in the open,' David agreed when he had finished reading. 'Who knows what's being said in private.'

'I'll call Alex and Lucille, tell them I've received their letters, and say I'd like to discuss the whole thing face to face.' Cathy looked down, swilling the wine in her glass. 'If only I had a crystal ball. It's just so hard to know what to do.'

'Well, I predict that this will drive a wedge between you and your brother,' concluded David. He flicked the volume of the TV back up.

***

The meeting at the penthouse started amicably enough.

'I'd like to talk about relationships and what's gone wrong,' began Cathy. 'I'd like us all to be fair and honest in our dealings with each other and keep an open mind.'

'Honest! I like that!' snorted Alex, sarcastically.

Cathy ignored him and continued. 'Lucille, you were with me when Dad gave me a cheque for £50,000. You heard him explain how he regretted that he hadn't been able to help me in the past and how he now wished to do so.'

'Have you got anything in writing stating Dad's wishes?' interrupted Alex.

'No, but Lucille was there; you remember, don't you? We had coffee with him in the bedroom that day. Remember, Lucille, it was your and Dad's idea to give me the money,' Cathy looked directly at her stepmother as she spoke, but Lucille only cast her eyes down and fingered the star emblem on her necklace.

'It was ten years ago, how am I supposed to remember all the details?' she said, with a flustered glance at Alex. 'Heaven forbid! I can't even remember where I played bridge last week. But I do know this, I'd like my money back.'

'But surely you read your bank statements, Lucille,' Cathy reminded her. 'What did you think...' Cathy was rudely interrupted.

'You've heard Lucille,' growled Alex. 'She wants her money back, NOW!' He banged his fist on the dining room table, then stood up abruptly and strode to the window, gazing out over the bay. Though thickened with age, his body was still taut and powerful. He turned back to the gathering, his tone authoritative. 'My financial advisers will invest that money for Lucille. I'm quite sure this arrangement will be in her best interests.' Alex softened his voice and fixed his dark eyes on Cathy. 'What I need you to do now, Cathy, is get out your cheque book. We need to settle this matter.'

'With all the best will in the world, Alex, I can't write a cheque for tens of thousands of pounds. I've put some of that money into our property and the rest is invested. I don't have a large sum like that just sitting about in my account.'

'Then we'll have to come to some other arrangement for payment,' Alex said curtly.

Lucille piped up, 'Look, I really need £10,000 pounds straight away. I've borrowed money from Bertie and he wants me to repay him.'

Cathy quietly doubted the truth of this story. She knew that Bertie was wealthy, generous and besotted with Lucille. Cathy had always given Lucille any funds she required and she was prepared to continue doing so. She could feel herself getting riled by Lucille's lies, but she forced herself to speak calmly.

'Lucille, it seems strange that you're suddenly penniless and in debt. You certainly don't act like someone on the breadline. You live in a beautiful apartment, you wear lovely clothes, you throw lavish parties and go on holiday each year. I know you've got your old age pension, plus a disability pension and income support... that must all add up.' Cathy stared at her stepmother, her blue eyes candid.

Lucille looked down, fiddling with a hanky in her lap. It was David who broke the silence, speaking for the first time. 'Perhaps since there's such a big difference of opinion here, we should try to reach an agreement we can all live with.'

'Yes, we have to get this settled once and for all,' agreed Cathy. 'Let's talk figures and reach a settlement. Alex, why don't you make some calculations and work out how much per year Lucille needs to live on? We're going away for a few months to Australia and New Zealand, but when we get back in April we can finalise the settlement. Lucille, I'll write you out a cheque now for £5,000 – that will tide you over.'

'Thank you. I'd like to go to my cousin's wedding in Melbourne.'

Cathy noted her stepmother's story had changed yet again, but chose not to comment. She pulled her cheque book out of her handbag. 'Alex, how about I write out a cheque to repay you for the glazier's bill? How much was it?'

His reply was prompt. 'Three thousand, five hundred and forty-four pounds and sixteen pence.'

Cathy did a double-take, but proceeded to write out the cheque. She handed it over to her brother, glancing at the white face of the French clock – discussions had gone around in circles for almost two hours. Her stomach rumbled. Lucille had offered them only tea and plain biscuits, which was no doubt a show of austerity.

Alex closed his notebook, then slipped out of the room to turn off the tape recorder in the pocket of his navy blazer. Cathy watched him leave. He was acting like he was in the MI5. Next he'd be hauling her into some back room at the station for further interrogation.

***

A few days later, Cathy held the home phone tentatively to her ear. It was Alex. His tone was menacing.

'I think you can forget about your little trip to New Zealand. It won't be happening. I don't see why you should go gallivanting around the world, leaving a fat unpaid debt behind you. There's a court injunction against you and your bank accounts will be frozen. So if you don't want to be stopped at passport control, you'd better pay up.'

'That's just not possible, Alex. I've done nothing wrong!' Cathy said, incredulous. 'Look, let's not let this whole thing snowball. We'll get together and talk about it again when I'm back from New Zealand. Goodbye.' She hung up quickly.

A week later, Cathy popped into the bank to see her old work mates. She had been chatting with Tony for a few minutes when he surprised her by asking, 'Does your brother Alex work for Surrey Police?'

Cathy nodded, her heart jumping. 'Why do you ask?'

'He rang this morning, wanting to talk about you and your accounts. Of course, there's no way I'm discussing your private affairs with him. I got the impression he's trying to make trouble for you. I thought I'd better warn you. He made an appointment to see the boss last week. But then he rang up and cancelled it at the last minute.'

Cathy drew in her breath sharply. 'Thanks for telling me, Tony. It's a long story and I'm embarrassed he called you – it's a private, family matter.'

'That's okay. I just thought I'd better warn you... Didn't you say he was in the SAS?'

'Yes, and he seems to have picked up a few bullyboy tactics from his years in the Middle East. Right now I bet he wishes he could drop me off in the desert somewhere with an empty water bottle and no map.'

Tony shook his head. 'He sounds like a tough sort to be up against. I wouldn't want to be in your shoes. You take care, Cathy.'

Chapter 12

Alex strode into the police lunch room carrying his sandwich bag. Half a dozen officers were sitting or standing around the long wooden table. He sat down next to Sergeant Dawkins, who was doing the cryptic crossword.

'Six across, a king's recipe for salad. The sixth letter is "l",' said Dawkins by way of greeting.

Alex stared at the light green wall opposite for a couple of minutes, thinking about the clue. 'A king's salad... salad... hmmm.' He had it! 'Coleslaw!'

Dawkins clicked his tongue. 'Nice one.'

Alex knew Dawkins had recently been involved in some inheritance battles in court, so after they had worked on the cryptic crossword together a while longer, he asked casually, 'Got anything interesting on at the moment?'

'I've been up at Guildford listening to a case where a son was cut out of his mother's will. She left everything to the RSPCA and he was contesting it. The old lady was mad about cats – had about 15 of them when she died.'

'Really? That reminds me, a friend of mine was asking me the other day if one of those homemade wills you can buy at the stationer's will stand up in court. He wants to leave his daughter his cottage in Wales.'

'Yeah, a homemade will is legally binding so long as it's been witnessed by two people who are *compos mentis*. But you'd better warn him that the will may not stand up in a court of law if it's contested by the family. Tell him you can download really good wills from the internet these days.' Dawkins then made another suggestion to help Alex's "friend" make things watertight.

'Thanks, I'll tell him.' Alex pushed back his chair. 'Well, guess I'd better get back to the firing range for the next session.' He dropped his empty sandwich bag in the bin and walked out.

On his day off, Alex sat at the computer in his dark study; he preferred to work with the venetian blinds closed. From a cupboard, he pulled out a grey lever arch folder, opened it, and studied Lucille's will. It was very basic. He thought he should look for a more official looking document on the internet. Trawling through numerous legal websites, some information caught his eye. 'So this is what Dawkins was talking about,' he mumbled.

Sonia appeared at the doorway bearing the coffee tray.

'Come and read this,' he said.

Sonia took his place in front of the computer and scrolled down the screen, carefully reading the information. 'That's just the ticket,' she said. 'Well done.'

'It's surprisingly easy to get this all sorted. No need for any busybody solicitors or hefty legal fees,' Alex remarked, taking the mug of black coffee. 'If you get these documents typed up and printed for me, I'll drive down to Lyme Regis in the morning.'

***

'Come in, Alex. Can I make you a cuppa?' Lucille held back from a bear hug, instead pecking her stepson on the cheek. She felt some trepidation about this meeting, as Alex had warned her that he wanted to discuss financial matters. The weekly income support payments were now weighing heavily on her conscience; she missed Cathy's financial support, but most of all her friendship.

'How was the trip down?' she asked.

'No traffic, the Range Rover flew along, I made good time. Are you ready then?

Lucille chose to go to an Italian restaurant nearby. Alex ordered mushroom risotto for both of them, which Lucille washed down with two large glasses of chardonnay. When she slipped her bread roll onto his plate, Alex studiously ignored the offering. Lucille spent most of the meal chatting to the waiter, a balding gent from Sicily.

'Let's go back to the penthouse; I've got a couple of legal documents for you to sign,' Alex told her at the end of the meal. They stood up and he helped her into her fur coat.

Lucille sat at the dining room table reading her new will. Alex pointed out that he was the sole beneficiary, but if he died before she did there was provision for other relatives to inherit. She was pleased with this change and wrote down the names of six relatives. Then Alex laid a second document on the table.

Lucille read the first few sentences and immediately looked up at Alex, her eyes widened in horror. 'What's this?'

'Lucille, it's necessary, believe me,' murmured Alex, soothingly. 'It's just a way to avoid inheritance tax. You can still live here – everyone will think you still own the apartment.' He took a couple of newspaper clippings out of his satchel. 'I've got something to show you.' Slowly and deliberately he laid the articles in front of Lucille and proceeded to read the first aloud:

Prison for Pension Cheat Grandad

A grandfather in Portsmouth has been jailed for eight months after falsely claiming nearly £20,000 in benefits, despite having £65,000 in the bank…

Lucille sat motionless, hands clasped in her lap, head bowed. A few weeks ago, she had read the same articles in the paper; since then she'd been waking in the middle of the night to an imaginary clang of prison doors in her head.

She eyed Alex, realisation dawning slowly as she processed this information. Alex was financially savvy and knew the law, but could she trust him?

'It sounds awfully familiar, doesn't it, Lucille?' he said unpleasantly, looming over her. 'You're in a real pickle now. You've been cheating the system. You haven't been honest about your financial circumstances. Did you show the bank statements for the Jersey account to the lady from Social Services who visited? No? Do you know that deliberately failing to disclose your true financial position constitutes benefit fraud? You could be had up in court!' He poked a finger at the article. 'That old man paid back the debt, but they're still throwing him in the slammer!'

Lucille's face crumpled. She covered her face with one hand.

Alex leaned down and whispered, 'One phone call is all it takes to start an investigation.'

He paced back and forth in front of the windows. The harbour looked desolate – the tide was out, revealing mud flats, and the sea was a dirty grey. When he returned to the table, he spoke more gently. 'I've got the documents right here. Are you ready to sign?'

'Well all right, if you think it's for the best…' muttered Lucille. She watched with a sense of dread as Alex wrote the date in black fountain pen on the will and then on the document titled "Assignment by Way of Gift". She felt overwhelmed. It was hard for her to think straight.

'We'll need witnesses, so how about asking Bertie and one of your neighbours to pop in for a nice cup of tea? I'll put the kettle on.'

'All right, Alex,' Lucille said, sounding resigned. 'Just let me take one of my pills before I call them.' She stood up and walked heavily to the kitchen.

***

That night Lucille couldn't sleep; she was distraught. Round and round the memories circled. She recalled the first night she had slept in the penthouse with Renton; they had been like a pair of excited kids on a sleepover, and then Cathy had arrived the next day with a bottle of bubbly and a bunch of sunflowers… The happy memories were suddenly blotted out by an image of Alex standing over her shouting, 'You could be had up in court!'

In desperation, she called Bertie.

A sleepy voice answered.

'I'm sorry, Luvvy… I know it's late. I'm all upset about signing those documents today. My chest's hurting and I feel terrible.'

There was a pause. Finally, Bertie replied, 'I can't see you had any choice, sweetie. He's got all the trump cards. Do you want me to come over?'

'That would be wonderful. I'll make us some hot cocoa.'

Soothed by Bertie's visit, Lucille finally fell asleep on the couch at about 4 am. *At least I won't be reported for fraud*, she thought as she dozed off. But she was wrong.

Chapter 13

Lucille's own worried face stared back at her from the heavy gilt-framed mirror. The skin under her eyes formed soft puffy pouches and her eyelids sagged over bloodshot eyes. There's no way I can go to bridge looking like this, she thought. Buttoning her pink dressing gown, she went into the kitchen to look up her friend Daphne's phone number.

'Hi Daphne, Lucille here.'

'Good morning Lucille, how are you?'

'I'm not feeling too chipper, actually. I've hardly slept a wink. I'm sorry, but I won't be able to come to bridge today.'

'That's a shame. Your voice sounds a bit hoarse, are you okay?'

'Oh, I'll be right, I just need to rest.'

Lucille put the receiver down. Opening the fridge door, she considered what to have for breakfast. Worry and lack of sleep had made her feel slightly queasy. Perhaps a poached egg on toast would settle her stomach, washed down by a comforting cup of tea? The familiar actions of filling the kettle and putting a small pot of water on the stove for the egg soothed her frayed nerves.

Yesterday she had been fully prepared to sign the new will Alex had brought her the day before, but his springing the deed of gift on her like that had been a bolt out of the blue. At the time, she'd felt like she had no choice in the matter – the shame and trauma of going to prison for benefit fraud would be unbearable. But now she wondered if she had done the right thing. Perhaps she should have stalled for time until Cathy came home, then tried to mend their relationship.

Cathy and David had visited her before they had left for their trip Down Under. Cathy had sat on the couch, looking perky in navy three-quarter pants, a striped t-shirt, her blonde hair freshly blow-waved. The conversation had been a little stiff due to their recent spat, but in spite of that Cathy's excitement about the trip kept bubbling up, just like froth rising on a freshly made ice cream soda. David had been quiet as usual; he was a dependable sort. Lucille recalled that Renton had been fond of his son-in-law, and, of course, Cathy was the apple of his eye. The topic of Lucille's finances had been avoided. They had chatted about their stopover in Singapore and the prospect of staying with Emma in her flat at Manly.

After breakfast, Lucille took the lift down to the lobby to check the post. Under a couple of bills and an advertising flyer lay a postcard. She put on the spectacles, suspended by a chain around her neck, to study the picture. It was of Sydney Harbour Bridge, the opera house and a sparkling blue ocean. She flipped it over.

> *Dear Lucille,*
>
> *Sydney Harbour is a magnificent sight on a beautiful day. Yesterday Emma took us across on the ferry from Manly. We visited the Harbour Bridge, the Opera House and then went for a walk in the Botanic Gardens. The tropical flowers were beautiful and we saw lyre birds with long curly tail feathers. Emma took us shopping in David Jones, which is the Australian version of Harrods. She has taken a few days off work to show us around. Hope you are keeping well.*
>
> *Love,*
> *Cathy & David*

Lucille propped the postcard against the silver-framed photo of Alex in his SAS uniform. For a moment, she studied his handsome square face and unsmiling mouth. Then she picked up the faded sepia photo of Renton and herself. How she missed his strength and support. Could she trust his son?

***

Lucille drew back the curtains. It was the softest of spring days; the blue sky was dotted with small wisps of cloud and the sea was silken. She had slept late, but that didn't matter, as she wouldn't be picked up for bridge until 11:00. After breakfast, she dressed in a pair of navy slacks and a long blue and white patterned blouse and settled in a wicker chair on the balcony to paint her nails. She was just applying the second layer of pink nail polish when the doorbell chimed. Lucille screwed the top on the bottle. Too early for Sylvia, she thought. Who could it be? She padded off to open the front door.

A clean-shaven man with friendly blue eyes was standing on the threshold.

'Good morning, are you Mrs Coleman?'

'Yes, I am.'

'My name is Derek Sanderson and I'm from the District Council. Some information about your benefit eligibility has come to light and I've got a few questions I'd like to ask you. May I come in?'

Lucille took the card that Sanderson was holding out and propped her glasses on her nose to read it.

Derek Sanderson
Senior Investigating Officer
West Dorset District Council

To Lucille, this was the equivalent of an axe murderer, and he wanted to come in! Her heart pounded madly, she looked from the card to Sanderson's face. Sanderson smiled encouragingly. 'Just a few questions – it won't take long.'

'Well...I suppose you'd better come in,' Lucille said reluctantly. 'I've got a bit of time before I go to bridge.' She led him through to the lounge.

'What a lovely apartment you have, Mrs Coleman. Stunning views on a day like this. How long have you lived here?' As he spoke, Sanderson's gaze expertly swept the interior, taking in the richly coloured carpets, Lladró ornaments, and antique furniture.

'I've lived here for 13 years. My husband died ten years ago. Please, take a seat.'

Sanderson opened his leather briefcase and took out a black spiral bound notebook. He flipped back the cover. 'Now, Mrs Coleman, I won't beat about the bush. The reason for my visit today is that we've received an anonymous call alleging that you have a large sum of money in an offshore account. Can you tell me anything about this?'

'No, that account was closed many years ago because it was empty.' Lucile paused to collect her thoughts, then continued. 'My late husband gifted all the money from it to his daughter and asked her to use the money to look after me in my old age. Well, I've hardly seen a penny of it! I think she's planning to take the whole lot to New Zealand and make a new life for herself.' Lucille lifted her chin in defiance, warming to her story. Sanderson jotted down some notes.

'I see you've been on holiday recently.' He nodded in the direction of the gilt framed holiday photos standing on the octagonal table. 'Looks a bit like Austria, with those onion domes…'

'Yes, that was a holiday we had in Salzburg a while back… in better times.'

'How long ago?'

'It must have been about eight years or so,' lied Lucille. 'My friend kindly paid for that holiday. It's been very hard to make ends meet since my husband died. I've needed the income support, that's for sure.' She looked down at the Persian rug.

Sanderson raised one dubious eyebrow, but said nothing. His gaze fell on a theatre programme lying on the coffee table. 'I've seen the "Phantom of the Opera" too,' he said casually. 'Did you enjoy the show?'

Lucille shook her head quickly. 'No, a friend gave me that programme. I couldn't have managed that on my budget.'

'Mmm.' Sanderson scribbled something in his notebook. 'Now, I see you're on a disability pension for your feet. How is your mobility these days?'

'I struggle to get about. You see, I've got this foot condition called Charcot-Marie-Tooth. It was caused by wearing army issue boots that were too tight in the war – my toes are all curled up – do you want to have a look?' Lucille reached down to take off one of her slippers.

'No, it's all right, thank you. I'm not a medical person. I need to assess your current financial position. Could I please have a look at the bank statements for all your accounts?'

Lucille looked apologetic. 'Oh, it would take me a wee while to get those together, I'm afraid, and I'm being picked up for bridge soon.'

Sanderson's eyes hardened, a shrewd look had replaced his earlier affable expression. 'I must remind you, Mrs Coleman, that you are legally bound to fully disclose your financial position to the investigating authority and not to do so would be a criminal offence of a most serious nature. Please have this information ready for my next visit. If I return in two weeks' time, it will give you time to assemble your accounts. Would that suit you?'

'Yes, that should be fine,' agreed Lucille.

Sanderson snapped his notebook shut. 'That'll be all for now, then. No, please don't get up – I'll show myself out.' But Lucille insisted on creaking to her feet and hobbling with him to the door.

Back at the council offices, Sanderson began typing up his notes:

The penthouse flat Mrs Coleman lives in is very palatial and I find it hard to believe that she can keep it to its current high standard just on Income Support and her pension.

Chapter 14

'Lucille, slow down, I can't understand you,' Alex interrupted the hysterical stream of jabbering and wailing coming down the telephone line. On the other end, Lucille took a deep breath and began her tale of woe again.

'Someone's dobbed me in. An investigator from the council was just here. They suspect me of benefit fraud. He's coming again in two weeks' time. Oh Alex, what shall I do?' Lucille broke off, howling.

'Lucille, calm down!' snapped Alex. 'Did you show him your bank statements?'

'No, I still have to show them to him.'

'Well, for goodness' sake, don't let him see anything relating to the Jersey account – shred it all! What you've got to do is play poor – put him off the scent. Dress in something from the ragbag; hide the Persian rugs and some of the antiques in the garage. Tell him you've been selling some of your possessions to make ends meet. Now, what is this chap's name? I'll give him a call as your "attorney", mentioning I'm with the police, and vouch for your good character and lack of funds.'

'Thank you, Alex. Who do you think is behind this?'

'I don't know, but I've got a fair idea who the troublemaker is. I'll find out – don't you worry.'

***

On Monday, Lucille bustled about preparing for the officer's visit. She boxed up any precious ornaments, rolled up the Persian carpets and stowed them in a corner of the garage under an old tarpaulin. A strapping young man, who lived two doors down, carried the Italian inlaid marble side tables to the garage. She threw a tartan rug over her chintz sofa and replaced the fine bone china and silverware in the display cabinet with cheap knickknacks unearthed from a box in the back of the garage. It was a good week to skip doing the housework. She noted how shabby the cream carpet appeared when it was strewn with bits and pieces.

On Tuesday morning, Lucille pulled on some baggy track pants with saggy knees and a shapeless old cardigan with a button missing. Normally she wouldn't have been seen dead in such a get-up. With the help of some soap, she wriggled her diamond engagement ring over the enlarged knuckle of her finger. She decided not to remove the gold star medallion necklace, which she firmly believed brought her luck; instead, she slipped it out of sight under her t-shirt. Alex arrived half an hour before Sanderson was due to arrive.

'This is my stepson, Alex Coleman,' Lucille said, as the investigator stepped inside.

'Oh yes, we've talked on the phone,' said Sanderson. 'Good morning, Mr Coleman.' The two men shook hands.

'Would you like a cup of tea?' said Lucille, filling the kettle.

'I'd prefer coffee, if it's not too much trouble?' replied Sanderson.

'As long as you don't mind recycled coffee grounds. I don't like to throw them out after just one use – such a waste.'

'Actually, a cup of tea would be nice.'

'Right you are – one bag between two is my motto. I'll give you the first dip.'

'Thank you – ever so kind,' said Sanderson, a touch sarcastically.

His eyes looked here and there at the apartment, thinking that it appeared somehow tawdry today, and Mrs Coleman decidedly shabby. Was that a hole in her slipper? Perhaps it was the overcast day that made everything seem so dreary, more like the usual hard-up pensioner's flat he was accustomed to visiting. But hang on a minute, he suddenly wondered, weren't some of the furnishings missing?

'Errr, Mrs Coleman, I seem to remember some rugs on the floor?'

Alex answered, 'There was one, but my stepmother has been selling off things to help pay the maintenance bills for the apartment. It hasn't been easy for her since my father died.'

'It's very hard,' continued Lucille, 'It breaks my heart to flog off the family heirlooms.'

'I see.' Sanderson swallowed some tea to help wash down the dry biscuit. 'Have you got your financial statements ready for me? I need to see everything, so please don't forget any building society statements, bonds, share dividends or statements from any offshore accounts you might happen to have.' He put special emphasis on the words "offshore accounts".

Alex handed over an orderly file of papers. 'As I mentioned on the phone, I have power of attorney for my stepmother and I have gone through all the accounts. My father did have some savings, but he lent the money to my sister to buy a new house, and she now refuses to repay Lucille. I'm afraid that puts my stepmother in a difficult position. You can see for yourself.'

Sanderson spent some time carefully studying the statements, occasionally using his calculator and referring to a table. Finally, he looked up.

'Mrs Coleman, I don't see any reason to pursue this investigation any further. Your benefits will continue to be paid.'

'Thank you.' Lucille beamed at him. 'Here, you must have another biscuit.'

'No, thank you, Mrs Coleman.'

Alex shook Sanderson's hand. 'Well, I'd better head back to the station. Thank you for coming.'

Back at the council offices, Sanderson typed the conclusion to his report:

On looking at the flat a second time, I could see that the flat was living on past glories and I am not so sure now she does have additional capital. I have decided to take the matter no further and Mrs Coleman is aware of this.

Chapter 15

Cathy snipped the crackly brown flowers off the hydrangea bush, dropping each stem into her wheelbarrow. There was a nip in the air, heralding the arrival of winter. Since she had stopped work, she had found herself working more and more in the garden. It was a good place to think and try to make sense of what was happening in her family. The snipping sound of her secateurs, and the progress she was making in pruning the row of hydrangeas along the side of her house was satisfying. Things never seemed so bad after a morning working in the garden.

For 25 years, they had lived in England; it was time for David to return to his homeland. Emma was still living in Sydney and had no intention of returning to England to live. It seemed as though all road signs were pointing in the direction of the Southern Hemisphere. Cathy loved New Zealand, and if she was honest with herself, the breakdown in the relationship with her stepmother and all the vitriol from her brother were making it easier to leave the UK.

After the fraud investigation, Lucille had refused to speak to her, slamming the phone down in her ear. Alex had sent her another nasty letter demanding money. Cathy felt she could no longer help her stepmother. In her eyes, Lucille had chosen to side with the devil. Speaking of the devil… Cathy straightened up and looked towards the road. A black Range Rover was stopping outside her white picket fence. Was it Alex? Her senses were suddenly alert. It looked like a male driver in the front seat, his face half-obscured by sunglasses. He was staring at the house. What did he want? A shiver of apprehension went through her. She turned and walked quickly up the side of the house and through the back door, locking it behind her. She knew all the downstairs windows were closed on account of the chilly weather, but now she pulled the curtains, too, in case he walked around and peeped in. Then she dialled David's work number.

'Hello, David speaking.'

'David, there's someone sitting outside the house in a Range Rover,' Cathy whispered urgently. 'I think it's Alex. What shall I do; call the police?'

'No, I don't think you should,' David said after a moment's thought. 'After all, it's not an offence to sit in a car on a public road.'

'But he's stalking me! What does he want?'

'I don't know, but I'll come home right now.'

The Range Rover sped off as David pulled into the driveway. He hurried inside. Cathy met him in the hallway and he put his arms around her, holding her tight.

'He scares me,' she whispered.

'I know. I just can't wait to move to New Zealand to get away from all this.'

'Me too, I've had enough.'

***

On Saturday morning, they drove north to visit Cathy's mother, who lived in an apartment in the old part of Scarborough. David was silent most of the way – he enjoyed driving – leaving Cathy, who preferred to be driven, to hand out the peppermints and think her own thoughts. It was mid-afternoon before their Escort joined the traffic winding into the centre of Scarborough. Thankfully, it was off-season, so the seaside town was comparatively quiet; during the summer months it would have been heaving with tourists. As they approached a main intersection, the corner site once occupied by Milnes Department store came into view. The four-storey white Georgian building with its bow windows and square dormers had been demolished and replaced by a pub. *My grandparents would have turned in their grave*, thought Cathy as she recalled the grand old store where once the wealthy ladies of Scarborough had shopped for their fur coats. When her mother had joined the family business, Grandfather Milne had insisted his daughter work her way up through the business

– or in this case from top to bottom, according to the store's layout. To her credit, Margaret had knuckled down and worked hard, six days a week, moving from lingerie on the top floor down through the various other departments, until eventually she had found herself seated behind the manager's mahogany desk on the ground floor.

Cathy recalled visiting Milnes as a little girl. It was a scene straight out of the television programme *Are You Being Served?* Milnes had its very own "Mrs Slocombe" complete with purple hair, and its own "Mr Lucas" in menswear, while "Captain Peacock" patrolled the floors. Cathy would be ushered into the spacious lift, where the uniformed male attendant drew the double grills closed before politely enquiring if customers were "going up or down?" Then his white gloved hand would press the right floor buttons.

Material for Cathy's dresses and coats was chosen from the haberdashery on the second floor and made up by the dressmakers in the sewing department. For a moment, she saw herself as a little girl again, standing in a new red, velvet dress while the dressmakers gathered around in a circle to admire her.

'Give us a twirl,' one of them would say. Cathy found it most embarrassing.

On Saturdays, she would stay home, tidy her bedroom, and do her homework. Then she would bus into Milnes to meet her mother for lunch. Her mother would be smartly dressed in a tweed suit. They always went to the same tea rooms, across the road from the store. Cathy liked to order a sausage roll and tomato soup. During lunch, her mother would ask her about school and Cathy would talk about her week. Maths was her favourite subject. She got plenty of practice at arithmetic in real life. After lunch, they would return to Milnes, entering through the big plate glass doors, and Cathy would follow her mother past the jewellery department to her small back office on the ground floor. Her mother would lay the ledger books on the desk and Cathy would help her with the bookkeeping, carefully writing the figures in her even, rounded hand. Then they would count the day's takings together, locking the money in the safe to be banked on Monday.

As David drove the Escort round the brow of the hill, an expanse of sea appeared before them bringing Cathy back to the present. Her mother's second husband had died. She now lived in an apartment overlooking the harbour in the old part of town.

'Now, tell me all about your plans to move to New Zealand,' said Margaret, once her daughter and son-in-law were comfortably seated in the elegant living room of her home.

'We're going to hire a motor home and travel all over the North Island. The idea is to find a place we'd like to retire to,' David told her.

'Well, I'm going to miss you both. But I can't imagine leaving Scarborough,' her mother said. She let the spout of the teapot hover over Cathy's cup. 'Would you like a top-up?'

'Yes, please. How are you keeping, Mother?'

'I'm feeling old,' said Margaret wistfully, looking beyond her daughter and out to sea.

'You look like you've lost a little weight,' commented Cathy, concerned. In fact, her mother looked as if she'd shrunk a couple of sizes, and her face had taken on the hollow-cheeked, bird-like look of the aged.

David chatted for a while about his favourite places in New Zealand, while Cathy's mind drifted back a few years to an occasion when her mother had been ill and she had rushed up to Scarborough to be by her bedside. It had been just before Christmas, and when Alex had arrived at the weekend to find his mother fretting about getting her Christmas cards and gifts delivered to friends and family; he had made it clear he wasn't prepared to help.

'I'm not hanging around here delivering Christmas presents, like some kind of Santa Claus,' he said to Cathy. 'I've got to get back to work.' It hadn't seemed to occur to him that Cathy had a job too.

Cathy had stayed to deliver the Christmas presents, post the cards, decorate the tree and nurse her mother back to health. She had travelled back to Glastonbury to hastily organise her own affairs, before returning with David to Scarborough for Christmas. The illness had been a sobering experience for Margaret. Once she had fully recovered, she had arranged for Cathy and Alex to have joint enduring power of attorney.

86

Margaret interrupted her daughter's reverie. 'Come into the kitchen. I want to give you some things to take to New Zealand.'

Cathy followed her mother's hunched figure to the kitchen. There, Margaret opened a few cupboards. 'Please, take whatever you fancy. I have too much crystal and china. There's a nice Royal Doulton tea set in this cupboard.'

'I won't take much, Mother. We've got too many things already to ship to New Zealand.'

'I'll go and get some newspaper and boxes.'

Cathy chose a Waterford crystal candy dish that had stood on her grandmother's sideboard. At Christmas time, it would always be filled with chocolate bonbons.

'I should probably get this in writing; otherwise I might be accused of stealing,' Cathy muttered to David.

'I heard that,' said Margaret, re-entering the kitchen just at that moment.

'Well, your hearing's still good, then,' replied Cathy.

'It is. And, I must say, I don't like some of the stories I'm hearing about you.' Margaret fixed suspicious eyes on her daughter.

Two bright spots burned on Cathy's cheeks as she faced her mother. 'I don't know what Alex has been telling you, but I haven't done anything wrong!' She stormed out of the room.

Cathy had avoided talking to her mother about the feud because she had been reluctant to draw her into the fray. She was an old lady and she didn't want to worry her. Now, as she lay sobbing, hot, angry tears on her pillow, she saw her mistake. Alex had fed his lies to her mother and the result was that Margaret doubted her daughter's integrity. The loss of her mother's trust wounded Cathy deeply.

In the living room, she dabbed her eyes with a tissue and forced herself to regain her usual composure. She resolved to try and talk to her mother after dinner.

When the meal was over, David tactfully retired, pleading exhaustion from the long drive. Cathy offered her mother an after dinner mint from the box she had brought with her.

'Mother, I'm in a really difficult situation. Dad and Lucille *gave* me that money a few months before Dad died. They wanted me to have it. Lucille has no right to demand it back.'

'That's not what your brother says.' Margaret's voice had a hard edge.

'Well, he wasn't there at the time, so he doesn't know what happened. He's been really nasty to me, Mum, threatening me and –'

'I don't want to hear any more,' interrupted Margaret, covering her ears. 'It's got nothing to do with me. I just wish you'd sort it out with your brother.'

'I've tried,' said Cathy in a small voice.

Her mother reached for the TV remote.

The next morning, Cathy popped out to buy date scones – her mother's favourite. She and David planned to head back home after morning coffee.

'Well, I suppose I'll see you two next at Charlotte's wedding,' said her mother, presiding over the silver coffee pot.

'I didn't know Charlotte was getting married,' said Cathy.

'Didn't you get an invitation?' asked Margaret, 'Mine's over there on the mantelpiece.' Cathy crossed the room and picked up the thick cream-coloured card. The happy couple were to be married in a castle in Berkshire. Cathy shook her head, feeling confused and hurt. Charlotte had been her favourite cousin; they were a similar age and had played together at family picnics at the beach, or in the Yorkshire Dales. Margaret took in Cathy's pained expression, but looked away without a word.

On the way home, Cathy and David drove for a long time in silence. Then Cathy finally blurted out, 'I feel like I've become the black sheep of the family!'

'Just as well we're moving to New Zealand, then,' said David drily. 'You'll be right at home. Great place for sheep.'

Chapter 16

Cathy popped her head around the French door. 'Are those steaks nearly ready?'

'Five more minutes,' said David, expertly flipping the Scotch fillet on the gas barbecue.

Cathy set the coleslaw and new potatoes on the little table covered by a sky blue cloth. She sat down, took a sip of her sauvignon blanc and gazed at the lake at the bottom of the garden. A boy in a yellow kayak paddled past, slipping behind the branches of a weeping willow.

'I'm so glad we bought this house. It's such a serene spot.'

'And Lake Rotiti is far enough away from Rotorua that we can't smell the sulphur,' said David, 'but it's still handy to town for shopping.'

They shared the silence for a few minutes, until Cathy said, 'I thought it would be fun to take the boat to the hot pools tomorrow.' This was one of Cathy's favourite outings. David would load the chilly bin onto the launch moored at the bottom of the garden, start the motor, and they'd cruise out of the inlet, following the shoreline around to the hot mineral pools. The pools were only accessible by boat.

'That's a good idea. I feel like a good soak. It's meant to be a fine day tomorrow.' David served the steak and sat down. Cathy spooned some coleslaw onto her plate.

'I had another nasty letter from my brother this morning asking me "not to send any correspondence" to Lucille. It's ridiculous. I only send her the odd card just to keep in touch.'

'Have you tried phoning her lately?'

'Not since she hung up on me a few weeks ago. It's hard, because even after what happened, I still care about her.'

David chewed on his steak quietly.

'Would you like some more coleslaw?' asked Cathy, holding out the bowl.

'No, that will do me, thanks.'

'You haven't eaten much.'

They sat outside long after the meal was finished, as the cool, calm twilight descended. Together they listened to the croaking of frogs and chirping of crickets, enjoying the quiet companionship of a long married couple.

David was the first to speak. 'I think I might need to see a doctor.'

'Why?'

'I've been passing some blood. I don't know why.'

Cathy looked at him quickly. Though he spoke calmly, his eyes were dark and staring. 'How long since you first noticed it?' she asked anxiously. 'You definitely need to get that checked out. Perhaps it's a haemorrhoid? Why don't you see the doctor tomorrow and we'll take the boat out another day? We've been on a lot of outings lately. I'm happy to stay home.'

Cathy thought of all the activities they had shared in Rotorua since arriving a few months ago... she and David had been trout fishing, bathed in a hot stream, massaged warm, grey mud into each other's shoulders, dropped coins into the crystalline waters of a deep spring and rubbed their hands over the chunky, ridged bark of redwood trees. Cathy had even dared to go skydiving and jet boating.

***

Two weeks later everything changed. David had been sent for an emergency colonoscopy. Cathy stared in shock at the smooth-faced young doctor in the hospital consulting room. It was hard to take in what he was saying in his Oxford accent; it was all so unexpected.

'I'm afraid the tumour on your colon is quite large,' the doctor was telling David. 'It will require surgery followed by a course of chemotherapy.' He turned to his computer and hit a few keys. An ultrasound scan appeared on the screen. 'This here is a tumour,' he said, pointing to a grey shape about the size of a peanut, 'and this here is a smaller one.'

Cathy squeezed David's hand. It was sweaty.

'What are my chances of survival?' he asked huskily.

'The good news is that there are treatment options, in your case surgery, to remove the tumours we can see on the scan, followed by chemotherapy. With that treatment regimen, you have a 50% chance of being here in five years' time. It's very hard to detect colon cancer early, as symptoms such as pain in the abdomen do not present themselves until the later stages of the disease. But the good news is that you are otherwise fit and healthy; you should make a good recovery from the surgery and you're more likely to be able to tolerate the chemotherapy.'

They drove straight home in shocked silence.

David sat numbly on the couch. Cathy brought him a mug of tea and sat down next to him.

'We can get through this,' she said. 'Lots of people have cancer and survive.' *And lots of people get cancer and die*, said a little voice inside her head. The landscape of their retirement had suddenly shifted. A large crack had appeared and threatened to swallow them up. 'We'll just have to put our plans on hold and concentrate on getting you better.'

David nodded. Cathy leaned against his chest and he kissed the top of her head. Inside, she wondered how she was going to survive with David in hospital, no family nearby and only a few acquaintances to speak of.

***

Within a few weeks, David was operated on. Cathy spent her days at the hospital and her nights at home. One evening, she came home from a long day at the hospital to discover that Rhonda, a woman she had met at croquet, had left a meal on the doorstep. Cathy popped the beef and noodle casserole straight into the oven. There was enough for two nights. For the first time in weeks, she finished everything on her plate.

She set the dishes in the sink, then picked up the phone. 'Hi Rhonda, I'm just ringing to thank you for the delicious casserole.'

'My pleasure. I'm glad you enjoyed it. We've missed you at croquet. How's David?'

'Well, they think they've got all the cancer out. He's coming home tomorrow and soon he'll start chemotherapy.'

'That's good. It'll be hard going while he's on chemo. Has your daughter gone back to Sydney?'

'Yes, Emma had to go back to work. It was great having her over.'

'How are *you*?' asked Rhonda, with real warmth and concern in her voice.

'I'm hanging in there – just trying to stay positive for David's sake. It's not going to help him if I'm mooching about the place with my bottom lip on the floor.'

After each bout of chemotherapy, Cathy nursed David through the after effects at home. Each morning she took him breakfast in bed. The room was always dark, the way he wanted it. She placed a tray with tea and toast on the bedside table, nudging aside the bottles of pills.

'How are you feeling this morning?'

David turned his head to the side. 'I feel like I'm being slowly poisoned. No, please don't pull the curtains.'

Cathy hesitated, her hand on the green curtain, then twitched it open just a crack and opened the window. 'Well, try and get that toast down. I'm popping out for a walk along the lake. I'll be back in an hour.'

David closed his eyes.

This morning the lake was silken and grey, the sky a dome of soft cloud. Cathy's sneakers crunched over the gravelly sand of Okawa Bay. She stopped next to a wooden picnic table and watched a mother duck paddle by with four little brown and gold ducklings in her wake. Cathy pushed back a strand of hair. She thought about how her life was dominated by medical appointments and nursing duties. It wasn't how she'd envisaged retirement.

She turned to follow the shoreline home. Rounding the bend, she saw David's small launch moored at their jetty. It had been his first purchase when they had arrived in Okawa Bay. She wondered if they should sell it. But no, she steered herself away from such a negative train of thought; David would get better. He would beat the cancer.

Leroy treaded lightly towards her across the lawn. He'd been flown over in the plane's cargo hold and happily settled into a new life of catching crickets, and even the odd mouse. Cathy looked up at their two-storey house with its dark stained wood and white window frames, nestled between English oaks. At this time of year, the trees were a lush, lime green.

She opened the French door quietly to find David sitting on the couch with the newspaper. She was surprised to see him fully dressed, even though there was no need.

He looked up. 'Oh, there you are. You had an unexpected visitor this morning.'

'Who?'

'The police!'

'The police? Why, what's wrong?' Cathy's thoughts flew immediately to Emma.

'You won't believe this, but a complaint has been filed with Rotorua Police. Apparently you've been harassing your stepmother.'

'You're joking.'

'No, I'm not. But the policeman who turned up knows it's all rubbish. He didn't even want to see you, just wanted to clear the paperwork from his desk.'

'This is ridiculous! It's Alex and Lucille who have been harassing *me* with letters and emails demanding money. I can't believe he got the police involved. This is such a waste of police time!'

'I know,' agreed David. 'The policeman said the file's been sitting on his desk for three months. He visited us so that he could get rid of it.'

'You'd think Alex would leave me alone now that I'm living on the other side of the world. But no, he's still chasing me. I'm going down to the police station.'

'What for? There's no need. The policeman said the matter's dealt with now.' David raised a glass of water to his lips, his hand unsteady.

'No, I'm going down there. Fancy harassing us at a time like this! I want to get to the bottom of it.'

She hurried down the hallway to change out of her walking clothes. Ten minutes later she picked up her ivory shoulder bag and car keys.

'Would you like me to come with you?' asked David.

'No, darling, you rest. I'll be fine. It's only a 15-minute drive.' She bent down and kissed him.

As Cathy backed her blue Toyota Corolla down the driveway, she narrowly missed the letter box. 'Careful now…' she told herself. Anger charged through her. Alex knew that David had cancer, yet he continued to bully them from afar. Her mind flashed back to her last months in England. She had met with Lucille and Alex a few times to try to reach an agreement. But Alex had been seething with anger and remained adamant that Cathy must repay the £50,000. She had hoped to leave the whole sorry saga behind her, but instead the demands by letter and email had only escalated. And now the police were involved.

***

Detective Bruce O'Connor gestured with a large, tattooed arm for Cathy to enter the interview room. She perched on the edge of a navy plastic seat. O'Connor looked down at the papers on the table, then directly at her.

'As you know, I spoke to your husband, Mrs Stewart. I'd like to reassure you that we're not taking this complaint seriously. It's obviously a private family matter, but we were obliged to visit because the complaint was made via Interpol. Now, did you have something further to tell me?'

'Interpol?' echoed Cathy in disbelief.

'Yes, the original complaint was lodged by the Surrey Police.'

'My brother works for the Surrey Police. I think he's abusing his position by making complaints like this, which are a total waste of police time. I mean, it's a family matter and he's got two police forces involved and now Interpol as well! I should think the police have far more important matters to attend to.'

'We certainly do,' nodded the detective.

'This is a family argument that's been going on for years – it's not a matter for the police and he knows it. He's just stirring up trouble. What exactly was the complaint about?'

O'Connor looked back down at the file for a minute or two before answering. 'It says here you reported your stepmother to social services, wrote nasty letters to her and sent anonymous letters of a defamatory nature to her neighbours. The letters were allegedly posted in New Zealand.' O'Connor couldn't help raising one eyebrow as he looked up.

'That's outrageous. My husband's got cancer. I haven't got time to write to all my stepmother's neighbours, and even if I did I wouldn't be silly enough to post the letters from here!' Cathy raised her chin. 'I'd like to lodge a complaint that my brother is abusing his police powers and wasting police resources. How do I go about doing it?'

'I'll make some enquiries, Mrs Stewart, if you'd like to make an official complaint.'

'Yes, I would. I also believe my brother is preying on my elderly stepmother with an eye on the inheritance. Is it possible to have someone in the police visit her and ask a few questions? I have good reason to believe my brother is a bully and is blackmailing her.'

Cathy left the station with contact details for Surrey Constabulary and the Community Police Liaison Officer in Dorset tucked into her handbag.

***

That night she had trouble sleeping. Her mind was troubled by images of Alex creeping about her garden in the dark, carrying a pistol and memories of David on a hospital bed as they poured chemicals into his body via a tube. She didn't want to disturb David with her tossing and turning, so she got up, put on her sheepskin slippers and crept down the hallway. Leroy meowed in the kitchen. He rubbed his furry body against her bare legs. Cathy opened the French door to let him out. Moonlight glittered on the lake.

She padded into the lounge with a mug of warm cocoa and turned on the TV. The warm, plummy tones of David Attenborough narrating a documentary about lions soothed her. Leaning her head back on the armchair, she watched luminous images of a pride of lions living in Africa. Suddenly, the story took a cruel twist. A male lion viciously attacked a young lioness. He asserted his authority in the pride as the new leader by tossing her out. The lioness limped off, leaving behind her family to somehow survive alone in the wilderness. Cathy sat up. She no longer felt sleepy. *It even happens in nature*, she thought. *Well, this lioness is going to fight back,* she vowed. She flicked the TV off, walked into the study and switched on the computer. After collecting her thoughts for a moment, she began to type a letter to the Surrey Police. Forty minutes later, she had finished the first draft. Tomorrow I'll finish it and send it off, she promised herself, switching off the computer and heading back to bed.

Chapter 17

Two months later, Cathy flipped open the door of her brown wooden letter box. She pulled out a long white envelope bearing the emblem of the Surrey Police. She tore it open and quickly read the letter. It recommended that she take her complaint to their Professional Standards Department. Shaking her head, she stuffed the letter into her handbag. She was on her way to visit David, who was back in hospital with a nasty chest infection.

Cathy caught sight of herself in the rear vision mirror as she was manoeuvring the Corolla into a space in the hospital parking ground, next to a large four-wheel drive. Frown lines marked her forehead and her eyes were circled by dark shadows. The weeks of worry had taken their toll.

Arriving at the ward on the third floor, Cathy noted that the nurse's station was empty. *That's odd*, she thought, continuing down the long corridor, her sandals clacking on the lino. Suddenly, a red light at the end of the corridor caught her eye. Hearing footsteps running behind her, she stepped aside to let an orderly pushing a machine rush past; a nurse hurried in his wake. All at once she realised the red light was flashing right above David's door. Cathy began to run.

In the doorway, Cathy stopped in her tracks. She could see a group of doctors and nurses crowding around David's bed. Her heart began to thump. She stepped towards the bed. David was making terrible gasping noises. A mask obscured his face.

'Pump, please nurse,' said one of the doctors. As the nurse wheeled the machine around, she saw Cathy. 'I'll be with you in a minute, Mrs Stewart,' she said. 'We've got an emergency. We need to drain your husband's lungs of fluid.'

Another nurse, a small woman with meek brown eyes, stepped forward. 'Are you Mr Stewart's wife?' Cathy nodded mutely.

'I'm Sue Gray. I've been nursing David. Let me take you down to the waiting area while they assist him.' She laid her hand gently on Cathy's arm and guided her down the corridor. 'I'm afraid your husband has developed pneumonia. Fluid has built up in his lungs and he's going to need intensive treatment to clear it so he can breathe properly.'

'Will he be all right?' asked Cathy, with a tremor in her voice.

'We hope so. But he's being moved to critical care. He's very ill.'

The following days passed in a blur as Cathy watched David fight for his life. Every day she sat by his bedside and constantly encouraged him. 'Don't give up. You'll get better. I know it.'

Coming home from hospital one rainy evening, she found another foil covered plate from Rhonda on the doorstep. She peeked under the foil – beef lasagne.

Cathy scraped the last morsel of lasagne from her plate and drained the last ruby droplets of merlot from her glass. Leaning back in her chair, she felt replenished by the hearty fare. Reading the letter again made her blood boil, and she resolved to write to the Professional Standards Department the following day. *I mustn't let this go*, she thought. *Alex has got to be stopped.*

Next morning, Cathy arrived at the hospital in an anxious state, wondering what she would find.

'Your husband's looking a lot perkier today, Mrs Stewart.' Nurse Gray smiled up at Cathy from the nurse's station. 'Go and see him. You'll be very pleased.'

Cathy found David sitting up in bed, eating his breakfast. He put down his bowl of cornflakes when he saw her.

'You've turned the corner!' She gave him a peck on the cheek. 'Your colour's good. What an improvement.'

'I'm still weak, but I feel *so* much better.

In a few days, he was home, seated in his favourite armchair, watching the rugby. Each day he walked a little bit further inside the house, until Cathy, standing next to the kitchen window, observed his tall gaunt figure venturing out to the letter box. He had even started drinking coffee again.

'There's a couple of letters here for you from England,' said David, sitting down at the polished dining room table. Cathy set the tray of coffee and date scones on the table and sat down. She picked up one of the letters.

'It's from Alex.' She read a few lines and shook her head, incredulous. 'Listen to this:

As you are aware, it is Mother's 80th birthday in February next year. It is a significant milestone and quite an occasion for her to celebrate. I would like to think that, as her family, we can make it memorable and enjoyable for her.

I just wish to assure you that whatever our differences in other areas, I am sure they can be put aside for this special occasion, and should you (and I obviously include David and Emma in this invitation) wish to join us at the Majestic in Harrogate for the celebration, I will make the necessary arrangements.

'Well that's big of him! One minute he's putting Interpol on my tail, the next he wants us to travel to a posh hotel to sit around playing happy families. Not bloody likely!'

Cathy passed the letter to David, who read it silently. After a few minutes, he spoke, 'I think he's sent you this letter so he can tell your mother he's invited you to the party. She probably asked him to invite you.'

'I won't bother replying. I'll send Mother a present and call to wish her a happy birthday.'

Cathy noted that the second envelope was from the Surrey Police. She tore it open and scanned the letter.

'Another wild goose chase… It says here "the Professional Standards Department has reviewed the case and found no fault." If I'm not happy with their decision, I can appeal to the Independent Police Complaints Commission.' She frowned. 'I'm totally fed up with the buck passing and the amount of correspondence going nowhere.' She held the letter out for David to read, but he shook his head.

'Why don't you give up? The Police Complaints Commission will never come down on your side, you know that.'

'I know, but I'm not letting it go. I always remember Dad saying, "fight for what you believe is right. Never give up."'

Some months later, Cathy learned that her complaint had been forwarded by the Police Complaints Commission back to Professional Standards in Surrey. After over a year of writing letters and emails, she was almost back to square one. This time an Inspector Andrew Hill was being assigned to the investigation. She doubted the inspector would find any evidence of her brother's wrongdoings.

Chapter 18

'Is that you, Alex?' Margaret blinked sleepily, turning her head on the plump hospital pillow to see her son.

'Yes, Mother.' Alex stood up and moved to the side of her bed. He bent to drop a light kiss on her soft, wrinkled cheek. Margaret reached up and grabbed the sleeve of her son's jacket.

'It's good to see you.'

'I drove straight up when I got the message that you were in hospital.' He unlatched his mother's fingers from his coat and laid them on the smooth coverlet.

'It's my heart – it must be wearing out like the rest of me. They've done some tests and I should hear the results today.'

'Good. I'll make sure I'm here when the doctor comes.'

Margaret closed her eyes. A few minutes later, she looked directly at Alex. 'Have you told Cathy I'm in hospital?'

Alex stared at her, his face stony as a Yorkshire wall. 'What would be the point of that? She's on the other side of the world. Do you want her here, stirring up trouble, after what she did to Lucille? I've severed all ties with her and so should you.'

Tears welled up in Margaret's blue eyes, and as she stared forlornly at the curtain rail surrounding her bed, Alex's face softened. 'I'll look after you, Mother.'

Neither said anything more. They listened to the sound of a trolley, with cups and saucers clattering, being pushed down the corridor.

'Will you stay at my apartment, then?' Margaret asked.

'Yes, Mother. I've taken a few days off work.'

'The keys are right here in the drawer. There's a pot of vegetable soup in the fridge. You could have it for your supper. Just drain off the fat.'

'Thank you, Mother.' Alex looked back down at his cryptic crossword. 'Here's a clue for you: "Dorset eccentric walked with a long step." I think "Dorset" is an anagram.'

'I'm too tired for crosswords,' said Margaret.

Just then, a woman with a grey-streaked pony tail entered the room.

'Good morning, Mrs Milne…' she greeted Margaret.

'Good morning.'

'…and this must be your son.' The woman smiled briefly at Alex, then looked down at her clipboard.

'Yes, I'm Alex Coleman. I wondered if the specialist might be visiting my mother soon.'

'I'm the cardiologist,' said the woman, extending her hand, 'Barbara Walker – pleased to meet you.'

'Oh! How do you do?' said Alex, half-rising to shake her hand.

'I have your mother's test results right here.' Barbara Walker patted the clipboard in her hand and turned to address Margaret. 'Mrs Milne, you have a blockage in your right coronary artery. We'll need to insert a stent to widen the artery. This is a straight forward operation, not requiring a general anaesthetic.'

Mrs Walker explained the procedure in detail, before asking Alex, 'When your mother comes home from hospital, will you be in a position to stay with her for a couple of weeks until she's back on her feet?'

'Er, no, I'm afraid not. I may have some pressing business in the Middle East – high level mediation talks for the British Government. A caregiver will have to be arranged.'

Later, as Alex marched out to the car park, the answer to the crossword clue popped into his head. "Strode" – walked with a long step, an anagram for "Dorset".

***

He slid the key into the lock and turned it. The door opened easily. Stepping into the small hallway, he fumbled for the light switch, just as the grandfather clocks chimed six o'clock in unison. He hung up his coat, dumped his bags in the guest bedroom, and turned on the central heating. Then he went to the living room and walked straight to his mother's antique writing bureau, where he began a systematic search, opening every cupboard, pulling out each drawer and ferreting through the contents. As expected, his mother kept her paperwork in an orderly manner. He pulled on the handle of the top right hand drawer. It was locked. Kneeling, he examined the lock.

'That shouldn't take a minute,' he muttered. He hurried to the bedroom and came back holding a small, flat piece of metal. He inserted it into the lock, jiggling it about as he turned it clockwise. The drawer opened in seconds. Inside lay a large brown envelope. Alex opened the envelope and pulled out his mother's will. Only the tick-tock of the clocks disturbed the silence as he stood reading it.

After a few minutes, he tossed it down on the desk in disgust. 'I can't believe it!' he fumed. 'I need a drink.'

A large, half-drunk bottle of Scotch stood in the drinks cabinet. Alex twisted off the cap and poured himself half a glass. After knocking back a few gulps, he called Sonia.

'How's your mother?' asked his wife.

'She'll be fine. She needs an angioplasty – just procedure.'

'Are you staying at her apartment?'

'Yes, and I'm totally pissed off.'

'Why?'

'I've just found Mother's will. She's split her estate equally between Cathy and me – no surprises there, and it'll need to be changed now Cathy's buggered off. But what really gets me is that she's left the best grandfather clock to James!'

'James Stafford? Really?'

'Yes – it's ridiculous!'

'She had two grandfather clocks, which one are you talking about?'

The Nathaniel Burt in the hallway. It dates back to the 17th century. There's no way she's leaving it to him. I'm putting a stop to that.'

'It belongs in the family,' said Sonia.

'My thoughts exactly.'

'In fact, it would look very nice at the bottom of our stairs.'

***

Alex was back at the station on Monday morning. He was stirring sugar into his black coffee as Dawkins walked into the kitchen and gave him a nod of greeting.

'How's your mum getting on?'

'She's recovering. I expect she'll be back on her feet soon. Any news here?'

'Old B.T.'s on the warpath again.' B.T. was their nickname for the new Chief Constable, Bridget Thompson, who wore a D-cup.

'What's she on about now?'

Dawkins folded his arms across his belly and leaned against the green wall. 'A few of the lads ducked across town for takeaways. The traffic was heavy so they flicked on the siren and flashed the lights for a bit of a lark. Well, she hauled them into the office and gave them a right bollocking. The woman's got no sense of humour.'

'I don't know why they put women in charge – they're so anal. She was on at me about sunscreen for the trainees – sunscreen! We're in Surrey, not the bloody desert!' Alex took a sip of his coffee, a sour expression on his face.

'I hear she wants to get more female officers in,' said Dawkins.

'More bloody dykes, no doubt!'

At precisely that moment, Chief Constable Thompson, a tall figure with cropped platinum hair, walked in. Alex nearly choked on his coffee.

'I heard that.' Thompson's eyes narrowed as she looked from Alex to Dawkins and back again. 'I expect my officers to keep a civil tongue in their heads when on duty and use appropriate, *respectful* language. You've been warned.' She turned on her heel and walked out.

As the Chief Constable strode down the narrow corridor to the meeting room, she thought about the two men. Dawkins seemed harmless enough, but there was something about Coleman that made her skin crawl. In her 25 years with the force, she had seldom been wrong in her instincts about people. Besides, hadn't she seen a complaint about his conduct recently? Something about harassing his sister? She made a mental note to check the file. It never hurt to let the dodgy ones know she was keeping an eye on them.

Chapter 19

The ringing phone woke Alex. As he fumbled for the receiver, he checked the time on the radio alarm clock: 4:28 am. He was instantly alert.

'Alex Coleman speaking… Yes, I'm her stepson.' He listened carefully before replying, 'I'll drive down this morning and make all the necessary arrangements.'

Sonia rolled over and looked up at him expectantly.

'Well, Lucille's gone. It's over,' he said matter-of-factly.

'That's a relief,' said Sonia.

As Alex got dressed and straightened his tie, he felt a grim satisfaction in knowing that he was well prepared for this day.

The matron was a tall woman with stooped shoulders. Alex followed her to her small, brightly lit office. Christina Agnew had worked in the sector long enough to know that for many the loss of "loved ones" was simply a relief, but she observed that this relative seemed particularly composed and dry-eyed. She decided not to linger on the details of the patient's last days and hours, but move on quickly to the practicalities.

'These bags contain Lucille's personal effects, Mr Coleman,' she told Alex once the paperwork was done.

'Is all her jewellery in there?' asked Alex.

'Yes, her rings were removed when her fingers got too swollen to wear them and they're in a white box labelled with her name, along with a few other bits and pieces. You'll find it's all in the bags.'

'Very good.'

'Did you wish to see your stepmother to say goodbye?'

'No, thank you. I've made arrangements for her to be transported to the funeral home.'

'Well, I think we're done then,' concluded the matron. She stood up and offered Alex her hand.

***

The keys to the penthouse were in the bag of clothes. Lucille had always refused to give him a set. He let himself in. He was struck by how empty the apartment felt. The door to the living room squeaked as he opened it; dust motes danced in a shaft of afternoon sunlight. He put the brown paper sacks holding Lucille's belongings on the sofa. Ignoring the sea view, he crossed the room quickly and crouched down next to the oak display cabinet that held the family's most precious heirlooms. Opening the glass door, he ran his fingers lightly over his father's war medals, then picked up the heavy gold fob watch that lay next to them. He held it in the palm of his hand for a moment, feeling its weight. He remembered how Grandpa Coleman had told him that it had been given to him by his own father. Grandpa had often flipped it over to show Alex the name engraved on the back:

William J. Coleman
For Bravery 1865

Grandpa had told him that his father, a policeman, had rescued a family from a burning paper mill. He had suffered burns to his face and hands during the rescue. Great-Grandpa had been riding by the mill on his bicycle when he'd smelt smoke and gone to investigate. He had banged on the door but no one had answered, so he had used a brick to smash a window. Fighting choking smoke and flames, Great-Grandpa had roused the family of eight, dragging some of them out of danger. They'd all escaped, except a 14-year-old boy in a back room who had perished in the blaze.

Alex placed the watch back on the glass shelf, coiling the heavy gold Albert chain around it – the chain that was missing the star medallion. It was now time to return the star to its rightful place, attached to the very last link of the chain.

He opened up one of the paper sacks. A white box labelled "Lucille Coleman" lay on top of her clothing. He took off the lid. Inside were two silver bangles, a gold wedding band and a solitaire diamond engagement ring. Alex scowled. Where was the necklace with the gold star medallion? He quickly rummaged through the rest of the clothing. It definitely wasn't in the bags. But Lucille never took that necklace off. It had been her talisman.

'Bloody hell,' he suddenly said out loud, '– it's around her fucking neck!'

He slammed the apartment door behind him, clattered down the stairs, the lift would be too slow, and jumped into the Range Rover. As he drove back to the nursing home he cursed every red light, and even a teenage girl in lycra who forced him to slow at a pedestrian crossing. Turning into the hospital driveway, he was stuck behind an elderly man in a wheelchair inching up the middle of the carriageway.

'Out of the way, you old git,' Alex muttered.

In the lobby, he had to dodge around two more old ducks pushing walking frames, before finally arriving at reception.

'I'm sorry, sir, Mrs Agnew is in a meeting,' said the receptionist, peering at him over her red spectacles. 'She can't be disturbed – grieving relatives.'

'Well, I'm a grieving relative and I'd like to see my stepmother now. Her name's Lucille Coleman.'

'Just a moment.'

Five minutes later the receptionist was back. 'I'm sorry, sir, you can't see Mrs Coleman. She's already on her way to the funeral home. But you'll be able to visit her there. I'll just look up the address for…' The receptionist's voice trailed off. Alex was already striding out the double glass doors.

He hurried up the steps of the funeral parlour, brushing past tubs of rosemary.

A further obstacle awaited him at reception.

'Well, er… Mrs Coleman has only just arrived. I'm afraid she won't be ready for viewing until this afternoon,' the funeral director wrung her hands together apologetically.

It's only a dead body, for chrissakes, thought Alex. A muscle worked in the side of his cheek as he said in a clipped voice, 'I understood there would be no embalming. I'd rather see her in her natural state, if you don't mind. I'm a former soldier; I'm familiar with death.'

'Let me speak to the undertaker,' said the funeral director.

***

It was shortly after noon when Alex was shown into a small room with pink roses on the wallpaper. Lucille lay on a raised bed, her large, knobbly hands clasping a sprig of rosemary. He glanced at her face – hollow cheeked, eyes closed. She wore a high-necked blue blouse, buttoned to the top. Perhaps the necklace was under the blouse. He looked about the room. There was no evidence of security cameras. Quickly, he undid the top buttons of the blouse – her white chest was bare. Then where on earth could the medallion be? He'd have to search the penthouse.

He applied his SAS training to the problem at hand, dedicating the entire afternoon to systematically and thoroughly checking every drawer, cupboard, cabinet and wardrobe in the apartment. The sapphire engagement ring and gold wedding band from Lucille's first marriage were easily located in a trinket box on the dressing table. Sonia planned to have these melted down and fashioned into modern, stylish pieces of jewellery. But where was the star medallion?

He knew he'd seen it when he had visited the nursing home. He remembered gazing at the five-pointed gold star, nestled in the folds of Lucille's nightdress as she lay sleeping. She hadn't had long to live and he'd wanted to ask her for it then and there. But he had held back. Alex knew it was very dear to her because of the connection with his father. She had often said it was a comfort to her and brought her good luck. Then he had realised that Lucille's eyes were half-open and she was shrewdly watching him. He'd sensed that she had known what he'd been thinking.

Was it possible she had deliberately schemed to keep the necklace from him?

Chapter 20

'I thought the wake was going to be at the Prospect Hotel, over the road,' Janice said to Bertie, as she surveyed the meagre spread of dry club sandwiches, cold sausage rolls and buttered scones on Lucille's dining table.

'Yes, I booked the Prospect – that was what Lucille wanted,' said Bertie, 'but his Lordship preferred to cut costs and have it at her apartment. He asked the bakery on the corner to do the catering. Lucille never used that bakery. She said they wouldn't know a decent scone if it bopped them on the nose!'

'Well, I suppose it's Alex's call if he has to pay for it,' said Janice, brushing crumbs off her smart grey jacket.

'Him pay – that'll be the day!' Bertie snorted. 'He'll be scooping the pool, and yet he hasn't even got the good grace to give her a halfway decent send off. Money is all that bastard cares about. I think I'd better sit down. It upsets me, thinking about how he's treated your godmother.'

Janice noticed Bertie's three-piece suit hung loosely off his thin frame as she gently guided him to a chair. She had travelled down to Lyme Regis from Derbyshire with her father, Tom, who was Lucille's cousin.

'I like your tartan bow tie, Bertie,' she told him.

'It was a favourite of Lucille's – it reminded her of our trip to Edinburgh to see the Tattoo – those were happy days.' His voice was hoarse.

'Can I get you another drink?'

'Yes, I seem to have lost mine. I'm drinking chardonnay – Lucille's favourite.'

Alex and Sonia were standing apart from the main group, next to the drinks table. As Janice approached, she saw Sonia whisper something to Alex.

'Bertie would like another glass of chardonnay, please Alex, and I'd like a pinot noir.'

Alex looked down at the bottles of wine standing on the table. 'Sorry, there's none open. It's a waste to open a bottle when we're just finishing up.' He glanced at his Rolex. 'Goodness me, 2:30! I'd hoped to have all this wrapped up by two o'clock.'

Janice gave him a withering look and turned on her heel.

'I'm sorry, Bertie. It appears the bar is closed. Alex wouldn't open another bottle.'

'The stingy bugger! We can go back to my flat and have a drink.' The pair stared sullenly at the grey waters of the bay, then Janice turned her attention back to the crowded room. She saw Alex leave Sonia's side and approach her father, who was standing nearby.

'Just before you go, Tom, I was thinking perhaps you or the girls might like a small memento to take with you.' Alex threw his arm out expansively. 'Something to remember Lucille by.'

There was a pause before Tom replied, his voice gruff with disapproval. 'I don't think this is the time or the place to be divvying up her belongings. Best to wait a while.'

'As you like. Perhaps you could visit another time,' said Alex. 'Excuse me, I must see to the drinks.' He decided not to approach any other family members on the matter. If they were silly enough to want to wait, let them. He would be moving swiftly to empty the apartment. There was no point in losing out on rental income.

After the last of the guests had dribbled out, Alex decided he might as well pack a few of the valuables into an empty wine box. He bent down to open the oak display cabinet, then stopped. The war medals were there, but where was the gold fob watch? He stared in disbelief at the empty space on the wooden shelf. Had it been there when they arrived? He had been too distracted, welcoming the hordes of friends and relatives, to check. With a sick feeling, he realised it was too late to fingerprint the house – anyone's prints could be on that cabinet. One or two small children had insisted on running about touching everything.

'Sonia – the fob watch is gone!'

Sonia came running. 'It can't have been taken this afternoon.'

'No, I think someone must have been in here before that. Who else has a key?'

Sonia thought for a moment. 'Would Bertie have one?'

'I'll have to pay him a visit,' said Alex.

But Bertie did not answer the loud knocking at his door, nor the telephone.

'I'll ring him this evening,' Alex told Sonia as she helped him carry the boxes down to the Range Rover. Frustrated, Alex locked the door of the penthouse behind him.

But when Alex phoned Bertie that evening, he brusquely denied ever having a key to the apartment.

'I'm reporting the theft to the police, so expect a visit from them,' growled Alex.

'Hmmph! Just try it, Alex. I'm a doddery old man with one foot in the grave. Let's see how interested they are in interviewing me. When they come over, I'll be dribbling on my bib and I won't be wearing my hearing aids! In fact, I might even have a little accident.' With that, Bertie slammed down the phone.

Alex looked at the receiver in surprise. *What had happened to the Bertie who was usually so mild-mannered and malleable?*

***

On a brittle blue morning in early December, Alex drove alone in his Range Rover up a sweeping driveway lined with bare trees. He had decided to drop in at the crematorium on his way to the penthouse, where he was meeting the painters.

At the counter, he flipped open his wallet to show his driver's licence, then signed the records for the "transfer of ashes". He had chosen a shiny black, biodegradable urn, not because he cared about the environment, but because at £32.75 it was the cheapest option.

Outside the crematorium, he stood on a patch of frosty grass, holding the urn in his leather gloved hands. He took a moment to survey the cemetery with its rows of gravestones, clipped hedges and woodland areas. His eyes settled on a large cone-shaped conifer tree at the end of a row of graves.

'That will do,' he muttered, his breath frosting in the chilly air. Alex strode over to the conifer, slipped off a black glove so he could prise the lid off the urn and then, without a moment's hesitation, tipped the ashes around the base of the trunk. Job done, he thought. He checked his Rolex. Still time for a coffee before I meet the painters. Alex tossed the empty urn into a nearby rubbish bin, then sped off in the Range Rover for Lyme Regis.

Chapter 21

'Well, this is a surprise,' said Margaret, in a tone that indicated it was not a pleasant one. She stood in the doorway eyeing her daughter, who had a small navy suitcase at her feet. 'You won't be able to stay here.'

Cathy felt a stab of pain. 'I've booked into a B&B,' she said quickly. 'I don't want to put you to any trouble.'

'Well, I suppose you'd better come in, then.'

As Cathy passed her mother, she reached out and gave her a small hug. Her mother's body felt stiff and unyielding.

'I'll put the kettle on,' said Margaret.

Cathy looked about the living room. The wooden furniture was covered by a light layer of dust and the room smelt of old books. She walked over to the octagonal table and was relieved to see that the photo of herself as a little girl, riding a donkey on the beach, was still there. None of the recent photos sent from New Zealand were displayed.

Cathy noted that her mother's hands shook a little as she poured tea from the chrome teapot.

'I've wanted to come and see you ever since you called to tell me about the heart attack. How are you feeling?'

'Much better, thank you. I just get tired easily. I usually have a lie down in the afternoons.' Margaret handed her a bone china mug with a leaf pattern. 'Emma calls me from Sydney on the first Sunday of the month. I enjoy our chats. But tell me, how is David?'

As Cathy chatted about David's health and their life in New Zealand, she noticed her mother's face relaxing, as her initial frostiness melted. Soon they were laughing together like old friends. When the clock chimed two, Cathy looked up in surprise.

'I'd better go, Mother, and let you have your nap. I don't want to tire you out.'

'It's been good to see you.' Margaret looked at her daughter with warmth in her eyes. Cathy stood up and went to her mother's side. She bent down and gave her a kiss. Margaret reached up and grabbed one of her hands, holding it in her cool grip.

'Why don't you come over this evening for dinner? Your Aunt Dorothy would like to see you. I've got a shepherd's pie I could heat up.'

'That would be lovely, Mother, thank you.' Cathy felt tears form in her eyes. It was what she'd hoped for – a return to their previous good relationship.

A light wind ruffled her hair as she walked along, pulling her small suitcase behind her. On one side of the road stood three-storey terrace houses, while on the other a green reserve dropped away steeply to an expanse of sand and sea. Cathy stopped outside "The Seabreeze", a cheerful red and white bed and breakfast with a "Vacancy" sign in the window. She pushed on the door bell.

***

At her mother's house that evening, she was pleased to see Aunt Dorothy, a tiny, fair lady with a widow's hump. Aunt Dorothy gripped her in a fierce hug. 'It's good to see you visiting your mother, my dear.'

Margaret handed around glasses of sherry. The conversation revolved around various family members, but tactfully skirted any mention of Alex or Sonia. A delicious aroma of shepherd's pie wafted through from the kitchen.

'I'll check if the pie's ready,' said Margaret.

'Let me help you, Mother,' said Cathy, following her to the kitchen. Together they set the small, rectangular mahogany table, with its elaborate centrepiece of porcelain flowers. *It felt just like old times*, thought Cathy.

'Remember the picnics we used to go on in the Yorkshire Dales?' said Aunt Dorothy between forkfuls of shepherd's pie.

'I remember having to walk for miles and miles through fields, and up steep tracks, until Mother was satisfied we'd found the perfect picnic spot. We'd all be lugging rugs, deck chairs and, of course, the picnic hampers with us.' Cathy smiled at the memory.

'It was well worth it. I've always loved the Dales,' said Margaret.

They were interrupted by the telephone ringing.

'Excuse me,' said Margaret, getting slowly to her feet.

Cathy had a feeling it would be her brother. She was pleased she hadn't given advance warning of her visit, as no doubt Alex would have travelled up to Scarborough to make sure she didn't see her mother on her own. Cathy's hands, holding her knife and fork, rested on the table as she listened intently to the conversation in the other room. Aunt Dorothy was listening too.

'Everything's fine. We're just having dinner.'

There was silence while Margaret listened to the caller for some minutes. Then she said sharply, 'Is that so? I'd better go. I'll call you tomorrow. Bye.'

Margaret returned to the table, her lips pursed. A tense silence settled over the table. Aunt Dorothy and Cathy exchanged worried glances. It wasn't long before Margaret put her knife and fork neatly together, though her pie was only half-eaten.

'I've had enough,' she announced.

Cathy swallowed the last forkful of pie – it was suddenly dry and tasteless, sticking in her throat. Feeling tense, she helped her mother clear away the dishes. Neither of them spoke. After wiping down the bench, she joined her mother and aunt on the settee.

Her mother's foot tapped on the floor – a danger sign Cathy recognised from childhood. 'Tell me, Cathy,' she began abruptly, 'why did you take Lucille's savings? You took all her money and she struggled to make ends meet in her last years. Alex had to support her.'

'Hang on a minute, I think you've got the story wrong. I think you're confused about what actually happened.' Cathy's heart was pounding, but she forced herself to speak in calm, measured tones. There were so many times she had wanted to explain everything to her mother. If only she'd hear her out this time.

'I'm afraid I've got to go,' said Aunt Dorothy.

'No, please stay. I know Alex has been spreading lies about me around the family and I'd like you to hear my side, too.'

'I'm sorry, Cathy. I've got an early appointment tomorrow. I really must go.'

At the door, Aunt Dorothy hugged Cathy and whispered, 'You've got to sort this whole thing out with your brother. I don't like to see rifts in the family.'

'I've done nothing wrong, I promise you.' Cathy wiped her eyes and took a deep breath before returning to the lounge to face her mother. She desperately didn't want the discussion to deteriorate into a slanging match.

Her mother's face looked very small and wrinkled. Cathy sat down in the armchair next to her and leaned forward. 'I feel very sad about all this. Dad *gave* me the money just before he died. Lucille was there when he wrote out the cheque. I was free to do what I liked with that money. Dad suggested we buy a bigger house, which we did.'

'But you were meant to look after Lucille in her old age and you didn't. Instead, you selfishly left for New Zealand, and that was after you had dobbed her in for benefit fraud!' Margaret's voice shook with anger.

Cathy looked at her mother in horror. 'That's not true! I looked after her for ten years until *she* cut off all communication with me.'

'I saw the letter Lucille wrote about how you stole her money. I'm ashamed to call you my daughter. You're a disgrace!'

There was a fraught silence as Cathy tried desperately to quell her rising emotions. After a minute or two, she replied, 'Was this letter, supposedly written by Lucille, typed or written in her own hand?'

'I wouldn't know what her handwriting looked like, but she signed it.'

'And who was standing over her when she did, I wonder?'

Margaret looked out the window at the cloud banks rolling in from the North Sea. 'Why didn't you or Alex tell me Lucille had died, Mother? Why keep that a secret? I visited the penthouse a few days ago and got the shock of my life when a strange man answered the door.'

'Do you really think your brother wanted you rushing back for the funeral and causing trouble? What are you doing here now? Upsetting me. Have you come here to sniff around for your inheritance? Well, I'm better now, sorry to disappoint.' Margaret stood up, her eyes fiery. 'I don't need you here, stirring up trouble like a nasty little hornet.' She pointed at the door, 'Off you go – out!'

Chapter 22

Cathy picked up her watch from the bedside table. It was seven o'clock. She sank back into the pillows and closed her eyes, feeling utterly exhausted and hollowed out from all the crying and fretting of the night before. There was no way she could face the "full English breakfast" downstairs. Just the thought of runny egg yolks made her queasy. Not even her favourite – fried bread – could tempt her.

The memory of her mother pointing at the door and her harsh words, *Off you go – out!* echoed in her head. She had believed a mother's love was unconditional, but apparently not. Cathy had never felt like this before. The thought of being cut off from her mother's love was like a tsunami threatening to engulf her.

Today was the day she had intended to visit her cousin, Charlotte. Well, that wasn't going to happen. She felt deep shame knowing that the letter "by Lucille", calling her a liar and a thief, had been circulated around the family by her brother. Little wonder she had received so few Christmas cards from them last year. No, she wouldn't get up today. She just couldn't face it.

At about ten o'clock, there was a tap on the door. It was Kevin, the B&B's bearded, stocky owner.

'Sorry t' disturb ye. I just wundered if ye were staying another night?'

'Yes, I'll stay another night – maybe longer.' The thought of packing and leaving was impossible at this stage.

Kevin took in her bloodshot eyes and night gown. 'Yer okay?' His kindly blue eyes were full of concern.

'Yes, I'm just a bit under the weather. I need to rest.'

'If there's owt ye'd like, summat t'eat mebbe, ye call me at reception.'

Cathy closed the door and slipped back under the covers.

At four o'clock, there was another knock on the door. It was Kevin again. This time he was holding a tray with a bowl of soup and some toast. 'Me wife's made a bit of broth for ye. 'Appen it'll make ye feel better.'

'Thank you,' said Cathy, 'that's so kind.'

The thick vegetable soup made her feel a little stronger, and knowing that someone cared was comforting. The room grew dark, but she didn't bother to put the lights on. She watched television until she fell asleep – anything to distract her mind from the endless reel of recriminations and accusations playing in her head.

Just after dawn, the rubbish truck emptied the bins outside her window. Cathy cried out and woke up with a jolt. It was the second time she had dreamt that her brother had pushed her off a cliff, down to the rocks and sea far below. It took her a moment to realise where she was – safe in the hotel room. She lay quietly for a while, then got up and pulled back the heavy maroon drapes. Dark clouds broiled over a surging slate grey sea. Her stomach rumbled reminding her she'd barely eaten anything the day before.

She still couldn't face a cooked breakfast, but, thankfully, a continental breakfast was laid out on the buffet in the dining room. Cathy half-filled a bowl with stewed apple and plain yoghurt. The only other diners were a big athletic man and a dark-haired woman she assumed was his wife. She chose to sit at a small table with her back to them, looking out over the ocean.

Kevin appeared at her table. 'How's ye feeling today?' he asked, concern in his eyes.

'A bit better. Please thank your wife for the soup – it was just what I needed.'

'Ye welcome, lass,' said Kevin, dipping his head. ''Ave ye any plans for today. 'Tis a bit muggy. P'rhaps a walk along t' beach… some fresh air? Do ye t'world of good.'

'Yes, I think I'll walk along the beach to the cliff top walk.'

'I know yer from 'ere, but ye tek care up there, lass.'

'I will.' Cathy looked back down at a copy of *The Scarborough News* to discourage any further conversation.

Back in her room, she stuffed a few complimentary biscuits and a small bottle of water into the pockets of her bright blue rain jacket and headed out the door. A steady breeze blew into her face as she walked south along the beach. It looked like it might rain, but she didn't care. In fact, she welcomed a downpour. She wanted to be purged by the elements – released from all her suffering. Leaving behind the seaside hotels, she began the slow ascent to the cliffs. She was panting by the time she reached the barren, grass-covered summit. Her white shoes crunched over the gravel pathway that, today, was empty of all other walkers.

After a while, she stopped at a red warning sign that read:

BEWARE
DANGEROUS CLIFFS

An anguished, reckless feeling came over her. Would anyone care? The path was well back from the cliff's edge. She left it and walked slowly and deliberately towards the edge. Her feet tingled with fear. She looked down into the abyss, where the waves pounded the jagged rocks. If she let herself fall, her bones would shatter and her body would be washed away or lie broken on the rocks to be pecked at by gulls. Her knees began to shake. Slowly, she backed away.

On she walked, losing all track of time, until she came to a place where the land jutted out in a narrow peninsula with steep cliffs on either side. Cathy decided to take a shortcut. It was starting to rain. She left the main path and cut across the grass to the other side of the peninsula. Once again, she felt compelled to approach the edge. But as she gingerly stepped forward, her eyes on the sea, her foot suddenly slipped into a hole. Instantly her legs buckled beneath her and she fell towards the cliff edge. Her hands groped desperately for something to hold on to, but found only long wet grass slithering through her fingers. She began to slide forward. Then she was falling, tumbling down the cliff face like a rag doll. Cathy screamed. Within seconds, it was all over.

Chapter 23

It was the cries of the seagulls wheeling above that first penetrated her consciousness. Cathy opened her eyes and blinked a few times. Above her loomed the cliff. It was not sheer, but a steep incline. She had fallen on to a grass covered promontory of flat rocks stacked like sandwiches, jutting out from the base of the cliff. Dazed, she rolled slowly and painfully on to her side and dared to look down. Far below, the waves surged against the rocks.

'Oh my God.' Her head pounded, her mouth was dry and her whole body ached. She began to shake.

Cathy pulled herself into a sitting position. *Well, at least my back's not broken.* She didn't trust herself to stand. But once she had regained her wits fully, survival instincts kicked in. She unzipped the pockets of her raincoat jacket and pulled out her plastic drink bottle and took a few sips. Then she ripped open one of the cellophane packets and ate the pieces of a broken oatmeal biscuit. She would save what was left of the other biscuits and the rest of the water until later.

Now, what to do next? She hadn't brought her cell phone with her. It lay on the bedside table in her room. Cathy looked back up at the cliff face. She had fallen a distance of about 20 feet. The surface of crumbly rock and patches of grass yielded no foot or hand holds. Her ankle throbbed painfully – she must have twisted it. It seemed she had no choice but to sit and wait to be rescued. The light was slowly fading and it began to drizzle. Cathy put up her hood. Thank goodness I'm wearing my merino jumper under my coat, she thought, realising she could be spending a long, uncomfortable night on the promontory. At least she had told Kevin where she was heading. He might miss her at breakfast. And when she didn't check out at ten, he was bound to go to her room to find out if she was staying another night. She had to hope he would raise the alarm.

Her dream of the night before came back to her. In a flash of understanding, she realised that though her brother hadn't actually pushed her off the cliff, the repercussions from his actions had driven her to such despair that she had almost saved him the trouble. She had nearly let him win. Cathy vowed that if she made it out she would carry on fighting him. He should be held accountable for his actions. She would investigate her brother's dealings with her stepmother, talk to Lucille's relatives and start asking questions. It shouldn't be too late to save her relationship with her mother, either. In the half-light, she felt the shadowy presence of her father next to her, nodding and encouraging her. "Don't give up, girl – never give up."

Back at The Seabreeze, Kevin was wondering about the whereabouts of the little blonde lady in no. 4 who had seemed so unhappy. When no one answered his knock on the door, he slipped his key into the lock and turned the handle. The bed looked unslept in. But it was the cell phone and brown wallet sitting on the bedside table that aroused his suspicions. He thought back to his conversation with Cathy the morning before. The cliff walk! A dangerous place for a nervy older woman. He would never let his wife walk there on her own. Kevin hurried down the steep staircase to call the police.

When he had spoken with the local constable, he put the phone down and frowned. The constable had been too laid-back for his liking. He had said they would send a couple of officers up "to have a look-see" in the afternoon, and if she still hadn't returned by evening then he should give them another call. Kevin looked at his watch – 11:00 am. He decided to go to the cliffs himself. He quickly gathered together an emergency first aid kit, some snacks and a rope... just in case.

Every so often, Kevin left the path and peered over the edge of the cliffs. Below, he saw only sea and rocks. It was a cloudy, overcast day and he was sweating a little from the exertion. He stopped to peel off. The barren cliff tops were familiar to him; he was a Yorkshireman and fond of hiking. He trudged on, stopping every twenty paces or so to look over the edge.

It was the bright blue raincoat that caught his eye. She was sitting motionless on one of the large flat rocks halfway down the cliff, staring out to sea.

Kevin put his fingers in his mouth and gave a shrill whistle.

Cathy looked up and saw him peering down at her. Relief flooded over her. She staggered to her feet, waving both arms excitedly. 'Kevin! You came for me!'

'Are ye rieght, lass?' he hollered.

'It's just my ankle.'

'I'm gunna throw ye down a rope, ye put it round yer waist, then I'll help pull ye up, right?'

Cathy gave him the thumbs up signal.

Kevin tied the rope around his waist, then quickly tied a slipknot on the other end. He threw the rope down to Cathy and she slipped it over her shoulders and around her waist. Kevin hauled on the rope, helping her scramble and crawl her way, bit by bit, up the incline.

It was slow going and Kevin was breathing hard and sweating by the time she got to the top. He reached down, grabbed her arm and hauled her up the last little bit. She flopped down onto the grass, shaking with exhaustion.

'Well dun, lassie! Ye've made it! Ye just lie there for a minute and I'll tek a look at yer ankle.'

He knelt down and gently examined her bruised, swollen ankle. 'I don't think ye can walk on this. I'll bandage it. Then, if I put me arm around ye, I can help ye 'op 100 yards back t' main path. I'll call me son and he can meet us yonder and tek ye back on his motorbike. Think ye can manage?'

Cathy nodded. 'Yes, I'm sure I can make it. Thank you so much; I'm so sorry to be such a troublesome guest. I hope the others are less work than me.'

Kevin grinned as he coiled up the rope. ''Tis good to 'ave a bit o' excitement. 'Tis not every day I 'ave to do a search 'n rescue!'

Cathy spent the next few days recuperating at The Seabreeze, drinking bowls of delicious beef broth. Once the swelling had gone down in her ankle and she no longer looked like a car crash survivor, she visited Social Services and Age Concern to express her concerns about her mother's situation and her brother's predatory nature. A staff member with tight grey curls and a quick smile noted down Margaret's details and assured Cathy that arrangements would be made for a social worker to visit her. Age Concern could organise volunteers, known as "friends of the elderly", to drop by regularly.

She had done what she could. Next day, she took her leave from the bed and breakfast, with Kevin and his family waving her off.

Now I must find out what happened in the last months of Lucille's life, thought Cathy as she steered her rental car on to the highway heading south.

Chapter 24

They took tea sitting at a table under the huge gnarled pear tree in Janice's back garden. *This would be very pleasant*, thought Cathy, looking up at the light green fruit, *if it wasn't for the topic of conversation.*

'As you know, Lucille was my godmother and I was very fond of her,' began Janice.

'I visited her many times after she had a fall and went into hospital.'

'Do you mind if I take notes about what you're telling me?' Cathy asked her.

'Yes, go ahead,' replied Janice. 'Anyway, I saw Auntie Lucie get progressively weaker. I'm a physiotherapist, so I'm familiar with hospitals. She had very swollen ankles and trouble with her breathing. Bertie was wonderful – he was 95, but he visited Auntie every day, driving to the hospital in his little Renault.' Janice smiled at the memory.

'I remember asking the nurse about her treatment plan. The nurse said Lucille didn't have long to live, possibly only days or weeks. They wanted contact details of her next of kin – your brother. Apparently, Alex had only visited once and then he'd brought a will with him for her to sign. The nurse he'd asked the matron to witness it – the cheek of it! – but she refused.' Janice looked down and shook her head, her straight coppery fringe glinting in the sunlight. Cathy waited for her to continue.

'It upsets me, even now, to recall your brother's treatment of Auntie. I know you've fallen out with him and I can understand why.'

'Were you ever with Lucille when my brother visited?' asked Cathy quietly.

'Bertie said Alex only visited her once during all those months she was sick. I saw Auntie a couple of days after Alex's visit and I can tell you she was very ill by that stage.'

Janice went on to tell Cathy how she had arrived at the ward on the third floor to find that her godmother's bed had been shifted next to a window looking out over the garden. Lucille was on oxygen. When Janice had asked if Alex had been to see her, a look of pure hatred had crossed her godmother's face.

'That bastard makes my back curl,' Lucille had spat out. Then she had begun to gasp and cry out. 'Help me... nurse! I can't breathe.' A nurse had rushed over to check the tubes in her nose and calm her down. Bertie had explained to Janice that Lucille was suffering from what he called "panic attacks". She got very agitated and felt as if she couldn't breathe. Afterwards she needed to rest.

Bertie had whispered to Janice, 'Please don't mention Alex's name again. It just upsets her. He's a nasty, nasty piece of work. Look how ill she is – imagine pushing her to sign a new will! It's a disgrace.'

'The last time I visited Auntie I gave her a pamper session,' continued Janice, smiling at the memory.

'I remember how she loved her visits to the hairdresser's,' said Cathy. 'Dad used to joke she had the fastest growing hair in Lyme Regis.'

'I know. I took in a brush with soft bristles to do her hair for her. You could almost hear her purring. I massaged her hands and fingers with lotion, filed her nails and painted them pink to match her nightie. I remember she was concerned about Bertie that day. He was unable to visit her for a few days because he had to have an eye operation. After we had talked for a bit, I fed her some soup and she fell asleep. It was the last time I saw her. She died a week later.'

Janice waited as Cathy made her notes. When Cathy looked up, she continued. 'A few months later Bertie died. We went to his funeral and that's when I found out that Alex hadn't even bothered to put up a plaque for Auntie Lucie. When I asked him where her ashes were buried, he just pointed to a tree and said he'd sprinkled them under there – they'd be good for the tree. He was so callous. My sister Alison was in tears.'

126

Cathy shook her head and closed her notebook. She looked at Janice sadly. 'Thank you for talking to me today.'

'So what are you going to do now?' Janice asked.

'I'll talk to some more family members and then I'm going to see a lawyer,' said Cathy. 'I think my brother has a case to answer. Is there anything else you'd like to tell me?'

'Yes, there is one thing. Auntie Lucie always told us that she'd leave my sister and me some money and her engagement rings. You know she was married twice, so there was one engagement ring for each of us. I was to get the diamond solitaire and my sister the sapphire. We never got anything. You should talk to my dad about that. I know he has spoken to Alex… I don't really care about the rings, or the money for that matter. I've got my own rings, after all.' Janice touched the ruby on finger. 'But I do care that my godmother's wishes weren't respected.'

'I agree. And for me, this is also about my father. It was his money too. This is absolutely not what either of them wanted.'

'You ought to talk to my father, Tom. He was close to Auntie Lucie – they grew up together.'

They talked a while longer about other things. Then Cathy quickly hugged the younger woman and left. In her handbag, she had a phone number for Tom.

***

The first thing that struck her as she hopped out of the rental car was the fragrance wafting through the air. She had parked next to a stone wall and on the other side grew a row of pines. She gazed up into the dark green branches, inhaling the woodsy, resinous smell. Then she spotted Tom, wearing a tweed cap, coming towards her carrying a bundle of pine cones.

'Hello Cathy, I was just collecting some pine cones for the woodstove. Come inside.'

She followed him into the stone cottage. It was typical of the farm kitchens Cathy remembered from her childhood; stone flags on the floor, a big, scrubbed kitchen table and a black coal range. Tom filled a large black kettle with water and set it on the hob to boil. They sat down on either side of the range in spindle back chairs.

'So how's life in New Zealand? Have you visited any of those big sheep stations? I saw on the telly how they found a wild sheep out the back of one of them. Hadn't been shorn in years – could barely see out from under his great big woolly fleece.'

They chatted about New Zealand until the kettle made a low, whistling sound. As Tom threw a handful of tea leaves into the enamel teapot and poured in boiling water, Cathy sliced up the fruit cake she had bought at the village shop.

'Cake looks nice, Cathy,' said Tom, taking a hunk.

'It's a great place you've got here, Tom. I know Lucille used to love visiting you,' said Cathy, by way of introducing the topic.

'After you moved to New Zealand, Lucie and Bertie came here for Christmas. Every year, either Janice or my other daughter, Alison, would drive them up here. I'd cut a branch from the pine trees for my little granddaughters to decorate with lights and tinsel. Janice would cook a turkey. My girls were very good to Lucie. They waited on her hand and foot. She never so much as dried a dish while she was here.'

Tom took a sip from his mug of tea and looked into the distance thinking. 'Yeah, that's why we were all surprised when she left them nothing in her will. Many's the time I heard her say over the years that she'd leave them each some money and her fancy rings.'

'Did you ask Alex what happened to the rings?' asked Cathy, looking at Tom's lined, patient face.

'Yes, I did. He gave me a call one day. I couldn't rightly follow what he was saying about different wills, this and that. But I do remember him saying that after the funeral costs were taken out there was only about £3,000 left. Now, how can that be when her apartment must've been worth hundreds of thousands of pounds?'

Cathy jotted that down in her notebook. Tom watched her quietly, before continuing.

'I asked him about the engagement rings and he said Lucille had sold them.' Tom snorted. 'I said she'd *never* sell her rings. Then he rung me back ten minutes later with some story that one of the caregivers who dressed Lucie's leg ulcers had stolen them!'

'What rubbish,' said Cathy. 'Do you know what happened to all the antique furniture?'

'He told me he sold the lot at auction for £150!'

Cathy raised her eyebrows.

Then Tom told Cathy how, out of the blue, Alex had telephoned one Sunday afternoon to say he was in the area and would drop off some jewellery from Lucille for the girls. Half an hour later he had been on the door step, the engine of the parked Range Rover still running. Tom had invited Alex in for a cuppa, but Alex had said he "must dash – important business". He'd asked Tom if Lucille had ever given him a gold fob watch or a necklace. When Tom had said no, Alex had thrust a cardboard shoe box into his hands, leapt into the Range Rover and rumbled off up the driveway.

In the kitchen, Tom had opened the box up. Inside were some framed photos and a cloth bag tied with a drawstring. He'd tipped the contents of the cloth bag onto the table and a fake coral necklace, a pāua shell pendant, two tarnished silver bracelets and some tacky earrings had dropped out. Tom had decided not to pass the trinkets onto the girls – they'd be insulted. The photos in stand-up frames were of Janice and Alison, from babyhood to their wedding days. They had once stood proudly on Lucille's sideboard.

'I'll tell you another thing,' said Tom, looking Cathy straight in the eye. 'One time I visited Lucie and she said to me, "Tom, I think I backed the wrong horse. I've got my regrets".'

There was a long pause while Cathy thought about what Tom had just told her. She'd often wondered if Lucille had regretted switching her allegiance to Alex.

'She cut me off completely, you know, over a silly argument,' she said in a low voice. 'I didn't even know she'd died until two weeks ago.'

'She was a stubborn old duck − runs in the family. But she suffered in her last months. If she'd been one of me cows, I'd have sent her to the great pasture in the sky.'

Cathy checked the time. 'I guess I'd better get going before it gets dark. It's a windy road.'

'Just take a bit of care and you'll get there without any trouble.'

As Cathy crossed a little humpback bridge and zigzagged up a hill with stone walls on either side, she thought about Lucille's death and the funeral. Her talks with Tom and Janice were helping her build a picture of what had happened. Before returning to New Zealand, she planned to visit other relatives and the matron of the nursing home, to get their version of the events.

Chapter 25

Cathy thrust her nose into the soft pink rose petals and inhaled deeply. She closed her eyes, allowing the calming fragrance to waft through her. She took another deep breath. The heady floral aroma was almost intoxicating. As she drank it in, she felt the tension slip out of her body. It was good to be home.

Dressed in navy three-quarter pants, white shirt and white bucket hat, she straightened up and wended her way through the colourful rosebeds towards the green spread of the croquet lawns. She was struck by the beauty of the setting, just as when she had first seen it five years ago. It could have been a movie set. Her eyes rested on the half-timbered, gabled and turreted old Bath House, which overlooked the lawns. A group of players was standing in a huddle in front of the croquet pavilion, a low, yellow weatherboard building with an outlandish green pagoda-style roof. Behind the pavilion, long, thin trees thrust up into the air at angles like a bunch of fingers. Above it all was a brilliant blue sky.

Cathy smiled as she saw Rhonda waving a long arm, her friend's tall frame dwarfing the other women. Rhonda strolled over to give her a hug.

'How was your trip?'

'It had its moments, but I survived and I'm back in one piece – but only just!'

'You'll have to tell me about it,' said Rhonda in her husky voice. She gestured towards the croquet lawn. 'If you like, we can make up a pair.'

They joined their opponents and began the match. Cathy's mallet gave a satisfying "thwack" as she hit her first ball through the hoop.

'Well done,' said Rhonda. 'I thought you might be out of practice.'

'Probably just a fluke,' said Cathy. Rhonda was a far superior player, but always generous with her praise. Cathy had met her when she had only just moved to Lake Rotoiti. She had been standing watching the croquet after a visit to The Bath House, now a museum. Seeing her interest in the game, Rhonda had introduced herself and invited her to come along and join in the fun another time. Croquet on Wednesday mornings had soon become a firm fixture on Cathy's calendar. During David's struggle with cancer, she had stopped playing, but Rhonda's kindness in dropping off meals for her throughout the stressful time had cemented their friendship.

Now they sat on the green benches under the eaves of the pavilion, a little apart from the main group. Rhonda looked thoughtful as Cathy told her how she had found out her stepmother was dead and her brother had inherited everything.

'Are you going to challenge the will?' she asked.

'Yes, I am, because I heard from relatives that he pressured her into signing when she lay dying in hospital with oxygen tubes up her nose.'

'The bastard! How can you fight it?'

'Well, I know my stepmother had her own lawyers draw up a will naming me as a major beneficiary and mentioning other relatives. If I can find a copy of that will, then I can begin to fight this. I'm not a blood relative, so if I can't find a copy, then it's the end of the road.'

Rhonda gazed at the croquet greens as she considered this. Then she said, 'If you knew where her solicitor's office was located, you might be able to find some contact details for law offices on the internet. There's more and more information being put online these days.'

'I'm pretty sure she would have used a local lawyer in Lyme Regis, where she lived. So I'm going to give it a shot tonight.'

Just then a burly senior in a broad brimmed white hat walked by, clanging a large hand bell. Cathy and Rhonda picked up their croquet mallets, took their balls from the bucket, and headed over to the whiteboard to see who they were playing next.

***

That evening, Cathy sat staring intently at her brightly lit computer screen. A Google search had revealed just four solicitors in Lyme Regis. She jotted down their phone numbers in a notebook, then checked her wristwatch: Nine o'clock – good, the working day would just be beginning in England. In ten minutes, she would begin making the long distance calls. From the lounge, she could hear the cricket commentary blaring over the TV. David really was getting quite deaf, but he refused to wear hearing aids.

Slowly, she began working her way through the list of phone numbers, politely explaining that she was calling from New Zealand and asking if it would be possible to check the files for a will for Lucille Coleman. By the fourth call, she was beginning to feel her search might be in vain, but she waited patiently while a crisp voiced receptionist carried out her request.

'Did you say her name was Lucille Coleman?'

'Yes.'

'And is your name Cathy Stewart? Can you tell me your middle name, please, and Mrs Coleman's address at the time the will was made?'

Cathy supplied the information. The receptionist said, 'I can confirm that we do hold a will for Mrs Coleman, who you now say is deceased. If you send me through an email with the necessary details to this office, then I can send you a scan of the will.'

Thanking her profusely, Cathy ended the call. She jumped off her swivel chair.

'Yes! Bingo!' she shouted, punching the air with her fist. She burst through the double doors into the lounge. David had nodded off in his armchair. Grabbing the remote, she muted the television, then prodded him on the shoulder. He jolted awake.

'David, I've found it!'

'What…? What did you find?' He stared up at her, blinking.

'Lucille's will! Her lawyers drew it up in 1990, then she made a small change in 1999. It names me as executor and a major beneficiary. This means I can now challenge that dodgy will Alex forced her to sign!'

'So when do I get my super yacht?'

'C'mon, be serious. This is important to me. If I hadn't found this out, I'd have come to a dead end and he'd have won.'

'Let's see it then,' said David, reaching for his reading glasses.

'The law office is going to scan the will and email it through. I'll be able to show it to you in the morning.'

'Well, it's a start,' said David, 'but are you sure you want to start digging all this up?'

'Yes, I am. I can't let him get away with it.'

She was woken at 7:08 next morning by the phone ringing. Reaching for the receiver, she sat up in bed. It was Emma's husband, Dean. Cathy and David had travelled to Sydney for their daughter's wedding in the Botanic Gardens the previous year. Emma had looked elegant in a sleek dress of buff coloured satin, carrying a bouquet of red roses.

Pressing the phone to her ear, Cathy shouted, 'I can hardly hear you, Dean. Speak up!'

Dean's voice came through the static. 'It's a boy.'

'I know the baby's a boy. Emma told us after the ultrasound. Wait a minute, where are you calling from?'

'The hospital… Emma's had the baby.'

'You're pulling my leg. It's not due for another three weeks!'

'He's been born early. But he's fine. He's a good weight and Emma is holding him now.'

Cathy felt herself go hot and cold as the news sank in. 'David, the baby's been born!'

'What?' There was an avalanche of bed clothes as David leapt up. 'I'm a grandfather!'

'Congratulations, Dean. That's wonderful news. How did the birth go?' asked Cathy.

'She's exhausted because she's been up all night. But everything went well and we've got a healthy little boy.'

'Fabulous! Give Emma our love and congratulations. Tell her to text us when it's a good time to call. I'll just put David on for a quick chat now.'

Cathy put the phone down and wiped joyful tears from her eyes. Of course, a part of her wished she could rush up to the hospital right now, but they had decided it would be better to give Emma and Dean a couple of weeks to settle into parenthood before they descended.

Chapter 26

Cathy bustled into the hall fizzing with excitement. About a dozen people, mainly women in their sixties, had gathered for the Age Concern training day for volunteers. Cathy spotted Rhonda with her back to her, stooping to talk to Zoe, a diminutive lady with cropped white hair, who Cathy recognised from croquet. She hurried over to tell her the news.

'Congratulations! Welcome to the Grandma Club. I've got a nice pattern for a cross-stitch bib,' said Rhonda.

Cathy's eyes gleamed with pride as she pulled out a piece of folded A4 from her handbag. 'Emma emailed this photo through last night. He was born early, but all is well. He weighs 6 lb 3 oz.'

'Let me put on my glasses,' said Rhonda. 'He's adorable… look at those brown eyes.'

'What a darling,' clucked Zoe.

Just then a tall, plump woman with honey coloured hair clapped her hands together.

'If I could have your attention, please, we'll get started on this morning's programme. Please take a seat.'

Once they were settled, she began, 'My name is Carolyn Price and I'll be taking you through the training to become a visitor friend for the elderly. Social isolation is a huge problem for the elderly living on their own. Our clients tell us that having a visitor makes them feel happier and less lonely.'

Cathy nodded in agreement. She hoped her mother could benefit from the same service in the UK and wanted to give back to the organisation by volunteering in the Rotorua district.

After the morning tea break, Carolyn wrote the words "ELDER ABUSE" in big red letters on the whiteboard. 'Elder abuse is a global problem,' she began. 'International studies report that every year 30 % of older people experience abuse or neglect. And it's on the rise. In the past three years, over 50% of the cases seen in New Zealand have involved financial abuse, and sadly, three-quarters of that abuse has been carried out by family members.'

Rhonda nudged Cathy, who kept her eyes fixed on the speaker. 'The abuse often entails misuse of power of attorney or establishing a relationship to exploit an older person's savings or assets. You need to watch out for signs of financial abuse on your visits.'

Carolyn turned her back to the audience to write, "Signs of Financial Abuse" on the whiteboard, then continued, 'Is the older person anxious, worried about their finances? Perhaps they've told you that they find someone in their life intimidating or scary? Does the older person appear to be short of money for the basics, like food? If you have any concerns about the welfare of an older person you are visiting, then please tell us. We have staff who are trained to deal with these situations.'

As Cathy listened, she decided to seek the tutor's advice during the lunch break. At the end of the morning session, she walked over to the tutor's table next to the whiteboard. Carolyn was packing her papers into her satchel. She looked up and gave Cathy an encouraging smile. Cathy quickly outlined her concerns about her mother. Carolyn's soft fleshy face wore a thoughtful expression.

'Do you know the name of your mother's solicitor?' Carolyn asked.

'Yes, I do.'

'Then why don't you write to them and express your concerns that your brother may try to exploit your mother for financial gain? That way they could be forewarned.'

Cathy nodded slowly.

'Even though you said you had a row with your mother, you should write to her and tell her your concerns about your brother's motives. Remember, he may try to isolate her. You should try to keep up regular contact by phoning and writing to her.'

They chatted for a few minutes more, then Cathy joined Rhonda, who was waiting at the door to walk to their favourite café. The tables inside were all taken with the Friday lunch time rush, so they sat outside next to a row of potted red geraniums. Cathy told Rhonda about her discovery of Lucille's original will.

'Now I've got grounds to contest the new will. If I can prove he ripped my stepmother off, then maybe that'll stop him from taking advantage of my mother.' She popped a forkful of passion fruit slice into her mouth, relishing the exotic tang and jelly-like texture. Cathy knew it was calorie-laden, of course, but didn't she deserve a treat to celebrate the birth of her first grandchild?

'It must be hard to fight it from this distance,' commented Rhonda, stirring her flat white.

'It is. And I've only just started.'

***

Cathy tore another page off her writing pad and scrunched it up. She let out a heavy, dejected sigh and rested her head on her hand. Her desk looked out over the lake, a view she normally found soothing. Today it only taunted her. The desk fan whirred, blowing waves of tepid air through her hair, which had gone frizzy in the humidity. She was finding it very difficult to compose a letter to her mother warning her of her brother's duplicity and ulterior motives. Every word she wrote made her sound like a jealous, paranoid, scheming daughter after the inheritance herself. She wiped a light sheen of perspiration off her forehead with the back of her hand. Perhaps a swim in the lake would help.

Half an hour later, she stood on the bleached wooden planks of the landing, a small figure in a blue swimsuit, peering into the water. She could see the sandy bottom of the lake and some dark green weed-like strands of grass swaying gently. Plunging under the deliciously cold water, she surfaced to swim breaststroke through the water. The cool water cleared her head. For a while, she floated on her back, staring up at the lime-green willow leaves. She thought about the letter and decided it would be best to write her concerns down quickly and honestly.

15 February 2009

Dear Mother,

I'm just writing to let you know that Emma has had a baby boy! They've called him Ryan Thomas and he was born on 10 February. He weighs 6 lb 3 oz, which is a very good weight considering he was born three weeks early.

I'm very sorry my visit ended so unhappily. I want you to know that I do truly care about you and I've got your best interests at heart, even though I live on the other side of the world.

As you may know, Alex has inherited Lucille's apartment and all of her estate. I believe he abused his power of attorney and pressured Lucille into signing a new will when she was very ill in hospital, making him the major beneficiary. I have gathered evidence from relatives to that effect and intend to contest the will.

I would hate to see you fall into the same trap. Alex cannot be trusted. Acquiring wealth seems to have become his main motive in life, so please be aware of this. If you have any concerns about his behaviour, please talk to your solicitor, or your doctor, or a representative from Age Concern. There are people out there who can help you.

Cathy's pen hovered over the page for ten seconds before she signed the letter. At this point in time, *'Love from'* felt dishonest, so instead she wrote, *'Take care, Cathy'.*

Her next task was to write to her mother's solicitor. Taking down a beer glass from David's collection, she poured herself a large lime and soda with ice, before sitting down in front of the computer.

***

The plaintive call of the morepork cut over the loud thrumming of the crickets. Cathy took a sip of tea as she contemplated the lake at dusk. David was just a few feet away on his wooden rocker. They sat quietly, thinking their own thoughts and listening for the owl to call out again.

'What have you decided to do about contesting the will?' David said eventually.

'I think I'll find out if the lawyer who drew up Lucille's original will still works there. If he does, I can ask if he's interested in investigating the case for me. Alex said all the paperwork was above board and legal, but I doubt that very much.' A note of contempt crept into her voice. 'I smell a rat – a stinking big, devious one.'

'I guess that's a good way to go. The lawyer may feel some moral obligation to find out if the client's wishes were carried out.' David yawned and stood up. 'Well, I'm off to bed.'

'I'll join you after I've called the lawyer. I'd like to talk to him before we fly to Sydney on Friday.'

Chapter 27

'I had a call from your cardiologist's office last week, Mother. The secretary said you'd missed your appointment. Did you forget to go?' Alex looked up from the stack of bills on the table in front of him, studying his mother from under dark bushy eyebrows.

Margaret replied carefully, 'Well, we all forget things from time to time. Are you taking me to the appointment this afternoon?'

'Yes, I've driven all the way up from Surrey to do that, Mother. Since you *forgot* last week.'

'I thought you said you were up here giving a training course?'

Sharper than I thought, realised Alex. 'Yes, but it's hardly convenient to schedule in this appointment when I'm already busy. The fact is, you're getting forgetful, Mother. Your memory isn't what it used to be.'

Margaret said nothing, but only shrank into herself a little more. There was silence, then the grandfather clocks chimed once.

'These accounts seem to be in order. Now, what's for lunch?'

'I'll just see what I can rustle up. If you'd told me you were coming, I'd be more prepared.' Margaret went out to the kitchen.

'But I *did* tell you I was coming, Mother,' insisted Alex.

'No you didn't,' Margaret called out from the kitchen.

Nothing wrong with her hearing either, thought Alex.

As Margaret opened the fridge, he loomed up suddenly behind her, peering over her shoulder. 'There's not much in there. I don't think you're doing your shopping.'

'Well, I shop on Thursdays and that's tomorrow,' snapped Margaret.

'I see you've got some cheese. A toasted sandwich will be fine,' said Alex shortly.

While Margaret made the toasted sandwiches he went back to the living room and stood looking disapprovingly around at all the clutter. He ran a finger along the edge of a photo frame thick with dust and returned a stack of books to the bookshelf. Picking up a vase of dead flowers, he walked into the kitchen. 'Has your cleaner been this week?' he asked.

'She was here on Monday,' said Margaret, popping the sandwiches into the toasted sandwich maker.

'Well, she's not doing a very good job, and you can tell her I said that. The lounge is dusty and there's cobwebs in the corners.'

'Anything else not to your liking, sir?' asked Margaret, clearly irritated.

'As a matter of fact, Mother, there is. This apartment is really getting too much for you.' He purposely softened his voice. 'It's lonely for you, too, especially in winter. Sonia and I have discussed this and we'd much rather see you in a retirement home where you'd be well looked after, close to us in Surrey. That way we could visit you every week, take you out, and you wouldn't have to struggle here on your own.' He leaned back on the cupboards, arms folded.

Margaret lifted her chin and turned to face her son. 'I've always lived in Scarborough and I like it here by the sea.'

'We've found a very nice place with a big garden near us. I'll take you there one weekend to have a look.'

'No, thank you. I don't want to be surrounded by old ladies wearing nappies.'

'It's not like that at all, Mother. They'll take good care of you.'

'I don't like the smell of pee and cabbage soup, and as for those old biddies talking nonsense all day – I'm not ready for that. Now take these placemats to the table. I'll bring the toasted sandwiches. Enough about old people's homes.'

'I said "retirement home" mother.'

'Same thing.'

They ate their toasted sandwiches in silence, then Margaret said, 'I hear Emma's had a baby boy.'

'Really…? And how did you hear that news, Mother?

Margaret hesitated for a moment and then replied airily, 'Oh, Emma told me.'

'Is it wise to have contact with Emma after what her mother has done?' His voice rose in indignation. 'Stealing £50,000 is a crime in anyone's book.'

'Well, she just calls now and then… she is my granddaughter, after all,' said Margaret.

'Mother, I've warned you to cut all ties with them – for your own safety. It's no coincidence they're in Australia; they'll be right at home with the rest of that convict stock.' He smirked at his own joke. There was no more conversation for the rest of the meal.

While his mother cleared up in the kitchen, Alex took the opportunity to snoop about the apartment. His mother's bedroom smelt like moth balls. Pairs of shoes were lined neatly around the perimeter of the room (Margaret had always loved shoes), and her dressing table was cluttered with trinket boxes and bottles of French perfume. Then he saw it. Propped against a big brown bottle of pills was a letter with a New Zealand stamp. Alex picked it up, recognising his sister's handwriting, and headed straight for the bathroom to read it.

Five minutes later he strode into the living room, where his mother was seated on the couch with her navy coat on, ready to go.

'I've had enough of this, Mother!'

She looked up, alarmed. 'What…? Enough of what?'

'Enough of Cathy bad-mouthing me and filling you with her lies. I'll not tolerate it. Here I am busting my gut to look after you, and she bloody well slags me off. I've told you not to contact her.'

'But I haven't!'

'Don't read her letters then. Write "return to sender" on them. And if she rings – bloody well hang up!'

'Have you been—'

Alex cut her off, shouting, 'Yes, I have!' His face was inches from hers as he said in a low menacing tone, 'And I'll continue to check on you, as it is my right as your son, with full power of attorney. I'm warning you, Mother, – it's her or me. You can't have it both ways and if you insist on keeping in contact with her, then I'll cut you off. And then who'll visit you, take you to the doctor and check all the bloody bills?' He straightened up, 'Now, get in the car!'

Margaret felt completely despondent and helpless as she tottered after him to the lift. *What a time to see a cardiologist,* she thought. *They're bound to bump up my medication.*

Alex wondered what he could do to stop Cathy from making contact once and for all. He was reluctant to go down the Interpol route again, as B.T. had her eye on him. The chief wouldn't tolerate any funny business. But Sonia might have some suggestions.

***

Sitting in the lawyer's office in his smart navy suit, Alex held himself very upright.

'Are you sure this is what your mother wants?' Stephen Farrow looked at his client shrewdly.

'Absolutely. I would bring Mother in, but she's not feeling well today. But she's really had enough of my sister ranting and raving at her over the phone, ringing her at all hours and sending nasty letters. I'm afraid my sister is really quite delusional and paranoid. It's all too much for my mother, who does have a heart condition. That's why she's not here today – palpitations and anxiety from it all. It really upsets her. Do you know anyone with a mental illness?'

'Yes, I do,' said Farrow, looking down at his notepad for a moment. He thought of his sister, who was manic depressive and quite impossible at times.

'Well, you'd understand then.'

'But, it is her daughter we're talking about – quite a major step to sever all communication,' said Farrow.

My mother is in her eighties now and she's had enough. She just can't take the constant harassment any longer. The stress of it all is bad for her health. I believe a strongly worded letter asking her not to contact my mother will solve the problem. You're welcome to give my mother a call to check that these are her wishes.'

'Very well, then,' said Farrow. 'Your mother told me you were in the army?'

'Actually, I served in the SAS in Oman. It was pretty rough in the mountains... 40° heat, scorpions in our boots, and always on the lookout for a rebel hiding behind a rock with a machine gun.'

'Really? Sounds very exciting.'

'Yes, you could say that... I've got a bullet wound on my shoulder to prove it. I was flown home on New Year's Eve. One of my mates lost both legs.'

'How tragic,' said Farrow, shaking his head and looking at Alex with new respect. 'As a matter of fact, I saw an interesting documentary on TV about the role of the SAS in the Dhofar War. It was a very successful campaign.'

'Yes, it was probably the most successful war ever fought against communists.'

Farrow looked like he would like to hear more, but Alex looked away, reluctant to continue. He could see Farrow was impressed and that was all that was necessary.

Chapter 28

Cathy lay on the couch in the dark. She reached for the box of tissues and blew her nose. The letter from her mother's solicitor lay on the floor next to her. It hurt, really hurt to be rejected by her mother yet again, but it was not as painful as it had been when she had been ordered out of her apartment in Scarborough. That time Cathy had been pushed to the very edge of her mental endurance, whereas now all she felt was a kind of heavy sadness settle on her chest.

An image flashed into her mind, of her father sitting at the table with his head in his hands. It had been the day her mother had walked out on him, taking Cathy and Alex with her. She had wanted to stay with her father, but her mother had grabbed her hand and tugged her out the door. She thought how bad her father must have felt being rejected by her mother – now it was her turn. It had been a lot worse for him; he had lost his wife, his children and the house in one fell swoop.

Her parents' divorce had been a bitter one. At the time, she hadn't really understood the circumstances, but later, through talking to her aunt, she had pieced together what had happened.

Their marriage had floundered early on. The Milnes had continued to indulge their spoilt daughter by sending her boxes of crockery, fine linen, expensive rugs and other quality items from the department store. Renton could not afford to pay for the "gifts" on his wages as a cabinet maker. Soon debts were mounting.

Meanwhile, Margaret was distracted from the drudgery of housework and caring for two small children by an admirer. Cathy had a sharp image of her father, with his rifle on his shoulder, heading out for target shooting practice. As soon as he was out of sight, her mother would dart out of the house to the red telephone box on the corner. As an adult, Cathy had realised her mother had been calling her lover, knowing her husband would be away for several hours. There were clandestine outings to London, too, for "a day of shopping". Cathy remembered her mother taking her and Alex on the train to London, but bundling them off at an appointed station en route. Kindly Granny Coleman would be waiting on the platform, with Grandpa towering above her in his three-piece suit. Grandpa would take the gold fob watch out of his waistcoat pocket to check if the train was on time. Cathy would watch her smartly dressed mother hop back on the train. It didn't escape Granny Coleman's notice that her bright-eyed daughter-in-law never got back into the same carriage she had alighted from, but always entered the next carriage, where the same man would be sitting by the window.

Eventually everything had come to light and the game was up, but it was Margaret who filed for divorce on the grounds of mental cruelty, on the advice of her mother and family solicitor. Renton would have none of that and the grounds for divorce were changed to adultery. The Milnes extracted revenge for their daughter's besmirched reputation by forcing Renton to give up the house and chattels, claiming it had all been loaned to him by the family business. Renton had diligently repaid his father-in-law for the many "gifts", but had never been issued with receipts.

Her mother had fared well, eventually becoming the manager at Milnes. As a teenager, Cathy had often been left to her own devices while her mother was at work. She remembered how pleased she would be to hear the key turning in the lock, knowing that at last her mother was home. They had relied on each other for company when her brother left home. And there had been moments of real companionship. She pictured herself sitting in front of the fire while her mother brushed out her thick blonde hair before she went to bed. Sunday afternoons, too, had been another cosy time for the two of them. After Sunday lunch at her grandparents', they would go home and watch a black and white movie together.

Though she had lived with her mother, Cathy had felt a strong bond with her father; it was such fun at his house! She was remembering the noisy board games they would play in the evening, and the thrilling adventures out sailing, when the sound of the front door opening interrupted her reveries.

'Hel-lo!' It was David back from his trout fishing trip.

The light flicked on. 'Why are you sitting in the dark? Guess what? I caught a ten-pounder!'

'Really?' Cathy sat up.

'Yes, it was a beautiful night; the moon was so bright I could tie the flies on without a torch...' He suddenly noticed Cathy's red eyes. 'What's up with you?'

Cathy inclined her head towards the letter on the carpet. David picked it up and read aloud:

As your mother has stated on many occasions, she does not want you to make any contact with her of any kind. If you telephone again, she will inform me, and it will be reported to the police on the basis of harassment. Your mother is well and does not need your assistance in any way. I would urge you not to ignore this letter.

David shook his head.

'Of course I know who's behind it,' said Cathy in a flat voice, 'but it's times like these that I really feel like giving up.'

David sat down next to her and put his arm around her.

'You smell all fishy,' she said.

'Not as fishy as this letter.'

Cathy had to smile.

David gave her an encouraging squeeze, saying, 'You can't give up now. You've found the will and you've found a solicitor who is prepared to challenge it. Wait and see what evidence the solicitor can gather against him before you make a decision.'

***

The next day was Wednesday – croquet. Cathy was just lining up a particularly difficult shot through the hoop when the mobile phone in her pocket rang.

Rhonda frowned at her.

'I'll just see who it is,' Cathy said, pulling her little mobile out and checking the screen. 'It's Emma, I'd better answer it. She never calls my mobile – it might be urgent.'

'Emma – what's wrong? Is it Ryan?' There was a pause while she listened.

Rhonda looked concerned. Their croquet opponents, Elsie and Zoe, tactfully watched the game on the next lawn.

Cathy shouted into the phone, 'I got the same letter from Granny's solicitor. I'm sorry, dear, it's horrible, isn't it? We'll have to talk about it later because I'm in the middle of a croquet game.' She turned the phone off, slipping it back into her pocket and apologised to the other women.

'Sorry, Rhonda, ladies,' Cathy lined up the next shot quickly. She hit her blue ball way too hard and it sailed past the hoop, and rolled out of bounds.

'By the look of that shot that phone call got you riled,' said Rhonda.

'Yes, there's a good reason why they say no mobile phones during play. Phone calls are a distraction a player doesn't need. I'm trying to have a break from all these problems.'

They played on and Cathy duffed so many shots that they lost the game. The bell clanged for morning tea. As they sat under the eaves nursing mugs of coffee Cathy explained the situation to Rhonda.

'… so I got a letter from my mother's solicitor telling me if I contact her they will call the police. Emma got the same letter today.'

'What's Emma done wrong?' asked Rhonda.

'Nothing, that's why she's so upset. She had an arrangement to call her grandmother on the first Sunday of each month. My mother loved hearing from her… now that will have to stop.'

'Do you know if Age Concern got involved?' asked Rhonda.

'I don't know. I'll try to find out. I'll keep calling her but I don't know if she'll talk to me. My brother's a real bully.'

'He picked up some good bullying techniques from his time in the SAS, no doubt,' commented Rhonda.

Just then Zoe walked up holding out a plate with slices of moist, dark cake. 'Here, try a piece of Elsie's chocolate cake, it'll perk you up.'

Chapter 29

Alex scowled in annoyance at the trail of cars snaking down the road. Roadworks again! He would have to try another route if he was to reach the lawyer's office on time. He cut down a side street in his new silver S-Type Jaguar, only to find that it was choked with cars too. Nipping into a driveway, he doubled back up the road, then drove swiftly through a maze of narrow side streets. He hated being late. He turned onto a main road that was at last clear of traffic and gunned the Jag in the direction of Lyme Regis. He'd gone five miles when there was a burst of siren and blue lights flashed in his rear vision mirror.

'Fucking hell!' Alex pulled on to the road shoulder. He gave a grunt of recognition when he saw who was getting out of the police car: Chris Messenger.

He had taught Chris how to use a Glock pistol as part of his basic fire arms training. Chris was a nice kid and a quick learner, but an average shot. When he slid down the window, he immediately saw the glint of recognition in Chris's eyes.

'Good afternoon, sir. Do you know how fast you were travelling just then?'

'Hello, Chris, was I speeding? I am sorry.'

'You were eight miles above the speed limit... by the way, nice set of wheels.'

'Thank you. I'm just getting used to driving it – powerful engine and really smooth to drive. I didn't realise how fast I was going.'

'How about I let you off with a warning this time.' Chris gave him a wink.

'Thank you, appreciate that.'

***

Nigel Heathcote glanced at his wristwatch: 1:55 pm. He hoped his next client wasn't going to be late. He wanted to get away from the office at three and head down to his cottage in Wales for the weekend with his wife, two children and springer spaniel.

Precisely at two o'clock, the receptionist phoned him to say Alex Coleman was in reception. Smartly dressed in a three-piece navy suit, Alex stood up when Nigel entered the room. The two men shook hands. Nigel showed Alex through to the meeting room, where a floor to ceiling book case filled with legal tomes covered one wall.

'As you know from my letter,' began Nigel once they were seated, 'I have a will here naming your sister, Cathy, as executor and major beneficiary of your stepmother's will. This will was drawn up by our office in 1990. Have you brought with you any wills made at a subsequent date?'

'Yes, I have,' said Alex. He took some documents out of his black leather satchel.

'May I see them?'

Alex handed him the documents. Nigel looked at them quickly, then stood up.

'Just a minute,' said Alex, 'where are you going with those?'

'I'm just going to have them photocopied, then you may have them back,' said Nigel pompously.

'No, I won't allow that. You can take some notes but I won't allow you to photocopy them.'

Nigel looked at Alex in surprise. He opened his mouth to say something, but Alex said quickly, 'Sit down. I know my rights.'

Nigel could only obey. He quickly began to jot down the details of dates, names and addresses of witnesses by hand. He noted that the first two wills appeared to be homemade. All three wills appointed Alex as executor and sole beneficiary, the only difference being the beneficiaries named if Alex was to predecease Lucille. As he wrote down the dates he could feel Alex's eyes boring into him. He looked up, flicked back his straight blonde fringe, which had an annoying habit of falling in front of his eyes, and cleared his throat.

'Do you have any documents relating to the transfer of the title of your stepmother's apartment to your name?'

'I'm not answering questions about the transfer of the apartment. It didn't form part of her estate and therefore it's not relevant to your client's questions regarding the wills.'

'Yes, but it did form part of her estate in 1990. Could you tell me what date the transfer of the title was registered?'

'No, I can't. You can take the time to look that up yourself. The 1990 will is irrelevant, so I don't see why we should even waste time discussing it. But while I'm here, there is something you should know. When my stepmother and my father sold their apartment in Spain, they kept the proceeds from the sale in a Jersey bank account. After my father died, my sister drafted a letter to make that a joint account in her and Lucille's names. Then she transferred £50,000 to her own Barclays account. She fleeced my step-mother. That's why my stepmother fell out with my sister. She stole her money. At that point, she gave me power of attorney and changed her will. She needed someone she could *trust*.'

Nigel broke away from Alex's gaze and looked briefly out the window. Did the man ever blink? He looked back at Alex. His stillness was unnerving.

'My client has some valid concerns regarding the will and as she is named as executor in the 1990 will, she is entitled to contest the wills if there are questions regarding their legality.'

'I assure you that everything is in order with the wills and they are legally binding. If my sister thinks she has any claim on the estate after what she has done, then she is clearly delusional. I would not encourage her if I were you, even though it may be profitable for your business.'

'Now, just a minute,' said Nigel, standing up indignantly.

'No, I'm sorry, I've wasted quite enough time on this absurd wild goose chase.' Alex gathered the wills up from the lawyer's desk, slid them into his satchel and closed it. 'Goodbye.'

When Alex had left, Nigel shook his head. What a truly unpleasant chap. Now he would have to subpoena Alex to provide the wills, which would add unnecessary costs for his client.

He checked his watch, then updated the timesheet on his laptop: 2:45 pm. If he hurried, they could beat the Friday night traffic out of town. They should be in Wales by dinner time.

Chapter 30

Alex was shaving in the upstairs bathroom when he heard Bruno barking. He froze, the razor resting on his cheek, and listened to the noise of a car pulling into the gravel courtyard. He put the razor down, wiped his face with a flannel and crept into the dark bedroom. Sonia asked drowsily from the bed, 'Why is Bruno barking?'

'Ssh,' he said, sidling up to the window.

Lifting one edge of the curtain, he peeped out. A man in a blue denim jacket and a baseball cap hopped out of the brown four-wheel drive. Holding a large white envelope, he walked towards the front door. Over the din of the dogs barking, the doorbell jingled.

Alex sat down on the bed.

'Aren't you going to answer the door?' asked Sonia.

'No, it's the process server. He'll have a subpoena for me for the wills.'

They listened to the repeated loud knocking and the ring of the doorbell.

'Well, how many times is he going to ring that bloody doorbell? I'm going to go and give him a piece of my mind,' said Sonia, swinging her long legs over the side of the bed.

Alex rested a hand on her shoulder. 'Don't. Let's just wait, he'll leave soon.'

There was silence for 15 minutes, before the doorbell rang once more. Then they heard the four-wheel drive roar off.

'He'll come again. But just tell him I'm out or on holiday. We don't want to make things too easy for them.'

***

A couple of days later, Sonia was frying pork schnitzel for dinner when she heard the bell again. Bruno, their latest dog – a Rottweiler – leapt up barking from his place by the Aga stove and bounded for the door. Sonia shook her head and went on slicing mushrooms. She had no intention of going to the door. Again, she heard repeated hard knocking, followed by silence. Bruno ran back into the kitchen. He let out a menacing growl.

'I've got a good mind to let you out,' said Sonia, opening the cutlery drawer. Then she turned to follow Bruno's gaze. A man in his twenties wearing a baseball cap was looking in the window. He tapped on the glass. Bruno snarled.

In two long strides, Sonia was at the window. She unlatched it.

'What the bloody hell do you think you're doing peeping in windows? This is private property. Get lost! Bruno, shut up!'

The dog stopped barking.

'You must be Alex Coleman's wife. I've got an envelope for him. Is he home?'

'No, he's not,' said Sonia, brandishing the tongs. 'He's at work. Now get off my property before I let the dogs out.'

She slammed the window shut and walked swiftly to the lounge windows. Hidden by the net curtain, she watched the four-wheel drive leave. The smell of burning sent her hurrying back to the stove. 'Shit!' She flipped the blackened schnitzel. 'That guy's a bloody nuisance.'

Half an hour later, Alex walked in; Bruno bounded happily around him.

'You just missed your friend.'

'What did he look like? Male in his mid-twenties, slim build, six foot tall, baseball cap?'

'That's the one. The cheeky bugger rapped on the kitchen window. I gave him what for!'

'I bet you did.' Alex laughed. His wife's hostility to strangers was legendary.

'Dinner's ready.'

'I'll just get changed and then I'll be down,' said Alex, heading for the staircase.

They ate at one end of a dining room table which seated ten.

'I was in the antique shop down in the village today and they had a gold fob watch just like your father's, only without the star medallion on the end of the chain.'

Alex's fork paused mid-air. 'Was it engraved on the back?'

'No.'

'I often wonder what happened to that watch. I talked to the matron, the undertaker, rang around the family… but nothing. I know my father wanted me to have it. Grandpa always carried it in the pocket of his waistcoat. He was a policeman, you know.'

'I guess it was stolen. Sorry about the schnitzel – it's overcooked – I was distracted by my visitor.'

Alex looked thoughtfully into the middle distance, his mind still on the watch. 'But there was no sign of forced entry and nothing else was missing…'

'I'd keep an eye on the websites selling antiques, if I were you. Jonathon found his great-grandfather's war medals for sale online.'

***

The next morning Alex heard the rumble of a diesel engine coming up the driveway, just as he was about to walk down it with Bruno. There was no time to run back to the house. He grabbed Bruno's collar and ducked behind some big camellia bushes on one side of the garden.

'Sit! Quiet,' he hissed at Bruno.

From his hiding place he could hear the crunch of car wheels on the gravel, then the slam of a car door. He peeped out from behind the bushes. It was the subpoena man all right, but this time he was wearing a brown hoodie. Again, the man pushed the brass door bell and banged on the door. He waited a few minutes, then walked down the side of the house and peered through the garage window. Alex was glad he had put the garage door down. The man didn't go around the back of the house this time. He rapped once more on the door, then jumped into his four-wheel drive and drove off.

Once he had left, Alex took the dogs into the walled garden. It would be smarter to throw them some balls, rather than take them for their usual walk. The process server could be waiting at the end of the driveway. All this hiding out and disruption to his routine was getting annoying.

***

On Friday, Alex was on his way to the training room at the station to deliver a theory lesson on gun maintenance when Dawkins stopped him in the corridor.

'There you are. Terry was looking for you.'

'Why?'

'There was a process server at reception for you. Been a naughty boy lately?' asked Dawkins with a wink.

'No. And if you see Terry tell him I'm teaching and can't be disturbed,' said Alex.

'Oh, I think the guy's gone now. It was about 45 minutes ago.'

***

The last of the trainees in navy boiler suits filed out of the room. Alex was packing his briefcase when he looked up to see B.T. leaning against the doorway with her arms folded.

'Have you got a minute, Alex?'

'Yes, ma'am.'

'Come down to my office when you're finished.' Thompson turned on her heel.

Alex let out a big sigh. An interview with B.T. – it was bound to be trouble. Maybe she had heard about the process server visiting.

When he knocked on her door, Thompson looked up from her desk. Her short blonde hair stood up in even spikes on top of her head – *A typical haircut for her kind*, thought Alex.

'Sit down,' she said in a forceful, authoritative tone. Even on a parade ground, B.T. had no need for a loud hailer. 'I've asked you to my office because Inspector Hill is carrying out an inquiry into the complaint about your conduct and has brought a couple of matters to my attention. Getting Interpol involved in what appears to be a family quarrel is rather like hitting a ladybird with a sledgehammer – unnecessary. It's a complete waste of police resources here *and* in New Zealand.' Her blue

158

eyes were cold as she went on. 'I don't take kindly to our contractors using their knowledge of the law to harass members of their family. Have you got anything to say for yourself?'

'It won't happen again, ma'am.' Seething inside, Alex looked down at a black speck on the grey carpet.

'No, it won't. I see you're coming to the end of a three-year contract and I don't expect it to be renewed. I know there are plenty of ex-army or retired officers who would be pleased to take over your role. That will be all.' She flicked open a file in front of her and began reading.

***

Meanwhile, on the other side of town, a meeting was in progress at Abel's Process Servers and Private Investigators. Dave Abel, a heavy man with a double chin, stood arms crossed in front of his team for the weekly pow-wow.

'How are you getting on this week, Gary?' he asked a youngish man in a baseball cap.

'I've served six subpoenas successfully, but I'm stuck on two. One of them is for a woman living in a caravan in a camping ground. Last time I tried, her partner recognised my car and chased me out of the camp in his van. He sat on my tail for a few miles until I managed to ditch him.'

'Hmmm, sounds like you need back-up with that one,' said Dave. 'Go out there with Steve next time and take his car.'

Gary nodded. 'I'm really struggling to serve papers on that guy who lives out in the countryside near Godalming, too. His wife lies and says he's not home when I'm sure he is. He's got a big Rottweiler I don't like the look of. I'm getting tired of driving right out there for nothing. I've been to his work place – he works at the constabulary – but still no luck.'

'Sounds like a real Tricky Dicky. I think this might be one for you, Sam.'

Sam looked at her boss and nodded, her high blonde ponytail bobbing.

'Gary, you brief Sam on this guy's appearance, the car he drives, his wife and his daily routine.'

Dave looked back at Sam. 'You have my full permission to be creative in your approach.'

159

***

Alex was driving the Jag home. He was nearly at the end of his road when he saw a young woman in a short denim skirt, with long blonde hair, standing next to a red Volkswagen Golf with the bonnet up. He slowed to a crawl and slid down the window.

'Do you need some help?'

'Yes, my car won't start.'

'Give me a sec to park my car and I'll have a look.' Nice set of pins, thought Alex as he pulled up and switched off the motor.

He walked back to where she was standing. 'How long have you been here?'

'Probably about ten minutes.'

'Any idea what the problem is?'

'No, it just started making strange noises and then conked out.' She shrugged her shoulders.

Alex peered under the bonnet and checked a few cables.

'Thank you for stopping to help me. My name's Samantha Drury.' She held out her hand with a radiant smile. Alex shook it.

'I'm Alex Coleman.'

Smooth as a dancer, Sam reached into the pocket of her mini skirt, took out a folded sheet of paper and held it out. 'This is for you.'

Alex took it with a confused expression. Sam dropped the bonnet. 'Sorry, have a good evening.' She walked swiftly to the driver's door, hopped in and drove off.

'What?' said Alex, reading the subpoena. He looked up to see Samantha do a U-turn and drive by with a friendly wave. Alex shook his head in disbelief. He'd heard that process servers would sometimes go to great lengths to serve papers, and even though he was seething inside, he had to concede that this one had put on a class act.

Chapter 31

'What do you mean, my brother only delivered two wills?' Cathy said tersely to Nigel on the telephone. 'It's taken weeks and weeks just to deliver a subpoena and now you're telling me he hasn't even handed over all three wills!'

Nigel's rather posh accent made his reply down the long distance line sound more sleepy than she would have liked. 'Yes, it's a frustrating business, I agree. We supplied the dates of all three wills in the subpoena, but Alex claimed there was no will dated 3 March 2002, so he only produced two wills.'

'Strange,' said Cathy, looking thoughtfully at her white flowering orchid.

'Yes, it's most odd. But rest assured, I shall continue to urge him via letter and email to produce that missing will. We will also contact the witnesses to check they are bona fide. I do come across people forging signatures from time to time.'

'But I thought you'd already checked the witnesses,' said Cathy, frowning.

There was a pause, then Nigel replied, 'Er, one of the witnesses was different from the name noted earlier.'

'Really? How could that be?'

'Quite possibly a clerical error of some sorts.' He smoothly changed the subject. 'You will be pleased to hear we are making good progress with the statements from Lucille's relatives, who appear to be highly suspicious of your brother's antics. I hope to gather evidence that the final will, made only a month before Lucille died, was signed under duress.'

They discussed the case further. Nigel mentioned that Alex had complained about the behaviour of the process servers '... something about a woman in a mini skirt pretending her car had broken down and then springing the subpoena on him.'

Cathy laughed. 'I'd love to have seen that.'

Alex was sitting on the heavily carved hall chair tying his bootlaces.

'Where are you going?' asked Sonia, pausing under the stag's head with mobile phone in hand.

'I'm taking Bruno for a walk down to the village to post a letter to the Solicitors Regulation Authority.'

'Why have you written to them?'

'Just to keep up the sniper fire. It's an old combat technique. Make it as uncomfortable as possible for the enemy, lower morale and sow the seed of doubt.'

'Sounds fun… tell me more?'

Alex patted his leather satchel. 'This letter complains that my sister's lawyer has acted in an unprofessional manner and used my sister "a particularly sad and vulnerable pensioner", as a source of income in a quiet patch.'

Sonia smiled. 'That should put the wind up him.'

'Yes, I imagine it will take the edge off his zealous investigation and dampen his spirits somewhat.'

'Have you sent him the other will yet?' asked Sonia.

'No, I'll make him wait a few more weeks for that. If he can't even copy dates and names of witnesses down correctly, then he'll have to suffer the consequences – pompous git!'

Sonia glanced at her mobile and pulled a face. 'The cleaner's going to be late again. Some lame excuse about her daughter being sick. Really, if she can't get her act together and make it here on time then I'm going to have to sack her.'

'Fair enough,' said Alex, standing up. He grabbed the lead off the hook. Bruno went into a frenzy around his legs. 'Let's go, boy!'

***

Cathy and Rhonda walked side by side through the trees, along a path next to the icy Tongariro River. As they rounded a corner they came upon a beautiful flowering kowhai tree, its branches arching over the pathway like a golden waterfall. Half a dozen tuis were at work, sipping nectar from the pendulous flowers and taking turns to sing high pure notes, interspersed with throaty clicks. The two women stood, faces upturned, listening to the chorus and admiring the dark plumage of the birds against the yellow flowers and blue sky.

They were spending the weekend in Turangi with their husbands, who were trout fishing further upstream.

'How are you getting on with that inheritance battle?' asked Rhonda.

'Progress is slow,' replied Cathy. 'We've dug up so much evidence against my brother and got copies of some dodgy homemade wills, but my lawyer doesn't want to go to court.'

'Why do you think he's dragging the chain?'

'My brother's come up with another one of his special tactics. This time, he's complained to the Solicitors Regulations Authority that my lawyer was taking unfair advantage of me as I'm a "very vulnerable pensioner with delusional tendencies".'

Rhonda shook her head. 'He's a smart one, that brother of yours.'

'Of course the complaint wasn't upheld by the SRA, but I think it's put my lawyer off. He doesn't want to go to court. But what was the point of gathering all that evidence if we're not going to start legal proceedings?'

'Yes, you need to put pressure on your brother. I thought lawyers were good at bluffing to squeeze big settlements out of people.'

Just then they came upon a clearing in the trees and saw David in his waders, standing up to his thighs in water, his rod and line arching gracefully in front of him. Len was a little further upstream, jigging his line in the river.

'Caught my dinner yet?' called out Cathy.

'Have a look in the bucket,' shouted David.

Cathy tilted the bucket to admire the fat silvery trout. 'That will do me smoked.'

Rhonda had spread out the red tartan picnic rug; Cathy unpacked the thermos and cheese scones. Kneeling on the rug, she poured coffee into two red enamel mugs. She handed one to Rhonda and sat gazing at the serene blue-green river and the men fishing. Lulled by the spring sunshine and the pleasant sound of water trickling over smooth rocks, she closed her eyes for a few minutes. After a spell, she said to Rhonda, 'You know, it's moments like these that I feel like forgetting all about the inheritance. Is it really worth fighting for...? After all, we've got our health, touchwood, we're living in a beautiful place; we've got our friends, we've got a good lifestyle.'

'What, after all you've been through? No way! You can't give up now.'

Cathy looked at her. 'I know, you're right. But it's all got so ugly. Not to mention that I've already spent £6,000, and now it looks like I'll have to start again with another lawyer.'

'Do you think that's really necessary?'

'Yes. Nigel Heathcote isn't prepared to litigate. Like I said earlier, my brother's put the wind up him by complaining about him. Besides, I don't think he's good enough. My brother's bound to hire a Q.C.'

Chapter 32

On Thursday morning, as part of her Age Concern volunteering, Cathy played scrabble with Sylvia, an elderly woman who was rapidly losing her sight. The two women's heads were bent over a giant scrabble board, which Cathy had ordered from the Blind Institute. When it was Cathy's turn, she put down seven large plastic tiles: P-R-O-B-A-T-E.

'You've got a lay out – you clever fish,' observed Sylvia, her eyes magnified by her thick lenses. 'Now tell me, what exactly does that mean?'

'It means proving that a will is official.' Cathy reflected wryly that her legal vocabulary was growing steadily.

After they had finished the game, Sylvia asked Cathy to write out a cheque for her to sign. On the way home, Cathy stopped off to post it. As she slid the envelope into the slot, she thought again how vulnerable the elderly could be.

After lunch, Cathy sat down at the computer to search the internet for probate law experts in England. Beside her, a hefty tome on community law lay open, next to a stack of lever arch files. After half an hour she came across the Association of Contentious Trust and Probate Specialists. This could be just the kind of specialist lawyer I'm looking for, she thought. About 600 probate lawyers were listed alphabetically. She began clicking through their profiles, and then to save time she narrowed her search to those working in Somerset which was where she used to live and not too far from Lyme Regis. David came in, stepping around boxes of files on the floor.

'Are you ready for a cuppa?' he asked.

'A bit later.' Cathy didn't take her eyes off the screen. David stood there, motionless, until Cathy spun around in her swivel chair.

'What is it?'

'I just wondered if you'd be interested in going to the Antique and Classic Boat Show next week.'

'Where is it?'

'Near Nelson. We could drive to Wellington and take the ferry over to the South Island.'

'I don't think so. I really need to concentrate on this. I want to find another lawyer.' She turned back to the computer screen.

David sat down on a wicker chair. He looked at his wife's back and said, 'Cathy, this is taking over your life. You've given it a good shot. Why not let it go now? You're holed up in here for hours on end. You've spent £6,000 on a lawyer, if you find another one you'll just end up spending even more money, and if you go to court it'll cost a fortune.'

Cathy half-turned around, leaning back in her chair and resting her hands in her lap. Her voice was flat. 'I know, but I just can't let it go. It's not right that Alex is getting away with it. He got all my father's mementos, the gold fob watch, his autobiography – the one I was supposed to type up – not to mention the penthouse. The way things are panning out with my mother, he'll take everything she has too.' A hint of hope lifted her voice. 'If I can challenge Lucille's will successfully, then maybe I can save my mother from his clutches.'

David was silent.

'Come and look at this… I've found the Association of Contentious Trust and Probate Specialists. I think one of these lawyers should be able to help me.'

David stood up and went over to her, leaning with one hand on the desk as he peered at the screen.

'I think I'll email a few of these lawyers in Somerset to see if one of them is interested.'

David straightened up. 'Well, it's your retirement fund you're spending on this, my dear. Personally, I'd prefer a cruise around South America, with perhaps a side trip to Machu Picchu, but it's up to you.'

'You'll have to go without me. I don't like heights. Besides, I hear those llamas like to spit.'

***

In Taunton, Somerset, probate lawyer Frank Henegan shoved aside folders, a stack of papers and an empty pizza box to make way for his breakfast: two fried eggs on toast and a mug of instant black coffee. Frank was tired. He'd been up at five to watch a K-League football game on the internet. He preferred to bet on games abroad in the hope of catching a bookie out. He'd waited until half-time to place a bet on the game in Korea because he was sure that at 2-0 up Jeonbuk Hyundai Motors were set to win. But Jeonbuk had a man sent off and Incheon United went on to score three goals in the second half. So much for an easy pay out. He might as well have shoved £200 down the waste master and ground it up with the potato peelings.

He was disgusted with himself. After his house had had to be sold to cover his gambling debts and his wife had kicked him out he'd sworn that he wouldn't gamble again… but sometimes the temptation of some easy money and an adrenalin hit was too much. He sighed. Even his eggs were overcooked; whites crackly and yolks dry.

Frank worked from home; home being a dingy basement flat with an entrance next to a row of smelly wheelie bins. He'd struck a quiet patch with work, but was hoping business might pick up now that the website, his son, Connor, had built him, was up and running. Connor had done a great job on photo shopping his image – without all the frown lines, he looked ten years younger.

After dumping his plate in the sink, Frank went over to the computer to check his emails. No point in crying over spilt milk, as his Ma always said. Best to get on with finding some work. He went through his emails, deleting the spam first, before reading his mail. The sixth email he opened was from a woman in New Zealand, who wanted help contesting a will. He read Cathy's summary of the situation with interest, then googled Lake Rotoiti to see where it was. For good measure, he also googled Cathy's street address at the bottom of the email. Google Earth revealed an attractive, two-storey house on a lake. She should have no trouble paying the bills. He was also pleased to have a client he could only communicate with via email, snail mail, phone or Skype. This suited him perfectly as there would be no need to make excuses about not having a secretary or posh offices. He certainly couldn't afford those overheads. Perhaps this was his lucky day after all. Frank was a great believer in Lady Luck. He began to type a return email.

Dear Cathy,

Thank you for your enquiry. I have considerable experience in probate law. I found your summary of the case very interesting. Judging from what you have written, I believe you may have grounds to contest the wills, but I will need more information before I can make a thorough assessment. Before I embark on an assessment of your case, I will require a retainer of £2,000. If you would like to discuss the matter further, please do not hesitate to telephone me.

Kind regards,

Frank Henegan

www.henegan.co.uk

Henegan & Co. Ltd.

PO Box 321, Taunton

Somerset TA1 3PW, United Kingdom

Phone: 01823 625838; Fax: 01823 625813

Frank read the email again, correcting the wording and a couple of spelling mistakes until he was satisfied, then clicked "Send". Right, that was done. Time to watch a recording of the big Chelsea-Man U game. He pattered out to the kitchen to make himself a cuppa before settling in front of the telly.

***

Cathy walked into David's upstairs study carrying a huge stack of papers. He was drooling over a computer image of a classic launch with a white painted hull and a varnished wooden cabin floating on a southern lake.

'Sorry to interrupt, but I was hoping you could scan these for me and email them to Frank.'

'What, all those? That will take me half the morning.'

'I'm sorry, but I need help. Frank has asked me to send him copies of wills, powers of attorney, any documents related to finances, witness statements and letters. He needs these papers quickly and I have to go through my Inbox and find some of the nasty, accusing emails big brother has sent me over the years. Then there's a few more letters I need to search for… the list goes on.'

'All right, I'll give you a hand,' said David, turning his head and eyeing the pile of documents Cathy had dumped on his desk.

'Thank you, darling,' said Cathy and dropped a kiss on the top of his bald head. She knew he didn't agree with her decision to keep fighting, but continued to support her out of loyalty. She picked up one of the wills lying on top of the stack. It was the final one, drawn up by Alex's solicitors St Pier Whitley & Co. and signed by Lucille in hospital a month before she'd died. She peered at Lucille's miniscule signature at the bottom of the page. It was suspiciously small. Was that really her signature?

Cathy addressed David's back as he busily scanned the documents. 'Because of the distance involved, I think a solicitor from St Pier Whitley probably never even visited Lucille to check these were her actual wishes. Alex most likely used his power of attorney to organise her affairs. Surely that was wrong when Lucille still had all her marbles. It seems negligent on the solicitor's part.'

Suddenly, it was as clear as a mountain stream what she should do.

'Hah!'

'What?' asked David, placing a document face down on the scanner?

'Two can play at that game. I'm going to complain to the Solicitors Regulation Authority about the conduct of Alex's solicitor.'

'So that'll be more work for your legal secretary, I suppose,' said David, lifting the cover of the scanner. 'At your service, madam.'

'I should hope so.' Cathy gave him a wink. 'And make it snappy or no lunch break!'

***

Carrying a box file under one arm and with a plastic bag of Indian takeaways dangling from his wrist, Frank struggled with the deadlock on the front door. He jiggled the key. The lock turned and he kicked the door open. A grey cat scooted inside. He dropped the takeaways on the bench, knocking over an old disposable coffee cup next to an empty McDonald's hamburger box.

'Here puss, puss, puss.' Frank shook some nibbles into the cat's dish. He glanced at the wall clock. Good, the UEFA Champions League game, Barcelona v Arsenal, was about to start. He could eat his takeaways in front of the telly and call his client in New Zealand when the game was over.

He grabbed a bottle of Guinness from the fridge to go with his takeaways. He'd read in the paper that it had less calories than trim milk, which was good news for his gut. Frank was feeling positive. He was on day 95 of the 100-day challenge for problem gamblers. There was money in his account, thanks to his new client, and the work was distracting him from the boredom and loneliness which often caused him to give in to the longing for a "buzz" from gambling. He was sleeping better, too, now he wasn't always thinking about watching football games at night on the internet. He'd go to bed after he'd called Cathy.

The game finished with the camera showing a close-up of the dispirited Arsenal coach as his team was knocked out of the League again. Frank burped, then padded over to his desk in his socks to fish out his diary from under a pile of papers. He flicked through it to find Cathy's number.

'Frank Henegan here, Cathy, how are you?'

'I'm just fine, and how are you getting on with filing the papers at court?'

'All done. The barrister has advised us to go to mediation first. Mediation is a good idea because the outcome of a case in court all depends on which judge you get on the day. Some judges are more sympathetic to inheritance disputes than others. We all know Judge Barrow's a softie, for instance. If we end up in court, a judge will look at a case more favourably if there's been an attempt at mediation.' Frank put his feet up on the coffee table and leaned back on his old brown sofa as they discussed the procedure further.

'Well, let me know as soon as the mediation date is set,' Cathy told him eventually. 'I'll need to book my airfare.'

Chapter 33

After a week in England the jetlag was wearing off, but on the day of the mediation Cathy still woke at 5 am. Rather than lie in bed gnawing over the possible antics of her brother and his lawyer, she got up, dressed, and went for a brisk walk. Taunton was quiet in the pre-dawn, with only the occasional jogger or car with headlights on passing by. She crossed over the cobbled road to enter a small park she'd spotted the previous day. It had rained overnight; she breathed the damp smell of the earth. She was drawn irresistibly towards the mottled trunk of a massive plane tree; looking up into its branches she saw layer upon layer of large brown and yellow leaves shimmering in the early morning light. The tree's quiet strength was just what she needed. Today was an important day; she would have to stay calm, focus on what was important, and resist the temptation to get sidetracked or intimidated by her brother's accusations. With this firmly in mind and feeling calmer, she turned to head back to the hotel for a hearty breakfast.

***

Frank hurried through the hotel's double glass doors at 8:50 am.

'Cathy, hello! Big day today, how are you feeling?' He shook her hand, heartily.

'Fine, thank you.' Cathy noted that though it was early, Frank's navy suit already looked rumpled and he'd applied too much gel to his wispy dark curls.

'Now, if you're all ready to go, I'm parked right outside. Frank Henegan at your service.' Frank pulled back the glass door and gestured grandly for Cathy to step through. Cathy smiled. At least he had a sense of humour.

Frank had borrowed his brother's new gold Lexus to drive Cathy to the solicitors' offices. There was no way he wanted her to see the old blue dunger with missing hubcaps he usually drove about town.

They headed to the business park on the outskirts of town. Cathy noticed that Frank was a twitchy driver. As they stopped for a red light, she asked, 'Have you got the seat warmers on, Frank?'

'Ah yes, I thought it was a bit nippy this morning. Cosy, isn't it?'

'Actually, it feels a bit odd... sort of like sitting in your own pee.'

Frank chortled. 'Don't worry, we're nearly there.' He didn't have a clue how to turn the seat warmers off, but he wasn't going to admit it. Soon the Lexus was cruising through streets lined with modern office buildings. He turned into a car park next to Alford & Bellingham.

'These are our mediator's offices,' he explained.

'I hope he's good at his job,' said Cathy, anxiously.

'It's always hard to know unless you've actually been in mediation with them, because, of course, mediation is confidential and conducted in private. But I've seen Mark in action once before and he seems a calm, competent fellow.'

'He'll need to be, my brother's got a filthy temper.'

Cathy followed Frank into the lobby. She scanned the grey interior and brown couches. Thankfully, Alex hadn't arrived yet. She was desperate to appear confident and in control, but in truth her nerves were jangling at the prospect of seeing Alex after ten years of feuding. Standing next to Frank at the reception desk, she kept her eyes fixed on the glass door. Two men in suits were approaching from outside. Her stomach gave a little flip and dropped. Then she realised it wasn't Alex.

'Just sign here, please,' said Frank, angling the sign in book towards her. Cathy signed her name in a tight messy scrawl that was barely legible.

'Our room is down the end of the corridor.'

'I'll just go to the bathroom, if you don't mind.'

'We're early, so take your time. I'll just wait here for you.' Frank was used to shepherding highly strung clients – the battered women involved in messy divorce cases were the jumpiest.

At the basin, Cathy cupped her hand under the tap and gulped down a few mouthfuls of water. Her mouth always got dry when she was nervous. For the hundred[th] time, she wondered why she was putting herself through such an ordeal. She straightened up and looked at her reflection in the mirror – dark marks under her eyes, her mouth a pensive line. Pulling out her foundation bottle, she smudged on another layer and added a touch of pink lipstick. In her head, she heard her father's voice, *You can do it Cathy, stay calm, girl.* She straightened her shoulders and pulled open the door. Still no sign of Alex. She followed Frank down a long corridor. On either side stood empty meeting rooms with glass walls, some of the sections frosted. Frank led her to a room right at the end of the corridor. Cathy had expressly asked not to sit in the same room as Alex. As they walked, Frank pointed out there would be two empty rooms between her room and Alex's, where he would sit with her mother and Sonia. Cathy had agreed to Alex's request to bring Margaret and Sonia to mediation as she hoped they might help him to see sense and be reasonable. Secretly, she hoped her mother would hear the truth at last. Cathy had asked Tom to come with her, but unfortunately Tom had had a holiday booked for the same dates.

Once they were seated, Frank recapped their arguments for reaching a favourable settlement. At ten o'clock, Mark Cunningham, the mediator, appeared to outline the day's programme.

'I hope to help you and Alex untangle the practical and financial aspects of this dispute to reach a satisfactory resolution,' Mark concluded.

Cathy nodded hopefully.

All morning the mediator commuted between Cathy and Alex's rooms, gathering and transmitting their versions of events.

'I feel it's unfair I haven't received any inheritance at all and no family heirlooms,' Cathy told Mark, 'I don't need money – I'd like my share of the inheritance to go to my daughter. As far as family heirlooms go, I'd like my father's autobiography, sports trophies and war mementos. My father was shot in France on D-Day. The hip flask he was carrying saved his life − a bullet bounced off it. He was hit by shrapnel and he always kept the pieces they removed from his body in a glass jar.'

When Mark had left the room, Cathy said to Frank, 'There was also a gold fob watch from my grandfather I'd love to have, but I don't think Alex will ever part with it. However, perhaps we could request that the watch goes to my grandson, Ryan, on my brother's death.'

'Yes, but it's probably better to try first for the mementos you think you have a chance of getting,' said Frank.

Sometime later, Mark returned from Alex's room at the end of the corridor. He looked frustrated. 'I'm afraid your brother's a very angry man. It looks like he won't give an inch.'

'What about my mother?'

'She looks rather tired and sad.'

'I'm sorry she's had to listen to all this,' said Cathy, ruefully.

A plate of club sandwiches was delivered for lunch. When Mark came back into the room, Cathy put down her egg sandwich and picked up a mini photo album. She held it out to Mark. 'Could you please give these photos to my mother? Tell her it's her great-grandson and she's welcome to keep them.'

Mark took the photo album down to Alex's room. He gave it to Margaret, explaining the photos were of her great-grandson. Margaret's face lit up. 'Thank you very much.' Mark left the room.

Her white head bent, Margaret slowly turned the pages of the album, carefully studying each photo. Alex glanced at the album over her shoulder. When she had finished looking at the last page, he put his hand out for it.

Mark appeared in the doorway.

'Please give this back to my sister.' Alex held out the album.

'Cathy did say your mother was welcome to keep it.'

'No, give it back to her, please.'

Margaret looked down at her hands clasped in her lap.

At the end of the corridor, Frank loosened his tie and unbuttoned his collar. 'Look, Cathy, there's nothing coming from him. I suggest we make the first offer.'

'Let's suggest we settle on the terms of the 1990 will – I get two-thirds, he gets one-third and Lucille's relatives receive their payments as stipulated in that will.'

'I suppose it's a starting point,' said Frank, jotting down the terms.

Half an hour later, Mark returned with news that the offer had been angrily rebuffed. Instead, Alex proposed that brother and sister each pay their own legal costs and walk away from the dispute.

At two o'clock, Mark said, 'We appear to be making no progress. I'm afraid your brother's wife is telling him not to budge. I'll suggest he comes for a walk with me around the car park to get him away from her. Then perhaps he'll be more amenable.'

Twenty minutes later Mark returned to suggest that Alex and Cathy try discussing matters face to face in the same room, without Sonia or Margaret present. Cathy agreed and followed Frank into the next room.

In one glance, Cathy saw that Alex was bubbling like a hot mud pool. She sat down opposite him and his lawyer, Whitley, a tall man with a belligerent scowl. Frank sat next to her, while Mark was at the head of the rectangular table. Mark had urged her to begin by expressing her regret over what had happened. Cathy forced herself to look into Alex's tiny glinting eyes as she spoke. Alex listened, his face set in hard, angry lines. When Cathy had finished, the solicitors looked expectantly at Alex.

'I regret nothing!' he exploded.

Mark and Cathy visibly jumped. Frank's eyes opened wide, and Whitley stiffened in his expensive looking pin-striped suit – he shot a concerned sideways look at his client. 'You stole all our stepmother's savings and then went off to New Zealand, leaving me to look after her in her old age,' growled Alex, 'Now she's gone and I'm left looking after our mother. Don't you think I deserve some recompense?'

Cathy replied in an even voice: 'We've been through this all before, many times. I did not take that money; it was given to me by Lucille and our father, before he died. What proof have you got that the money was stolen?'

'I've got all the details to prove you took £54,293.47. You set up a joint account with Lucille, then you transferred that amount to your own account.'

'Hang on a minute – I never had a joint account with Lucille, though she suggested one. It was *you* who had the joint account. And how can you come up with such a precise figure? Show me the evidence.'

'I'm getting it from the bank in Jersey and expect it any day.'

'That's impossible. Banks only keep records for seven years. If you're going to start accusing me, then what about the transfer of the ownership of the apartment?'

At the mention of the apartment, Alex flashed an uncertain glance at this lawyer. Then he looked at Cathy, hatred filled his eyes.

'That's irrelevant to this discussion of the will,' he said through clenched teeth.

But his nervous reaction hadn't been lost on Cathy. *Was there something wrong with the transfer of the apartment?*

At this point, Mark intervened, leaning forward in a conciliatory fashion.

'Cathy has indicated she would like the settlement to be for her daughter, your niece.'

Alex shot back, 'Emma doesn't deserve anything. She lived in my flat in London all those years.'

'Alex, how can you say that?' said Cathy in disbelief. 'Emma paid market rent for your flat.'

Alex simply shook his head.

'Lucille's relatives, including her goddaughters, have missed out on their inheritance, so I would like to see them receive settlements as per the 1990 will.'

Alex snorted. 'No chance when one of them's on drugs.'

'Who's on drugs?' asked Cathy.

'I can't say,' replied Alex.

Mark suggested that now they had some understanding of each other's position, they return to separate rooms for deliberations.

177

Cathy was tired and her head was pounding. She asked Frank to accompany her down the corridor so she could go to the bathroom. She was terrified of meeting her brother in case he lashed out and hit her and she wanted to avoid a possible slanging match with Sonia in the toilets. As they walked down the corridor, she caught a glimpse through the glass of Alex sitting with Sonia. Her mother, tiny and hunched, had her back to her.

'I think your brother's the only one likely to be on drugs,' muttered Frank. 'What planet is he on?'

A short while later, Mark conveyed to them an offer from Alex: £50,000 for Ryan when he reached the age of 25. The sum was to be shared with any future siblings.

'It's not nearly enough. The apartment was worth £650,000 five years ago. I think we should ask for £250,000.'

'I don't think he'll accept that,' said Mark quietly.

'Well, just try,' snapped Cathy. Frank nodded. Cathy felt exasperated. Weren't lawyers meant to be good at negotiating deals? She began to suspect Frank was simply hanging out for her to settle so the job would be finished and he could send an invoice. After all, he'd be paid the same whether they settled for £50,000 or £250,000. As for the mediator, hadn't she seen him joking with Alex's lawyer as they came up the front steps this morning? Frank said he'd seen them at the pub together.

A short while later Mark returned. 'He won't go above £50,000. Listen Cathy, in my experience, inheritance disputes are typically very difficult to resolve. I suspect the root of the problem is the money you were gifted by your father. You explained that your father asked you to keep it a secret. I think Alex saw that as a betrayal by those he loved and trusted and also as your father showing favouritism. The 1990 will favoured you, once again. Inheritance disputes inevitably awaken old sibling rivalries. He seems to believe he's entitled to it all. It may be wise to settle for a smaller amount than you hoped and some personal items of your father's.'

'I've been cut off from my own family because of him. So don't talk to me about rejection and betrayal. I'd prefer to go to court than accept such a ridiculous sum.'

'Now, Cathy, we've discussed this,' began Frank, 'if you go to court there'll be no change from £150,000. Evidence is thin on the ground and the odds are stacked against you. And I'm a betting man – I know my odds. We all know it comes down to which judge you get on the day. It might be better to avoid a costly legal battle.'

Cathy took a sip of water. There was a throbbing pain in her temples. She looked at the clock on the wall – almost six o'clock – they had been stuck in these hellish negotiations all day. When her stomach rumbled, she heard an echoing rumble from Frank's.

'He's a stubborn man. I've seen his type before – he won't budge,' said Frank, huskily. 'It's best to settle and be done with it. At least he won't have inherited everything, especially if we can convince him to give you those items of your father's.'

Cathy stood up and walked to the window. She saw the tiny stooped figure of her mother, holding Sonia's hand, tottering out to the car. Sonia was like a telegraph pole next to a gnarled bush. She was probably taking her mother back to the hotel for a rest, leaving Alex to conclude negotiations. Cathy knew Sonia and Alex were totally in control of her mother's life now. She had vainly hoped her mother would learn the truth about what had happened through an open, honest discussion, but now she realised her mother had only been needlessly exposed to more vitriol from her brother. She had been naive to agree to her mother and Sonia attending.

Frank and Mark took turns at nagging Cathy to agree to the settlement. Finally, she gave in to their wheedling.

Looking smug at the prospect of another successful mediation, Mark left the room with the acceptance note. Five minutes later he was back, his brown eyes wide behind his glasses.

'I'm sorry, Cathy, I've never heard this before, but your brother says that the offer is for £50,000 *without* interest. He will keep the interest and when your grandson is 25 years of age he will inherit the £50,000.'

Frank's mouth dropped open. Cathy leapt out of her chair.

'That's it! I've had it. Tell him he can take his £50,000 without interest and stick it! I've worked in a bank. I know that without interest accruing that sum could be worth next to nothing in 25 years' time. It's outrageous and it's insulting. I've had it with him. I'm taking him to court.'

'But Cathy, that's unwise,' said Mark in his most soothing tone, 'you could end up losing and paying big legal fees. Why don't we arrange another date for mediation – perhaps after a break he'll be more agreeable to a settlement.'

Cathy thought for a moment. Once again, she heard her father's voice in her head. *Don't rush, Cathy, give it time.*

'I'm fine to have another mediation day. But my bottom line is, I want the £50,000 plus interest and the heirlooms. Otherwise, no deal.'

Chapter 34

Eyes closed, Cathy rocked gently backwards and forwards in the old rocking chair beside the range, listening to the ticking cuckoo clock and the rustle of Tom's newspaper. The warmth of the range made her feel relaxed and drowsy. She had found mediation gruelling and it had left her feeling despondent. After spending a few days with friends in Glastonbury, she had decided to spend some time with Tom in the countryside. His quiet companionship was soothing and he was interested and sympathetic to her struggle.

'Another cuppa, Cathy?'

'That'd be lovely, Tom. Just a small one, please.' Tom busied himself setting the kettle on the hob and fetching the tea caddy from the dresser.

'You're worn out, lass, from all that mediation bother. I'm sorry I couldn't be with you, but I couldn't miss Annabelle's wedding in Scotland.'

'I know, Tom. I could've done with the support. It was like Alex, Sonia and my mother were all ganged up on me. But I'm not letting him bring them to the next mediation session.'

'Your stepmother was like a sister to me. I was always sorry she had no children of her own. It was a great sadness to her. Lucie suffered terribly as a child, y'know, when one of her twin sisters died... poor Betty died of scarlet fever when she was only nine. 'Twas Lucie who brought the fever into the house. She never did forgive herself.'

Tom handed Cathy a blue and white striped mug of hot tea. Cathy took it gingerly and sipped from the side that wasn't chipped.

'Would you like a hobnob?' Tom asked.

'Yes, please.'

'To think that after all those happy years with your father, poor Lucie was so poorly treated by your brother. Alex was like one of me neighbour's Jack Russell terriers with a rabbit – tore into her and wouldn't let up. The last time I saw your brother was when he dropped that bag of trinkets off. But he rang me up a while later asking about some necklace with a star on it. I remember it, but I don't know what happened to it. Maybe the same caregiver who swiped the fancy rings took it?' Tom smiled grimly.

'I'm really sorry your daughters missed out on their inheritance, and Lucille's other relatives. I wish I could make it right for them.'

'So do you think you'll end up in court then, Cathy, if Alex won't come to the party in your next mediation session?'

'I'd love to have my day in court, but I can't really afford to. The lawyers reckon it'll cost me £150,000 and the case could go either way, depending on the judge. David will be furious if I spend all my retirement fund on going to court and lose. He's getting antsy about me being away and spending so much time on it all. If I want to stay happily married, I'm afraid I'll have to settle.' Cathy looked down sadly at the tea leaves in her mug.

'Oh well, I wish you luck on Thursday, then, lass. At least it will be decided one way or t'other.'

The cuckoo clock striking 11:00 interrupted their conversation.

'Goodness, is that the time?' Cathy looked up at the little wooden bird bobbing up and down as the clock chimed loudly.

'I'm usually tucked up in me bed by nine,' said Tom. 'We'd best get to bed. You've got to take the train to Taunton tomorrow.'

Cathy lay awake in Tom's guest bedroom. She could hear him snoring softly in his own room further down the hall. For the umpteenth time, her mind ran over the last mediation session. Frank had mentioned the transfer of the apartment and for a second Alex's obstinate, angry mask had dropped and he had looked worried. What could that mean? She would give Frank a call tomorrow morning; perhaps he could do some more digging before mediation the following day. She rolled over, feeling her body relax as sleep gradually took over. That

182

night she dreamed about her father teaching her to sail in the little dinghy with the yellow hull and white sails. Fifteen-year-old Alex sat sulking on the shore, letting the sand run through his fingers, and refusing to go out in the boat. The onshore breeze ruffled her father's hair, his blue eyes shone. He looked so happy. Her father nudged the tiller towards her, 'You steer the boat now, Cathy. You're in charge.'

***

Cathy was in the shower in her hotel room when her mobile rang. She turned off the faucet, wrapped herself in a fluffy white towel and padded across the carpet, dripping. The phone stopped ringing before she got there. Looking at the screen, she read "One missed call: David". That's funny, David didn't usually ring her mobile, because of the expense. She would get dressed and then ring him back.

'Hi, David. Is everything all right?'

'Yes, everything's fine, apart from the fact that I'm getting tired of eating takeaways.'

'You could cook yourself a steak.'

'I have done. It's just not the same, eating on my own. But listen, a report has arrived in the mail which I think is important for your next mediation session.'

'What is it?'

'It's the report from… just a minute, let me take a look at it… the Solicitors Regulation Authority. The good news is that from what I can tell, they've come down hard on Alex's solicitors for poor conduct. St Pier Whitley seem to have breached the code of conduct by taking instructions from your brother and not checking with Lucille if the transfer of the apartment to your brother's name was actually what she wanted.'

Cathy's face lit up.

'David, you're a gem. Thank goodness you opened that envelope. This is really, really important information. Mediation is tomorrow. You're going to have to scan that report and email it to my solicitor's office right now.'

'Great. Just when there's no wind and I had a day's fishing planned.'

183

'You'll have to put your fishing on hold. It's only 9 pm here so I'll ring Frank now and tell him to check his emails in half an hour. I just hope he's not down at the pub.'

Frank, wearing his red and white striped football shirt, was sitting in his armchair, riveted to the League One match on television. His club, Exeter, was playing Bournemouth and the score was 1–0. He could feel his mobile vibrating in his pocket but he ignored it. Exeter was taking a free kick just outside the box. It grazed the crossbar and flew over. Frank pulled out his phone and looked at it; one missed call from Cathy. He decided to call her back in the morning. Thirty seconds later, his phone beeped with a message. That was the trouble with mobiles, people thought they could ring you after hours, not like the old days when they couldn't reach you after five o'clock. He'd learned to set his boundaries. Frank studiously ignored his phone and kept his eyes on the telly.

Chapter 35

Frank reached blindly for the phone vibrating on the bedside table.

'Hello,' he said gruffly.

'Frank, is that you?'

'No, it's the tooth fairy. Who's this?'

'It's Cathy, sorry to ring you so early, but I wanted to check you'd got the report.'

Frank groaned inwardly. He'd been up in the night betting on a football game in Chile and he couldn't imagine what report Cathy was talking about. He'd seen this kind of client before – full of notions of justice, bright ideas and wild goose chases which came to nought.

'So what's in this report?' he asked, sitting up in bed in his old black t-shirt.

'Some time ago I complained to the Solicitors Regulations Authority about St Pier Whitley, who handled the wills and the transfer of the apartment. I'd given up on hearing back from them. Well, they've done some detective work and released a report saying that St Pier Whitley has broken the code of conduct for solicitors by taking their instructions from Alex and not checking Lucille was in agreement with those instructions.'

'This sounds most interesting,' said Frank brightly, hopping out of bed to pull the curtains.

'My husband has emailed the report to you. Have you got it?'

'No, I haven't turned the computer on yet.'

'Oh! I rang you last night and left a message.'

'Er... I was out and didn't have my phone. Thank you, Cathy. I'll read it first thing and we can get together and discuss it before mediation begins.'

The call ended. Frank gazed out of his bedroom window at the mossy brick retaining wall. He was in a good mood after his win of £3,000 last night, though he felt a twinge of guilt because he knew he wasn't meant to be betting. He didn't feel overly optimistic about the report from the SRA. He'd seen this before. The SRA would probably give Alex's lawyers a slap on the wrist with a wet bus ticket. But it might just help them to squeeze a little more juice out of that SAS pillock.

He turned on his computer. It stalled, the screen flickering blue. Damn! It looked like it was crapping out. He turned it off at the wall and got out his laptop, which was slow to start up. While it was warming up, he cracked a couple of eggs into a hot frying pan. He typed in his password, then popped some bread in the toaster. When he opened his email account, he found David's email waiting in his Inbox. He opened up the attachment. To print it out, he'd have to get the old computer working, because it was connected to the printer. He switched the computer back on at the wall. Fingers crossed the old girl started... Yes! He was in luck. He buttered his toast, put the eggs on top, then returned to the computer to print out three copies of the report. The toner ink was running low, but the type was dark enough to read in spite of the odd blurry streak.

Frank pushed aside the litter of newspapers and hamburger boxes on the table to clear a space for his breakfast. The egg yolks hadn't broken and the toast wasn't burnt, so combined with his win last night he was off to a good start. He propped the report against an empty bottle of Guinness and began to read. His good mood only improved. It looked like his client had a good case for compensation. But they were running out of time. Shit! It was already 8:30 and mediation was supposed to start at ten. Shit! He should have answered his mobile last night. Shit!

Frank dialled Cathy's number.

'Hello, Frank?'

'Hi Cathy. I've just skimmed through the report. There are some things in here that may help us. We need to get together to discuss this, but we don't have much time. I'll ring the mediator to get the start time pushed out until 12:00 midday. Can –'

Cathy interrupted. 'Frank, there's something else I should tell you. Someone from the SRA has emailed me to suggest we should take a complaint of suspected fraud to the police. They'll write us a letter.'

'Great stuff! Do you think you can be ready in half an hour? I'll pick you up and we'll go straight to the mediation offices.'

'Yes, I'll be ready. See you then.'

Frank clicked off, thinking, shit, this is going to be tight.

Cathy and Frank were seated opposite each other in the mediation room at 9:30 am. Frank put on his black-rimmed glasses.

'I'd just like to go through this report with you and explain what it means. There are four major points. The first is that the power of attorney form was signed by Lucille, but she received no independent legal advice. In other words, no one at St Pier Whitley checked with Lucille that she wanted Alex to be her attorney and that the solicitors were to take instructions from Alex. Quite possibly the form was signed under duress.

'Secondly, the drafting of the wills. Once again St Pier Whitley took their instructions for drafting the wills from Alex, who paid the bill. The wills were signed by Lucille, but no one checked with Lucille that the instructions given on her behalf were actually what she wanted.'

Frank paused and took a sip of water. 'But the big one is the apartment, I think we should go for the jugular with this one.'

Cathy sucked in her breath. She sat motionless, her eyes fixed on Frank's unshaven face.

'The third point is that Alex instructed St Pier Whitley, in a typed letter dated 2006 and signed by himself, to register the ownership of the apartment in his name. Medical records prove that though Lucille was in a nursing home, she was still compos mentis. Lucille was never consulted about the transfer, nor did she authorise Alex to instruct his solicitors. His instructions to St Pier Whitley were therefore an abuse of power. He wasn't the owner of the apartment. Alex's solicitors should have reported him to the police and there would have been an investigation.

'The fourth point regarding the apartment is the impecuniosity principle.'

'Impecuniosity?' Cathy looked bewildered.

'I'll explain that to you later. It's important. But first let's talk about the will. In 2001, St Pier Whitely received a typed letter, signed by Lucille, requesting a new will. Her instructions were very clear: Alex was to be the major beneficiary, plus there were specific legacies to nine other people. The draft will was prepared and sent to her. It was returned with all the beneficiaries deleted – except for Alex. The solicitor did not express concern at the changes made within the space of a few weeks and did not confirm with Lucille that these were indeed her wishes. Instead, the will was executed and Alex paid the bill.'

'Yes, we all know who made the changes before sending back the will,' said Cathy grimly.

'In 2007, a few months before Lucille died, Alex lodged another request for a new will. A draft will was sent to Alex, which was signed by Lucille in the hospital, witnessed, and returned to St Pier Whitley by Alex, who paid the bill. A client care letter was sent to Lucille but it was returned signed by Alex.' Frank paused, and looked at Cathy over the top of his glasses. 'Do you know that despite all these transactions no one from St Pier Whitley ever met your stepmother in person?'

Cathy shook her head sadly.

Frank cleared his throat. 'Now, moving on to the deed of gift of the apartment. This was created a few months after your brother was granted attorney in 1999. The deed appears to be an offer from your stepmother to give your brother ownership of the apartment in exchange for him paying your late father's debts, namely a bill from a glazier for £3,500, because your stepmother was impecunious.'

Cathy raised her hand, a quizzical look on her face. 'Hang on a minute, I repaid him for that glazier's bill.'

'He's a real ratbag,' said Frank, shaking his head.

'But possibly there were other bills he paid; I remember something about a new boiler. What does impecunious mean?'

'A person declared impecunious means he or she has no money and is living in hardship, therefore they can't afford to pay their debts. Not long after your father's death, your stepmother was deemed to be impecunious – that's why she qualified for Income Support. Now the catch is, your brother didn't become the registered owner of the penthouse until 2007, even though the deed of gift was dated back in 2000. Why did he take so long to have the transfer of ownership registered?'

Cathy thought for a moment before answering. 'Well, the transfer of ownership would have had to go through the body corporate of the apartment building, so perhaps he didn't want to arouse suspicions as to why Lucille was giving away her beautiful penthouse.'

Frank nodded. 'That's one reason. Can you think of another?'

'To avoid paying tax?'

'Bingo. To avoid paying inheritance tax. If a person dies seven years or more after gifting a property, you don't have to pay tax. Also, there's the matter of the nursing home fees. Basically, the NHS isn't going to pay nursing home fees if you've just given away your luxury pad.'

'He seems to have thought of every eventuality,' said Cathy. 'Alex was always clever at working out all the moves. So what does this all mean for our mediation session? Can Alex be charged with fraud?'

Frank loosened his already crooked tie. 'We're in a much stronger position. Potentially, St Pier Whitley can be charged with negligence in the civil court or being party to the fraud from a criminal law point of view, so they'll be keen to keep this under wraps. I think they'll be very keen to settle out of court. As for Alex, yes, we could go to the police with the SRA backing us. That gives us some teeth. Do you know what the apartment's valued at now?'

'I've spoken to an estate agent and the market value is believed to be around £650,000.'

'Of course we'll need to get it valued by a registered valuer, but what say we go for £500k?'

Cathy thought for a moment – £500,000 – that was a lot of money. She looked through the glass wall into the empty hall way and considered this option. At last she replied, speaking slowly and firmly. 'No, what I actually want is for the 1990 will to be reinstated. That's what I believe is right. Then I can pay out all the beneficiaries who missed out. Money is tight for some of Lucille's relatives and they could do with a helping hand.'

Frank glanced at the clock on the wall – 11 o'clock. He could do with a coffee, but there was more to discuss and not enough time. Cathy had more questions and they continued to discuss the possible responses of their opponents, their own tactics and objectives for mediation. At 11:40 Frank and Cathy left the meeting room to duck to the toilets, grab a quick mug of instant coffee and return to the central meeting room where they had agreed to meet Alex and Whitley. Frank couldn't wait to wipe the smug expressions off their faces.

Chapter 36

Cathy's chest felt tight as she followed Frank into the meeting room. Alex and Whitley sat facing the door. Alex stared at Cathy coldly, while Whitley made a show of checking the time on his wrist watch before getting to his feet to shake hands with them. Alex remained seated.

'I'm sorry to keep you waiting, gentlemen,' said Frank.

'That's fine,' said Mark as he shook his hand.

Mark began by running through the general expectations and recapping on the last session. During Mark's introduction, Alex sat very straight in his immaculate three-piece suit, while Whitley leaned back in a casual fashion, one arm draped over the back of his chair. Cathy thought the pair had an air of arrogance about them, as if they were just filling in a few hours before heading to the pub.

'Now, Mr Henegan, you requested a later start time today because more information pertinent to mediation had come to light. Could you please talk us through this new material?'

Frank unzipped his black document folder and removed copies of the SRA report. He handed them around the table. Whitley glanced down at the report, then looked up, alarmed. Cathy had the impression that he had seen the report before but had hoped it wouldn't surface. Alex shot a worried sideways look at his lawyer. Frank began to outline the findings of the SRA. As Alex listened, his face grew dark with fury and a muscle in his cheek began to twitch involuntarily. Cathy could see he was struggling to control his temper, so she looked out the window into the car park. There was no sign of arrogance now in Whitley's demeanour. He studied the report with his head slightly bowed, like a chastened school boy. Cathy thought she detected a look of pleasant surprise cross Mark's face, just for a moment, before he resumed his neutral, conciliatory expression. She turned her attention back to Frank as he summed up the SRA's findings on the wills.

'The solicitor should be: "alert to abrupt changes in a will that leave all the assets to one family member. They should be particularly alert for abuse if instructions come from a third party who is to benefit from the will, and the vulnerable person is using the third party's solicitor when they previously had their own solicitor..."' Frank paused to eyeball Whitley, who kept his eyes trained on the report in front of him. Frank continued. '...where instructions are received from third parties, solicitors should obtain written instructions from the client that he or she wishes the solicitor to act. In any case of doubt, the solicitor should see the client or take other appropriate steps to confirm instructions.'

Alex let out a snort of disgust. 'This is just splitting hairs. I have Lucille's power of attorney and I was carrying out her wishes, and Whitley here executed the will in the correct legal manner – right, Whitley?'

'Er... there may have been a small oversight –'

'A small oversight? I'm paying you big bucks, don't talk to me about—'

Mark cut in. 'Gentlemen, please, there will be time to discuss this in private when Mr Henegan has finished. Please, Mr Henegan, continue.'

Cathy was careful to keep her face neutral. She kept her eyes on the solitary pin oak tree in the car park as she listened to Frank discuss the penthouse.

In his gravelly voice, Frank concluded his argument. 'Mr Whitley should have made personal contact with Mrs Coleman to satisfy himself she wished to legally register the deed of gift for the apartment. Mrs Coleman was compos mentis and we have evidence that she did not wish to leave the apartment to her stepson. The only conclusion that can be drawn from this report is that the transfer of the ownership of the apartment was, in fact, fraudulent.'

'Hah! That will be the day. I own that apartment!' shouted Alex, half-rising from his chair.

'Mr Coleman, please, contain yourself,' said Mark firmly. 'Please remain seated. Mr Henegan has nearly finished and

192

then you may choose to reply or deliberate this further, in private, with Mr Whitley.' He looked at Frank, seated at his right, with new respect. 'Mr Henegan, if you have finished discussing the findings of the report, could you please inform us as to your client's wishes regarding a settlement.'

Frank looked at Cathy and she gave a small nod.

'My client would like to be reinstated as executor of the 1990 will; the subsequent wills should be set aside. Since the transfer of the ownership of the apartment was fraudulent, the apartment should revert to being part of Mrs Coleman's estate. My client would like to see the penthouse sold in order to receive her two-thirds share and pay out the nine minor beneficiaries. She also seeks legal costs and expects some recompense from her brother's lawyers for the stress and financial losses she has suffered due to their negligence.' Frank paused for effect, then looked straight at Alex. 'I would like to add that fraudulently obtaining a property through abuse of power is a criminal offence.'

Alex sat rigidly to attention, but his eyes flickered dangerously. Whitley looked pale and uncertain.

'I suggest we break now for an hour to discuss the new proposal,' said Mark.

'Could we make it an hour and a half, please?' said Whitley, 'I need to contact one of the partners.'

Mark looked at his watch. 'I will see you all back here at three o'clock. Afternoon tea will be delivered to your rooms.'

Cathy was on her way to the bathroom when she heard the shouting coming from Alex's room.

'You've made a right mess of this, Whitley. You've made some real fuck-ups. You can forget about your fees or I'll sue you. You can help me fight this for free.'

Whitley growled, 'I warned you at the time it was risky… do you realise that you're criminally liable?'

Cathy looked straight ahead as she hurried past.

After the break, they all trooped back into the meeting room. Cathy noticed that Whitley had a tall, thin colleague with him. She tapped Frank on the shoulder and he followed her back into the corridor.

'Surely Whitley can't just bring another lawyer in without seeking prior approval?'

'Good point. I'll ask Mark.'

From the doorway, Frank caught Mark's eye and beckoned to him. He had a quiet word with him in the corridor. Frank and Cathy waited outside until Whitley's colleague left to wait in another room.

Mark looked at Whitley. 'Now, Mr Whitley, you have had time with your client to consider the SRA Report and the proposal put forward by Mr Henegan on behalf of Mrs Stewart. Do you accept this proposal?'

'My client considers the 1990 will to be no longer relevant. He rejects the proposal as it stands.' Whitley looked down at his notebook, obviously embarrassed. 'Instead, he proposes a settlement of £50,000 plus interest and delivery of the family mementoes as previously specified by Mrs Stewart. He proposes that each party pay their own legal costs and that Mrs Stewart sign an agreement that she will not instigate criminal proceedings against my client.'

The corners of Cathy's mouth lifted in a tiny incredulous smile. Mark seemed momentarily lost for words.

Frank spoke first. 'And what about your firm, St Pier Whitley? What recompense do you suggest for my client, who could quite easily take legal action alleging negligence on your firm's part for not checking that Mrs Coleman was in agreement with the instructions given on her behalf by her stepson? From a criminal law point of view, your firm of solicitors could conceivably have been party to the fraud. A case like this would soon be all over the papers. I'd like to remind you that in the space of seven years you executed wills and registered a property transfer for a vulnerable elderly woman you never even took the time to *meet*.'

There was dead silence. Whitley cleared his throat. 'St Pier Whitley is prepared to offer Mrs Stewart an out of court settlement of £60,000, providing there is no further civil action or publicity that will bring St Pier Whitley into disrepute. If Mrs Stewart is in agreement, I can have a contract drawn up immediately.'

Mark said, 'I suggest we break for half an hour to allow Mrs Stewart and her legal counsel to consider these proposals.'

'No need to, I've already made my mind up,' said Cathy firmly.

Frank touched Cathy gently on the shoulder. 'Let's have a wee chat in private first.'

Cathy shouldered her ivory handbag and headed for the door.

In the room at the end of the corridor, Cathy turned to face Frank, her hands on her hips.

'I am not giving in to that bastard. How can he have the cheek to offer me £50,000 *plus interest* – whoopty doo – when he stole an apartment worth £650,000? How dare he! He must think I'm a right idiot.'

'Okay, we know the offer's rubbish, even Whitley was squirming when he made it, but what about the offer from St Pier Whitley? You could look at it this way, if you accepted both offers you would have more than doubled your money in two weeks.

'Yeah, that's a more reasonable offer. Let's Google the firm – perhaps they can afford more.'

Frank searched the firm's website on his laptop. 'Hmmm, nice offices on the high street,' said Cathy, 'and it seems to be a good-sized family law practice. Let's try £100,000.'

'Sounds a bit on the high side,' warned Frank, eager to settle.

'What is it with you lawyers? Have you never run a stall at a car boot sale? Start high and be prepared to bargain.'

'I must admit, I've never worked at a car boot sale,' admitted Frank, though he considered himself a car boot lawyer. But car boot lawyer or not, he felt this case was going quite well and he could see a glimmer of respect in Whitley's eyes, which was gratifying. 'All right, let's try £100,000 for the law firm, plus they pay your legal costs. I don't like our chances of getting any money out of that brother of yours. For Alex, shall we propose…' Frank did some quick calculations on a pad, 'roughly two-thirds of the value of the apartment, which is £435,000, plus £30,000 to be divided among the nine minor beneficiaries. Shall we try for £465,000?'

'Round figures, please – £500,000,' said Cathy, 'to be paid into my lawyer's account by the end of November. And of course don't forget my father's autobiography and his war mementoes. I'll agree to distribute the money to the minor beneficiaries as per the 1990 will and most of my share will go to my daughter. That's what my father and Lucille would have wanted.'

Negotiations with the law firm were conducted swiftly, without Alex in attendance. After conferring with his lanky, bald partner in the corridor, Whitley agreed to settle for £75,000, plus pay Cathy's legal costs. In return, she agreed to a confidentiality clause.

Alex joined them to hear Frank's latest proposal. At the mention of the figure of £500,000, he exploded again. 'NO WAY!' He thumped his fist down on the table.

Cathy recoiled as if a gun had gone off. There was a shocked silence. Mark finally spoke.

'Please try to stay calm, Mr Coleman, your aggression isn't helping matters.'

'I don't give a toss. I've had it with that greedy bitch!'

'Remember the rules we all agreed to at the start of mediation,' said Mark sternly. 'Please use respectful language when addressing other participants.'

The only response from Alex was an ugly sneer.

Cathy stood up. 'Actually, I've had enough, too. Whitley – we've settled. Alex – I'll see you in court.' With that, Cathy picked up her handbag and stalked out of the room. Frank hurried out after her. He caught up to her in the lobby.

'That felt good,' she said.

'I bet it did,' said Frank. 'You were magnificent. I've got to go back and finish up.'

'Don't worry, I'll take a taxi.'

'I'm afraid we need you to hang around. Whitley will draw up the agreement straight away so it can be signed and witnessed before we all leave.'

Cathy sighed. It had been another long day.

'Why don't you wait in our room down the corridor, then after the agreement's signed, I can take you out for a curry. I know a good Indian restaurant just round the corner.'

Cathy nodded. 'Sounds a good plan.'

Chapter 37

It was a chilly evening and a curry was just what Cathy felt like. The restaurant walls were painted emerald green and decorated with elephant motifs; brightly coloured silks suspended from the ceiling created a canopy effect. Cathy ordered the lamb rogan josh and Frank ordered a beef korma.

'That was a smart move complaining to the SRA about your brother's lawyers. We never would have got anywhere without that report. Well done, Cathy. Cheers!'

Frank raised his glass. Cathy clinked her glass of Carling against his.

'Funnily enough, it was my brother who gave me the idea to lodge a complaint. Alex complained to the SRA about my previous lawyer. He said my lawyer had acted in an unprofessional manner and exploited me –,' Cathy leaned in and enunciated with emphasis, 'a particularly sad and vulnerable pensioner.'

Frank laughed. 'He complained about *your* lawyer! Talk about pot calling the kettle black.'

'I know. My lawyer was a moron, but that complaint wasn't upheld, of course. But it made me think that I should complain about Alex's solicitors, as they obviously hadn't acted in my stepmother's best interests. I suspected some sort of skulduggery.'

The waiter, dressed in white, delivered two steaming copper pots of curry to their table. Cathy sniffed the aromatic steam appreciatively.

'Do you come here often?' she asked Frank.

'I usually just get takeaways,' he admitted. 'I'm on my own – divorced. I've got two sons in their thirties living in London.'

'You're a bit of a lone wolf, then,' observed Cathy.

'Yeah, it does get lonely sometimes…' Frank looked at Cathy, 'but I've really enjoyed meeting you.'

Cathy picked up the basket of naan bread. 'Have a naan bread – they do look good. What made you become a lawyer?'

'Well, football is my first love, but with two left feet I was never going to make a career of it. At university, law seemed a good option, so here I am… helping you fight the good fight.'

They ate quietly for some minutes before she said, 'Now that my brother has refused to settle for a reasonable amount, what's next? How do we go about beginning criminal proceedings?'

'I'll write a letter for you to take to the police. Hang on a minute, doesn't your brother work for the police?'

'Yes, he does,' said Cathy. She put her fork down and sighed heavily. 'I've tried complaining to the police before about him, but got nowhere.'

'Yeah, they're not the best at investigating their own.' Frank rubbed his chin thoughtfully. Living on the edge had given him a wily streak. 'Your brother strikes me as someone who could ruffle a few feathers at times. Know anyone in the force with a beef against him?'

'I'll ask around the family – just the people I can trust.'

After the meal, they drove back to the hotel in silence. Frank parked outside.

'A nightcap?' he suggested hopefully.

Cathy smiled. 'No thanks, Frank. I'm really pooped. I'm going straight to bed. But thank you for the offer… and for the ride and meal.'

***

The next morning, Cathy woke at eight. Feeling stiff after the tension of the day before, she decided to do a few yoga stretches on the carpet before calling Tom.

'How are you, lass? Did that brother of yours get his comeuppance?'

For the first 20 minutes, Cathy filled Tom in on the previous day's negotiations. Then she explained their plan to get Alex convicted.

'I need your help, Tom. We want to instigate a criminal investigation so Alex can be charged with fraud. We have some information to help the police with their investigations but we have to make sure it falls into the right hands, otherwise there's a good chance it will get swept under the carpet. Have you heard on the grapevine if anyone in the police has a grudge against Alex?'

Tom was silent for a moment. Cathy could hear the BBC radio in the background. At last he replied, 'Alas, no one. I wish I could help you, lass.'

'Thanks, Tom, I'll try a few other people. It's tricky, though, because I can't call anyone who is friendly with him.'

She had just polished off a plate of bacon and eggs when her mobile rang. It was Tom again. She hurried into the lobby to talk to him away from the other diners.

'Cathy, it came to me when I was feeding me pigs, and I've hurried back up to the house to call you.'

'Take a few deep breaths, Tom – you're wheezing.' Cathy listened to Tom breathing deeply before he continued.

'Janice's husband has a friend in the Surrey Constabulary. I'll give him a tinkle and let you know what he says. I might not be able to find out for a day or two, but I'll do me best.'

'Thank you, Tom.' She clicked her phone off, smiling.

***

On Saturday, Cathy was staying with an old friend in Glastonbury when Tom called back.

'We've got our man, Cathy, or should I say woman.'

'Oh, tell me more… sounds promising.'

'My son-in-law's friend is a detective in Surrey. He knows Alex but doesn't like him. He sees him sometimes in the lunch room. He's heard Alex make the odd rude remark about the Chief Constable, a woman called Bridget Thompson. He can't stand the sight of her, and apparently the feeling's mutual. So there you go. Mark this complaint to the attention of Chief Constable Bridget Thompson and you might just find it makes its way over to the fraud squad for a full investigation. I don't think Alex will be working there much longer. It all sounds about right to me because I know Alex always hated female

199

bosses. Some lads can't stand it. They're stuck back in the Dark Ages.'

'Not like you, Tom – you're a modern man.'

'I sure am – did I show you me mobile phone?'

'No, you didn't. I didn't know you had one.'

'I've got one, all right. Janice bought it for me. But I never use it!'

They both laughed. Cathy thanked Tom for his help and ended the call. Once Frank had written a letter she intended to hand deliver it to the constabulary, along with the letter from the SRA. She wasn't taking any chances with the post. There were also one or two more things to see to, before she could at last fly home to New Zealand.

***

Alex was in his wine cellar when the mobile in his pocket vibrated. He looked at the caller ID – it was B.T. What did she want? He decided not to answer it. His phone beeped with a message. Frowning, he listened to it. It was a terse message from B.T. demanding he report to her office next morning, before he took his first class at nine. His pleasure at rearranging his wine bottles and selecting a French Bordeaux to go with tonight's beef bourguignon was swept away. A summons to B.T.'s office meant trouble.

***

Next morning, Alex tapped on Chief Constable Thompson's open door at 8:30 am. She looked up from her laptop. 'Come in.'

Her eyes were icy, her mouth a thin line.

The bitch, thought Alex, *she knows*. He stood in front of her desk. She looked up at him quizzically, raising one pencilled eyebrow.

'Do you know why you're here?'

Alex straightened up, squaring his shoulders. 'No, ma'am.'

'Six weeks ago I got a letter from a solicitor, Frank Henegan. The letter alleged fraud in relation to the acquisition of your stepmother's apartment. I've had the fraud squad

200

investigate this matter.' B.T. paused. She regarded him coldly before continuing. 'The result of their investigation is that you will be charged with appropriating a property by fraudulent means. This is a serious offence and it means you will be stood down immediately. According to the terms of your contract, you cannot work for us while you are under investigation. We expect *exemplary* behaviour from all our police tutors, who are supposed to be role models for our recruits.'

Alex didn't flinch. He could see B.T. was enjoying this.

'Go straight to your locker, take your things and leave the station *immediately*. Sergeant Walker is waiting in the corridor. He'll escort you from the building. You're free to go.'

B.T. went back to her laptop. Red with embarrassment, Alex turned to leave. He was in deep trouble now. Sonia was going to be very upset about this.

Chapter 38

Purple wisteria flowers hung like bunches of grapes over the trellis next to the deck. Cathy snipped off a few sprays of wisteria and popped them in one of her mother's Waterford crystal vases.

'Is it coffee time yet?' called David from his study.

'Yes, I'll make a pot. Let's sit outside, it's such a lovely day.'

Rhonda had dropped off a ginger loaf the day before to welcome her home. Cathy cut a couple of slabs and placed them on the tray with two green mugs, the coffee pot and a jug of milk. She carried the tray out to the cedar table and called David. She was standing gazing at the pale pink blossoms of the cherry tree at the bottom of the garden and the lake beyond, when David came up behind her, put his arms gently around her waist, and nuzzled her neck.

'It's good to have you back. It felt like you were away a long time.'

'Same here,' said Cathy, turning around and giving him a kiss. After holding each other quietly for a few minutes they moved apart, and Cathy poured the coffee. David picked up his mug, then set it back down again.

'I forgot – something came for you by registered mail. I'll just go and get it.'

Cathy sipped her coffee quietly, watching a bee hover among the wisteria blossoms. David returned holding a bundle of envelopes and a small white package from the UK.

'This looks interesting,' said Cathy, picking up the package and pulling at the sticky tape. David fetched the scissors. She snipped open one end and pulled out a bubble-wrapped, cube-shaped object and an envelope.

'Oh. I wonder what's inside.' With a few good snips, the bubble wrap fell open, revealing a sturdy navy box about 10 cm square.

Cathy took off the lid and removed a layer of protective padding. She gasped. 'Oh my God!'

'What is it?' asked David.

She tilted the box towards him so he could see what was inside – a gleaming gold fob watch encircled by a gold chain, lying on a cushion of white velvet. Picking it up, she turned it over. Sure enough, it was engraved with her great-grandfather's name:

William J. Coleman

Her thumb pushed down on the clasp and the watch sprung open effortlessly. Inside, lying on top of the dial face, was a five-pointed gold star and sitting beneath it was a tiny piece of folded paper. She looked at it in wonder. Gingerly, she picked up the star and the note. Someone had folded it many times until it was tiny. Carefully, Cathy unfolded it and read the spidery handwriting:

Dear Cathy,
Please accept this peace offering. I realise now we never should have fallen out. I heard that Emma has got married. Please pass this on to her firstborn child with my love. I'm sure your father would have wanted that.
Love,
Lucille

Tears blurred Cathy's vision. David, who had been watching her intently, came and stood behind her, laying a hand on her shoulder. Choked up with emotion, she passed him the note.

David read it. 'Well, well, well. That's nice. So Alex didn't get the watch or the gold star, after all. What's in the other envelope?'

Cathy wiped her eyes with a paper serviette, then opened the other envelope.

10 August 2007
Dear Cathy,
Today I visited Lucille, who is in hospital. She is very weak and her heart is troubling her. Lucille gave me the key to her apartment and told me not to give it to Alex. She never wanted him to have the penthouse, but she dug herself a hole so deep she could not get out of it. She asked me to fetch the gold fob watch from the cabinet in her living room and post it to you, along with the star she usually wears around her neck. She says the star belongs on the end of the watch chain. She made me promise to do this for her.
It's very sad to see her grow so weak. I try to visit her every day, unless I'm feeling poorly myself. I have happy memories of our holidays abroad with you and David. Thank you for those happy times, my dear. God bless you and I'm sorry for what happened but I was no match for your brother.
Take care,
Bertie

At the bottom of the letter someone had added a note in a different hand.

18.10.10
Cathy,
I am so sorry it has taken me so long to send you this fob watch. Uncle Bertie never got around to posting it to you because he fell ill and passed away a few months after Lucille died. He was 95. I found the package, addressed to you, in a cubby hole in his desk when I was cleaning out his apartment. I ought to have sent it earlier, but there was so much to do that I'm afraid I forgot all about it and it ended up in a box with some of his other belongings in my garage. I came across it again last week when I was looking for something. Please accept my apologies.
Hazel (Bertie's niece)

'Well,' said Cathy, leaning back in the deck chair, 'how amazing! I never thought I'd see Grandad's watch again. How lovely that I can pass it down to little Ryan. I'll have to ask the jeweller to attach the gold star medallion to the chain.'

David fiddled with the watch, setting it on the right time and turning the winder. It began to tick. Cathy sat in deep thought, watching him.

'Look, it still works.' He held it up so that she could see the white face with its black Roman numerals, and the hands pointing to the right time.

'That's great. I was just thinking we might be able to use this letter of Bertie's as evidence. If there's a trial, Frank's warned me that I'll probably be called up as a witness.'

'Hmmm… that means another trip to England. I'd hoped we'd go to South America next year.'

'Well, after this is over, I promise you we'll go on an overseas trip of your choice – Machu Picchu, perhaps? I guess I could put up with a few foul-mouthed llamas if they carried my pack and water bottle.'

Chapter 39

One Sunday morning the following spring, Cathy was feeling at a loose end. It was drizzling and David was pottering about in the garage. She decided it would be a good opportunity to try out Facebook. Emma had joined Facebook and told her snippets of news from old school friends she'd contacted in England. Cathy wondered if she might be able to use Facebook to find old friends she'd lost contact with over the years.

She sat down at the computer. The first hurdle was to sign up. Once she had negotiated the password business – always such a palaver – she was in. It was a dazzling glimpse of a whole global community; Cathy found the array of options a little confusing. Soon she was working on a Facebook profile. David didn't approve of Facebook and it felt odd, almost slightly subversive to be joining, though she knew Rhonda was a member. She'd talked about it at croquet. Cathy believed it was important to keep up with the times. She didn't want to be labelled a Luddite.

By selecting the "Find Friends" button, she was able to quickly identify a dozen people she knew, including Rhonda and Zoe.

'This is fun,' she said out loud, as she uploaded a photo of herself and David on a fishing trip. David was holding up a large trout. She added a photo of herself and Ryan at the Taronga Zoo, with the Sydney Harbour Bridge in the background. She had gone to Sydney because Emma had given birth to a second son. Smiling at the memory of the zoo trip, Cathy remembered how Ryan had been rooted to the spot by the Komodo dragon. The beast had seemed to spark imagination and when they'd got home he'd dragged out all his dragon and dinosaur books for her to read aloud. He'd also drawn a large dragon in green and purple crayon, which she had taken home and pinned to the notice board above her computer.

She browsed the public profiles of half a dozen old friends in England. Then, just out of interest, she typed in "Scarborough". Up popped a special interest group called "Scarborough: The Good Old Days". A sepia photo of the old town spread across the screen like a masthead. A wave of nostalgia washed over her. It was at times like these that she really did miss the sense of history in England. Scrolling through the photos, she smiled in delight. There was an old black and white photo of Milnes department store, standing proudly on its corner site. She couldn't resist typing a comment below the photo: "My family owned Milnes and I remember visiting every Saturday when I was a girl. My mother was the manager."

Next she looked at a few black and white photos taken at the beach. The striped beach huts and figures in black bathing suits certainly brought back memories of picnics with the family. She noticed that a woman called Dora had responded to her comment about Milnes:

"I remember your mother when she was alive, she was a lovely lady. She used to live across the road from me. I'd see her walking up the road to go shopping – she was always dressed very smartly."

That's strange, thought Cathy. She quickly typed back:

"My mother is still alive, but she has moved and now lives in a retirement home in Surrey, near my brother."

There was no reply.

Cathy felt unsettled by Dora's words, and especially by the lack of response to her comment. But when she glanced at the clock on the bottom right hand corner of the computer screen it said 11:12 am. Perhaps Dora had gone to bed. Anyway, it was time for coffee.

Seated on the cream settee, a mug of coffee in her hand, Cathy talked it over with David. 'I've got a funny feeling about this… it's strange that woman didn't reply. It's possible my mother could be dead.'

'Hmmm,' said David, 'I think you could be right.'

Cathy returned to the computer. She checked for any further comments from Dora on Facebook – nothing. Well, Dora was no doubt asleep.

***

That evening Cathy Skyped Emma in Sydney. She told her how she had joined Facebook and felt uneasy about the comment about her mother.

'Mum, you should send that person a private message,' said Emma, 'If you look at the top of the screen, you'll see two little speech bubbles... write this down or you'll never remember...'

'Hang on a minute, I'll just grab a pen.' Cathy dutifully noted down Emma's instructions. 'Thanks, sweetie. I'll try that.'

'There's something else that has just occurred to me. After Luke was born, I sent an email to Alex asking him to tell Gran she had a second great-grandson. He never replied. I didn't think it was that unusual at the time, but now I'm wondering.'

'It seems strange he didn't acknowledge the birth. After all, you have received the odd email from him from time to time.'

Cathy closed the Skype window and logged onto Facebook. Still no word from Dora, so she sent her a private message:

"Could you please tell me if you know anything about my mother. Unfortunately, there has been a family dispute and I haven't been in direct contact with her for some months. I live in New Zealand now."

She watched the screen for ten minutes. There was no reply.

Cathy got up and walked into the lounge. She sat in an armchair, staring into space. She knew mediation had damaged her relationship with her mother beyond repair. She thought how difficult it must have been for her mother, who had once enjoyed good relationships with both her children, to watch them clawing at each other. Some time ago Cathy had written a long letter to the rest home explaining that she suspected her mother was a victim of financial elder abuse, and that her brother was the perpetrator. She'd asked them to keep her informed of her mother's health and well-being. But the rest home hadn't even bothered to reply. Cathy checked the computer again – no message. She glanced at the clock. 11:00. It was time to give the rest home a call.

'Woodford Court,' said a woman's voice.

'Hello, my name is Cathy Stewart and I'd like to speak to Margaret Coleman, please.'

'Mrs Coleman? Just a moment...' there was a long pause while Cathy listened to the static. 'I'm afraid Mrs Coleman is deceased. Would you like to speak to someone else? Our manager would be happy to talk to you.'

Cathy felt her heart give a little jolt.

'Yes, please.'

'Hello, Raewyn Shepherd speaking.'

'Hello, it's Cathy Stewart, here. I live in New Zealand and I've just found out that my mother, Margaret Coleman, has died.'

'Yes, Cathy.' Raewyn hesitated. 'Your mother died a year ago after a long illness. I'll just look up the date... she died on 20 September 2012.'

'I'd like to know why the rest home didn't inform me of her death.'

'I'm afraid your brother gave us strict instructions not to inform anyone else. He said he would contact family himself.'

Cathy swallowed. 'You mean, even though I'm a next of kin, you saw fit not to inform me of my own mother's death?'

'We carried out your brother's wishes. Your mother was kept comfortable in the last weeks and she didn't suffer.' The rest home manager added gently, 'I understand there was a family falling out.'

'Yes, there was. My brother and I haven't talked for a long time, and my mother was caught in the middle.'

Cathy put the phone down. Mixed with her sadness was an overwhelming sense of relief. For a long time now, she'd had a nagging worry in the back of her mind. Was her mother being looked after? What schemes was her brother up to? Was she suffering? Would they ever be reconciled? Sometimes she'd suffered from pangs of guilt that she was living on the other side of the world. Now it was over. It was finished. She went to wake David and tell him the news.

She shook him gently.

'What is it?'

'I've rung the rest home. They said Mother died a year ago – on September 20th.'

'Oh, Cathy, I'm sorry.' He pulled her under the covers for a hug.

'I'm really annoyed that no one in the family thought to tell me. At the very least, one of my cousins ought to have let me know.'

'Your brother no doubt told them not to. I mean the last thing he'd want is you turning up at the funeral.'

'Yeah, but I'm hardly going to contest the will. He made mistakes with Lucille's will, and he wouldn't make the same mistakes again.' A note of bitterness sounded in her voice.

David stroked her hair, thoughtfully. 'Knowing your brother, it wouldn't surprise me if he passed your cousins over some of the family antiques, then asked them to stay mum.'

Cathy thought about this for a few minutes, then replied, 'I guess as long as they stay in the family that's the main thing. At least my mother will be spared seeing her son and daughter in court.'

Chapter 40

Cathy bolted awake. She had been dreaming about the trial. Alex, his face contorted with rage, had pointed at her and screamed across the court, 'This is bullshit. She's the one that stole the money!'

The thudding of her heart subsided. Feeling relieved it had been just a dream, she turned on her side, pulling the comforting cloak of the duvet around her. The red numbers on the digital clock display glowed 6:50 am – too early to get ready for court. She decided to dress and go for a walk along the River Wey.

October in Guildford is chilly. Heading along the towpath, Cathy relished the bite of the cold air, and the quietude. In her mind, she replayed scenes from the trial in the Crown Court. One of the direst moments had been when she had stood on the witness stand, her mouth dry and her legs suddenly wobbly. During cross-examination, the defence barrister, a tall, wigged and robed figure had said, 'You emigrated to New Zealand, I believe, and left your stepmother and mother in your brother's care. If you were such a loving daughter, then why did you choose to move to the other side of the world when your ageing stepmother and mother would obviously need more care in the years to come?'

Cathy had gripped the smooth wooden rails of the witness box to steady herself. She had swallowed, reminding herself that all she needed to do was tell the truth. The prosecutor had warned her that the defence would try to discredit her and she had prepared for this question.

'I left England because my husband is a New Zealander. We had lived in England for 27 years of our marriage and I had promised him we would retire to New Zealand – that was his dream. You must also remember that my brother sought to cut off all communication between my stepmother and myself. He even got Interpol involved at one stage.'

Cathy was proud of that reply. She'd looked at the jurors as she spoke. One or two had been looking down, but most of them had looked at her. She recalled an older woman with wavy white hair scraped into a bun and kindly eyes, and a younger woman with long dark hair seated beside her. She had sensed they were sympathetic.

A big black crow alighted on the path in front of her. Cathy stamped on the ground to shoo it away. It rose flapping and cawing, reminding her of her brother. He'd stood in the dock, dressed in a dark suit, his black wings of hair brushed with silver. She'd kept her eyes fixed on him during the chief prosecutor's summary, which she had to admit she had relished. The prosecutor was a heavy-boned, fair woman with a necklace of large multi-coloured beads over her robe. Her voice, strong and even, echoed in Cathy's head.

'When the defendant found out that his sister had been gifted £50,000 by his father and would inherit two-thirds of his stepmother's estate, he was very hurt, as he saw this as a measure of his father's and stepmother's affection. He was jealous of his sister, who he believed was the favoured child. So he set out to exact his revenge by pressuring, manipulating and deceiving his stepmother. Within a few months of his stepmother arguing with his sister, his stepmother had granted him general power of attorney, made him the major beneficiary of her will and gifted him her penthouse apartment estimated at the time to be worth £650,000. At the same time, the defendant fuelled the embers of his stepmother's disagreement with his sister, so his sister was, in effect, excommunicated from the family. Divide and conquer is a famous military maxim.'

The prosecutor had paused for effect, looking at the jury over her blue-framed glasses. 'The crux of the matter is, the defendant instructed his solicitors to transfer the ownership of the apartment to himself, without consulting his stepmother, the owner. In fact, a few months before she died, Mrs Coleman described her feelings for her stepson with these words: "he makes my back curl". Now if you felt like this about a person, ladies and gentlemen of the jury, would you want to leave them your most valuable possession in the world, your penthouse apartment?'

During the prosecution's summary, Cathy could see her brother's profile. She knew he must have been under enormous strain, yet he had sat perfectly still, looking straight ahead. No doubt he drew on the composure drilled into him by the army.

She stood still for a moment, studying the rippled reflections of the trees. Even with a crispy blue sky above, the river was murky. She cast her mind back to the defence barrister's final summary. He'd painted a picture of the former SAS soldier, the decorated war hero, the dutiful stepson with an unblemished military record. She had to admit his arguments had been convincing. She'd noticed the male jurors listening intently. At the mention of an MBE for services to the Police, she had given a huff of disgust. Tom had nudged her in the ribs. Tom and his daughters, Janice and Alison, had given evidence as witnesses, then sat in on various stages of the six-day trial to show their support. Sonia and her mother, a tall gaunt woman, had sat on the other side of the gallery throughout.

Cathy crossed over a narrow pedestrian bridge, and thought back to Judge Macdonald's summary. A few of the phrases, pronounced distinctly with his Scottish bur, came back to her.

'Members of the jury, fraud has a very special meaning. It means obtaining something by a statement of fact that the person making that statement knows to be false or knows might be false at the time that he made it... Now in this case it is said that the transfer of the ownership of the apartment was fraudulent. Has the prosecution proved beyond reasonable doubt that the transfer of the ownership of the apartment was fraudulent? Members of the jury, you may now retire to consider your verdict.'

Cathy turned to walk back in the direction of her hotel, picturing the jury trooping back into court after the recess. Once they had been seated the clerk had asked the foreman, an older man with eyebrows like ridges, to stand. Feeling for Tom's gnarly hand beside her, Cathy had clutched it tightly and held her breath.

The clerk had addressed the foreman, 'Do you find the defendant, Alex George Coleman, guilty or not guilty of the charge of obtaining his late stepmother's property fraudulently?'

'Guilty,' said the foreman in a deep, sonorous voice.

There were loud gasps from Sonia's direction. It was the one word Cathy had been so desperate to hear. Cathy and Tom hugged each other. Her main feeling was overwhelming relief that the jury had found him guilty, tinged with sadness for her brother. She saw Alex standing below her. He looked shocked, his mouth half-open and eyes glazed over in disbelief.

It was late afternoon, so Judge Macdonald had ordered that the court be adjourned until the next day for sentencing.

***

Back at the hotel, Cathy dressed for what she hoped would be her very last day in court. From a pouch in her cabin bag she took out a navy box. Inside lay the star medallion on its cushion of white velvet. It felt right that she should wear this necklace on the day she hoped her father and stepmother's true wishes would be fulfilled. She threaded the star medallion on a fine gold chain, slipped it around her neck and fastened the clasp. In the brightly lit hotel mirror, she stared at her reflection. The star seemed to glow as it lay against the navy merino top she had chosen to wear under her smart grey jacket.

Cathy met Tom, Janice and Alison on the front steps of the Crown Court, an ugly red brick edifice, built in the seventies, with an imposing high-pitched roof. They hugged each other briefly, then walked up the steps. Cathy led them through the security check, then straight to the court room. The public gallery was empty except for an older man and woman on the back benches whom Cathy didn't recognise. They sat down in the front row. The room was warm and stuffy. Cathy slipped off her grey jacket. The prosecution and defence barristers were already sitting at tables in front of them, busy with their paperwork.

A policeman led Alex to the dock; the irony was not lost on the gallery. Alex was carrying a black holdall bag and this time his head was bowed.

'All stand,' said the clerk.

They all stood for Judge Macdonald, who swept majestically in wearing blue robes, a red sash and wig. Cathy listened intently to the judge's summary. Then came the moment Cathy had been waiting for – the sentencing.

'I sentence you, Alex George Coleman, to two years in prison for fraudulently obtaining your late stepmother's property. The last three wills of your late stepmother are to be disregarded and the 1990 will reinstated. Furthermore, I order you to give your father's autobiography and war souvenirs to your sister.'

Alex stood, shoulders square, hands by his side, motionless. The constable tapped him on the shoulder and he picked up his bag and turned to follow. His eyes swept over the front row of the public gallery and found Cathy. For an instant, his gaze fixed on the star medallion, glinting in a shaft of morning sunlight. There was a flicker of recognition in his eyes, then he walked through the side door and was gone.

Cathy turned to Tom and they hugged each other tight. A huge burden had been lifted from Cathy's shoulders. Behind Tom, she glimpsed Sonia's back as she left the room. Cathy stood up to be congratulated by Janice and Alison. They wanted to take her out for lunch to celebrate. As executor of the 1990 will Cathy could at last ensure that the estate was divided fairly according to Lucille's wishes.

The mobile in her pocket vibrated. A text from David: "The sentence?"

She hastily replied, "Two years in prison." Then she answered a call from Frank.

'The odds were against you, Cathy, but you got him. Well done!'

'Thank you, Frank.'

'Are you going to talk to the papers? The journos are sniffing around – decorated war hero rips off stepmum and all that.'

'Maybe. I'll think about it.'

Holding her head high, Cathy walked out of the court house feeling jubilant. At long last, she could return to her life in New Zealand, free of the bitter family feud and finally able to enjoy her retirement, knowing she had fought for the justice her father would have wanted. Outside on the court house steps, she stood alone for a moment. She watched a police car pulling away from the kerb and thought to herself, *you never really know someone until you have shared an inheritance with them.*

Addendum

The Inheritance Thief is based on the author's autobiography *My Brother My Enemy* and draws on the true facts surrounding financial and psychological abuse in her family. Names have been changed and some aspects of the story have been altered for dramatisation.

The author's experience has given her an in depth knowledge of how elder abuse is dealt with in the United Kingdom and how this compares unfavourably with New Zealand's laws.

Below is an extract from a letter to the author from Hon Jo Goodhew, who was New Zealand's Minister for Senior Citizens in 2013.

Perhaps the United Kingdom should adopt some of these law changes.

'Sadly laws can never provide the community with 100 per cent protection from unscrupulous people. In New Zealand though we have made significant improvements to the laws and protections relating to Endurng Powers of Attorney (EPAs). The Law Commission's 2001 Review highlighted issues of misuse and abuse of EPAs and was the catalyst for the Protection of Personal and Property Rights (PPPR) Amendment Act 2007. The amendments came into force on 26th September 2008 and provide better protection for the rights and interests of people unable to manage their own affairs. I have highlighted some of the key changes which I believe better protect the welfare and rights of vulnerable people including:

- strengthened witnessing requirements, especially the requirements that the person creating the EPA (the donor) must receive legal advice on the effect and implications of the EPA before signing it and that the witness to the donor's signature be independent of any attorney appointed by the EPA.
- A new presumption of the competence for the donor.
- A clearer definition of mentally incapable in relation to the personal care and welfare.
- Authority for a personal care and welfare attorney to take into account advance directives given by the donor.
- That property attorneys are to provide personal care and welfare attorneys with financial support required to perform their responsibilities.
- Requiring attorneys to consult with the donor and others specified by the donor in the EPA and to act in the donor's best interests.
- That property and personal care and welfare attorneys are to regularly consult with each other in order to act in the donor's best interests.
- Restricting the ability of attorneys to benefit themselves except to the extent specified in the EPA.
- Requiring medical certification of the donor's mental incapacity before an attorney can act under the EPA (except where, in the case of a property EPA, the donor has authorised the attorney to act before the donor becomes mentally incapable).
- Providing easier access to the courts, and enhanced court powers in respect of EPAs.
- Requiring property attorneys to keep records of financial transactions and supply these to any person

nominated in the EPA. These records may be used in court proceedings under the PPPR Act.

- In NZ, if abuse of an attorney's powers under an EPA is suspected, a wide range of people can apply to the Family Court to review the attorney's decision.

There are also a number of helpful websites with good information on EPAs.'

Hon Jo Goodhew, Minister for Senior Citizens, Extract from letter dated 4 June 2013.

It is the author's sincere hope that her story will alert people to the dangers of all types of elder abuse.